THE
WHISPER
PLACE

Also by Mindy Mejia

The Dragon Keeper

Everything You Want Me to Be

Leave No Trace

Strike Me Down

To Catch a Storm

A World of Hurt

THE
WHISPER
PLACE

A THRILLER

MINDY MEJIA

Atlantic Crime
New York

FIRST EDITION

Printed in the United States of America

First Grove Atlantic hardcover edition: September 2025

Library of Congress Cataloging-in-Publication data is available for this title.

ISBN 978-0-8021-6539-8
eISBN 978-0-8021-6540-4

Atlantic Crime
an imprint of Grove Atlantic
154 West 14th Street
New York, NY 10011

Distributed by Publishers Group West

groveatlantic.com

25 26 27 28   10 9 8 7 6 5 4 3 2 1

For Logan and Rory.
You'll be a thousand things to a thousand people,
but you'll always be chaos demons to me.
Love you to the demon moon and back.

THE
WHISPER
PLACE

I used to love maps. As a kid, I'd follow the coastline and inlets, trace mountain ranges, and draw my finger along interstates that went from one side of the country to the other, seeing where they would end. I picked out spots I wanted to live, tiny towns perched on the edges of massive lakes or tucked away in a national forest. I never looked at the cities. Places like New York and San Francisco always sprawled too big, choked with grids of asphalt, turning the green of the landscape colorless. They looked like cancer, devouring the world around them. I liked places I could barely see, written in fonts so light it was like they were whispered onto the page.

The road map spread out in front of me, tented and creased in a way that brought back all those memories. God, I had missed maps. I almost cried when I saw this one in a truck stop stuffed with novelty items, plastic toys, and travel-sized everything. There it was, map of the USA, in a creaky turnstile full of paperbacks and travel guides.

"Don't sell too many of these," the ancient cashier commented as she rang it up along with my assortment of snacks and drinks. She smiled as she said it, friendly, just making conversation with the only other woman in the store. The greasy-haired kid on the other register probably wasn't much for company.

I made a *hmm* noise and said something like "I'm sure" as I counted out a few twenties and took my change, tossed a smile that landed somewhere between the counter and her face, and left before she could find another topic.

The backseat of my Mazda was crammed full of suitcases, bags, books, and pillows. I knew I'd forgotten things, but they were just things, and I'd packed the most important one: the dough cutter cradled in a stack of blankets on the passenger seat next to me. There was plenty of room in the trunk for some of this stuff, but I wasn't ready to open the trunk yet. It wasn't clean enough. It might never be clean enough, and I didn't want to contaminate anything else with the dirt and darkness of that trunk, not when there was so much I didn't know lying ahead.

Sitting at the gas pump, I found the whisper town where I was and traced the routes of all the whisper places I could go. For the first time as I spread the map over the steering wheel and felt the subtle gloss of the paper under my fingers, a spark of something like excitement rippled through me. I was tired and sore and wrung out from stress and adrenaline surges every time a door had opened or my phone had buzzed while I was packing, but I had the dough cutter, twelve thousand dollars stuffed under my seat, and possibilities stretching in every direction.

I drove west, toward the sun, which it felt like I hadn't seen in so long. I rolled up my T-shirt sleeves and put the visor up, letting the rays bake me as semitrucks and SUVs wove around my sedan and sped ahead to destinations known. Choices they'd already made. And with every mile, the spark of excitement in my chest grew.

Max

The guy looked broke.

In the year and a half since I'd left the Iowa City police and joined my best friend's PI firm, I'd learned to evaluate people through a very specific filter. As a cop I'd been trained to look for threats. Was someone a danger to themselves or others? Did the situation need to be de-escalated? That muscle was still there, underneath the veneer of my new private-sector loafers and laptop bag, but it wasn't the first thing I thought when someone walked through our front door. Not anymore. Now, I checked for money.

My six o'clock Friday night appointment, a prospect who'd messaged us through the website, could've been an extra from *Trailer Park Boys*. His stained flannel bulged over cargo shorts, his beard hadn't been trimmed since Covid, and he glanced nervously around the office with partied-out, bloodshot eyes. Early thirties. Beer gut. A classic failure-to-launch, directionless white boy. I put his bank account balance at three thousand, tops. If he invested, it was strictly Dogecoin.

"Charlie Ashlock?" I pasted a welcoming smile on my face and walked around the desk, hand out. He shook it with a clammy palm. "I'm Max. Have a seat. Can I get you a water?"

We had a Keurig, too, and some fancy mugs courtesy of my wife, who'd taken the office space on as her personal Pinterest-board challenge, but I wasn't wasting a K-cup on this guy.

He waved the water off and sat on the edge of the chair, setting an old backpack on the floor next to him.

I flipped to a fresh page in my notebook. "Your message said you're looking for someone."

He nodded and hesitated before speaking. "She's been gone for a week."

"She's missing?"

He nodded, offering zero additional details. I sighed inwardly. "Have you filed a missing person report?"

"No."

"That's your first step. The authorities need to be notified. They can conduct an official investigation whenever a person is missing."

He leaned in and met my eyes for the first time. His were red but lucid and I realized it might not be from late nights at the bar. He looked desperate. Hopeless.

"I can't go to the cops."

"Why not?"

"Because," his hands balled into fists in his lap, "she wouldn't want me to."

I put the notebook down.

"Start at the beginning."

* * *

Charlie told me he'd woken up at his house a week ago—a farm south of Riverside—and his girlfriend wasn't there.

"She'd started running in the mornings. Her running shoes were gone, so I figured that's what she was doing at first. Then I saw her car was gone, too, but she left her overnight bag behind. She's not at her place. She hasn't been to work in a week."

"How long have you two been dating?"

"A month."

"That's pretty new. Things going well?"

"Yeah." He swallowed. "She's the best thing that ever happened to me." He pulled up a series of pictures on his phone of the two of them lounging on a couch. He was clearly trying to get her to look at the camera while she burrowed under a blanket. Only one picture had a clear shot of her face, snuggled into his chest and looking half amused, half resigned. She was pale with long, dark blond hair, delicate features, and freckles over her nose. She stared at something above the camera, dissociating from the experience.

"Was she happy, too?"

He got up and paced the space between the two desks. "Yes. She was." He nodded, as if trying to convince himself. "I know she was happy."

"But?"

"But she never got comfortable. I tried to get her to move more of her stuff to my place, but she wouldn't. She wouldn't tell me why." He stopped pacing. "And she was scared."

"Of commitment?"

He shook his head. "No, not of us. It was something else. Something she wasn't telling me."

"Maybe she took off."

"Yeah. I hope so." He went to the front window and stared out at the parking lot of the office park. "That would be the best thing, right? That she was done with me, and left."

"What's the worst?"

He turned around. "That whatever she was scared of found her."

I sighed and flipped the notebook closed. "Look—"

"No, please." He came back to the chair, cutting off my rejection, and grabbed his backpack off the floor. "I just need her to be okay. It's fine if she doesn't want to come back. I'm not trying to stalk her or force her to do anything. I just need to know—"

He couldn't finish his sentence.

"We'd like to help you out. Really. But this could require a significant amount of resources, especially if she left and didn't want to be found. Our retainer alone is five thousand, and weekly billings on top of that."

He opened the backpack and pulled out two bricks of cash, setting them on top of my notebook. "Here's ten grand."

I stared at the money. Questions flew through my head, momentarily overshadowed by the realization that I'd pegged him wrong when he walked through the door. Charlie might be a lot of things, but broke wasn't one of them.

"I can pay weekly, too. The money doesn't matter. I need your help."

I ran a hand over my head. Red flags flashed like fireworks, impossible to ignore. In the eighteen months Jonah and I had operated Celina Investigations, we'd established a few ground rules.

Rule #1: Every dream required investigation, whether we got paid or not.

Jonah Kendrick wasn't just my best friend and business partner. He was a psychic who dreamed about lost people. I'd helped him discover his abilities when we were assigned to be dorm mates our freshman year of college. I was an insomniac. He was a sleep-talking loner with supernatural powers. We were a perfect match. And part of our purpose, regardless of starting this business together or being able to pay our rent, was to find those lost people.

Rule #2: No hard liquor at the office.

We established that one after a client brought us a thank-you bottle of peanut butter whiskey that we scoffed at and promptly drank within six hours, wrecking the office bathroom for days afterward.

Rule #3: We discussed every case before taking on a client.

Jonah had enacted this one, because I'd developed a habit of saying yes to anything and everything that came our way. And I got it. We were a two-person business. Our resources were limited and there were only so many hours in the day, especially when we spent a good number of them chasing Jonah's dreams. But the company hadn't exactly been an overnight success. We struggled to find clients, and the constant hustle and worry about making ends meet had made me a little hungry.

Charlie Ashlock's missing girlfriend seemed like a good case on the surface. We specialized in finding people and he needed someone found. But everything about it smelled wrong. His devoted-boyfriend story about a happy couple didn't lead to one party vanishing out of the blue. He refused to go to the police, conveniently blaming his reluctance on the missing woman. Then there was the money. It wasn't the first time a brick of cash had landed on my desk, and the last time it had I made a decision that still haunted me during the gray hours of sleepless nights.

"Look, my partner is out on an assignment right now. We can't take your case before we evaluate the scope and feasibility." Big words that basically meant I needed to ask Jonah's permission.

"How long is that going to take?" Charlie looked physically sick. "I can't wait any longer. I've been going out of my head this week, not knowing where she is or if she's all right. She's gone. Like she was never here. And I can't just keep living my life, you know? I filled out the online application. You've got everything you need to get started."

"Charlie—"

He pulled out another two bricks of cash, lining them up next to the first stack. "Twenty thousand."

I looked from the money—which could pay our rent and salaries for well over a month—to the red-eyed man who looked one step away from a complete mental break.

"Please," he said, and the amount of raw emotion packed in that single word overrode everything my gut was telling me about this case. "Your website said you specialize in missing people. I don't know where else to go."

The website was right. I'd written it myself, after spending half my life taking orders from superiors who told me what I was and wasn't allowed to investigate.

I offered my hand, which he shook fervently.

"Oh my god, thank you. Bill me for whatever you need, whatever it takes. Overtime, expenses, anything." He put the money back in the backpack and handed me the whole thing. It smelled earthy, like he'd dug it out of his backyard.

After brewing a few Keurig coffees, we sat down and got into details. I flipped the notebook to a fresh page. A fresh assignment.

"Let's start with the basics. What's her name?"

He swallowed a mouthful of coffee and looked down at the fancy mug.

"I don't know."

Jonah

Life was simpler before I knew her name. Not easier—my life had never mapped on the whistle-while-you-work spectrum—but objectively simpler before Dr. Eve Roth came into the picture.

I scrolled through the texts we'd been exchanging all night, rereading every word and trying to pretend I wasn't memorizing everything she said. Her last message was twenty minutes ago. I'd sent a picture of a nearby gas station sign advertising BUY ONE GET ONE RED BULLS, which she secretly loved and drank like an alcoholic trying to low-key slam tequila shots at the office. But she never responded to the picture. No emoji, nothing. And now I was obsessively refreshing the app, waiting for the nonexistent dots of her response to appear.

I put the phone down and looked around. The problem was I didn't have much else to do. I was on a job, doing fieldwork in Max's boring Toyota. An infidelity assignment. The cheating husband had left work and checked in at a hotel by himself, leaving me to sit at the edge of the parking lot taking pictures of every person who went in or out of the building, like a perv. The guy had to go home to his wife for dinner, which meant he and his sidepiece would be coming out again soon. If I was a different kind of investigator, I could've gone into the hotel and made friends with the front desk clerk, found out their room number, and maybe gotten a picture in a hallway where there was a better chance of catching them together. But hotels had people, and people were lousy with thoughts and feelings infinitely louder than any of them could imagine.

Out here, on the far side of the parking lot, I sensed almost nothing from the rotation of guests moving in and out of the hotel. A whiff of frustration from a dad packing his screaming kids into a minivan, but it was manageable. I could draw the boundaries of myself against the background static of humans living their lives. The farther away people were, the easier it was to tune them out, to remember where they stopped and I started.

Unless that person was Dr. Eve Roth.

I picked the phone up and refreshed the text feed. Nothing.

She'd been gone for over a month, in Australia studying tropical cyclones with a group of grad students. Flying into storms and probably learning Indigenous customs and wrestling giant snakes, although she only sent pictures of the storms. We texted daily. I gave her updates on her father-in-law, Earl, who was staying with a friend while she was gone. She gave me updates on the grad student drama—who was dating who and whose research looked promising—like I knew any of them. Her new PhD student, Chris, came up a lot and it was humiliating how much I viscerally hated seeing his name, the instant heat that boiled up at the idea of someone else being closer to Eve than I was. They'd arrived back in Iowa today and I could see Chris sitting next to her on the endless flights, discussing research methodologies and papers and all the data they'd probably collected together. Data was Eve's love language.

We weren't together.

I put the phone down and tried a few yoga breaths. Eve could date any brilliant twenty-something PhD student she wanted to. Not that she wanted to or seemed to think about—

I hit my head against the seat of Max's cheap car, hard enough to interrupt my creepy consent-less obsession. God, I hated myself. I needed this client's husband to appear so I could take a picture and leave. The freeway was in spitting distance and I wanted to bury the needle on this pile of beige scrap metal until bolts started shaking off. *Not healthy*, Eve had said. She'd been trying to get me to take up running lately, claiming it would be better than illegal street racing for my sero-adrenal whatever. She'd probably bookmarked studies and made charts about it. Most people's minds were a chaotic scattershot of random thoughts and whiplash emotions, but Eve's mind hummed. It was like being around a supercomputer, if supercomputers were bright and warm and—

The passenger door opened and I jerked, dropping the phone onto the camera.

"Hi." Eve slid into the passenger seat and smiled.

I looked behind the car, trying to figure out where she came from, which made her laugh. "Did I just surprise a psychic?"

"Omniscience isn't part of the deal."

"No, but you've claimed a radius of awareness. If someone were to test that hypothesis, sneaking up on you might be a valid method."

I hadn't felt her approach because I was already thinking about her. Listening to the whirr of her mind from what I thought was miles away. I couldn't tell her that, though. Just like I tried not to focus on the sudden singing in my chest.

"I'm sure I'd fail all your tests."

"There's no failure in science, only the elimination of possibilities." The grin hung on her face, but I felt an undercurrent of exhaustion. She had dark circles beneath her eyes. Her short, dark red hair was messy and her jacket was rumpled. She should've been in bed, sleeping off the jet lag. The fact that she was here, that she'd found me instead . . .

"Wait, how did you sneak up on me? Are you the omniscient one?"

Leaning forward, she peered up at the sky. "Altocumulus are moving in. Based on the progression of the system and the timestamp on your picture, it was easy to find the longitude of the gas station location."

Of course it was. For her. I'd seen her chase down a drug trafficking ring and hijack a plane. The list of things Eve would find challenging could fit on a Post-it note.

She sighed, watching the clouds. "I missed the sky here." Contentment hummed out of her as her eyes darted from cloud to cloud. I forced myself to turn back to the hotel entrance and focused on separating her emotions from mine, redrawing the boundaries.

"Isn't the sky the same everywhere?"

"No."

I waited for the explanations, the ionic molecular something that impacted something else to support her conclusion, but she was silent. Waiting. I looked over to find her watching me, studying me as intently as she had the sky.

"I missed you, too."

It was hard to breathe. The quiet words coupled with a cocktail of emotion emanating from her—happiness, fatigue, and a hint of longing—didn't leave room for oxygen. She slid her hand into mine and for an endless moment we just looked at each other. I feasted on the details, the sight, smell, and feel of her. I wanted to bring her hand to my mouth, to taste her skin and listen to what it did to her heart. Instead, I squeezed her palm and absorbed the flow of heat and energy.

"I was thinking while I was in Australia."

"You'd be thinking if you were in a coma."

I felt it coming. I heard it before she spoke it, and still it caught me like a punch in the gut.

"Would you like to have dinner with me? I want to go out. With you. Or stay in. I don't know how you date, but I'm flexible. I want to be with you, Kendrick." Her voice caught and went quiet. "I didn't like not being with you."

"Eve." I pulled my hand away and tried looking anywhere else, as if that would help, as if I couldn't feel the bright pulse of her intent shimmering behind my own ribcage. I wanted to say yes. My body was screaming at me to say yes. To ask her where and when and tell her how much I wanted it, too, that I'd been miserable while she was gone. That she was the best part of my day, the calm at the center of my entire stormy, complicated existence.

And I didn't know how to do any of it.

"What?" I could feel the debate brewing, her list of counterpoints at the ready.

"I don't date. It's not really . . . possible."

"We don't have to go to a restaurant—"

"It's not about being in public." I turned back, drawn like a moth to the light of those blue, questioning eyes and choking on the truth I had to finally—after months of fantasizing and denial—admit out loud for both of us to hear. "It won't work."

"How do you know? We've already established you're a pretty half-assed psychic." Her mouth tipped up at one corner. "And you don't have precognition. You can't see the future."

I didn't have to see the future to know how this would play out. My haunted visions, dreams that woke me screaming in the middle of the night, a constantly medicated, barely-hanging-on existence at the fringes of every situation, wasn't the kind of life I could invite someone into. Eve was brilliant, at the top of her field, rightfully in the center of every room, and beyond all that she was still recovering from her last relationship to an asshole who'd gotten himself—and her, almost—killed. It had been two years since her husband's murder, but you don't bounce back from a marriage like that and never with someone like me.

"I can't be what you deserve."

Her eyes narrowed as she processed that. The longing I'd sensed in her solidified into something more familiar, a silky and immutable determination. Holding my gaze, she leaned over the console until we were a foot apart and every fleck of her irises came into focus. Her heart thudded and mine picked up, matching her beat. Every good intention flew out of my head until all that was left was her—the smell of her, the pulse at her throat, the heat of her skin, and that shining whirr of her mind, ten paces ahead.

"Merit is an arbitrary, problematic concept. Completely untestable. I'm disregarding it because this isn't a question of what I do or don't deserve. It's a question of what I want. And I want you, Kendrick." She swallowed and her gaze dropped to my mouth. "Do you want me back?"

All the reasons we shouldn't be together dissolved into white noise. I forgot everything. I forgot my own name. I leaned in, pulled toward her like gravity, as voices murmured from outside the car. Then, out of nowhere, I felt a jolt of satisfied lust.

"What the—" I swung around to see my mark—our client's cheating husband—locked in an aggressive kiss with his sidepiece directly in front of the car, two rows ahead.

I grabbed the camera and snapped a dozen shots as the guy tried to keep his fling from leaving. "Sorry. Max will lose his mind if I miss this."

"It's hard to miss." Eve retreated to her side of the car and waited for me to complete the surveillance. The pictures were paid-on-delivery perfect. Clear shots of both faces, the whole scene in complete, prenup-negating detail before they both drove out of the parking lot.

I transferred the photos to my phone and backed them up on the company cloud, aware that I was stalling now. That Eve wasn't going to forget the question hovering in the air between us.

Do you want me back?

It was inevitable, probably. It had been inevitable since the day we'd skated across a frozen, abandoned world and she told me she believed in me, since I'd held her hand in a dark bathroom while she sobbed, since we'd brought down a building and survived, together. *Entanglement*, she'd called it, and there was never any hope of untangling, not for me.

"I do. Yes." Equal parts elation and terror ballooned in my chest.

Eve and I were officially dating.

Holy shit.

Darcy

The bakery stood in the shadow of downtown, across the street from a parking ramp and a steel and glass high-rise building that looked like condos or a bougie hotel. The old, converted house was tucked between two brick buildings and sat back from the street on a weedy path. I hadn't even seen it at first. It was the smell that drew my attention, wheat and sugar and cinnamon floating in the air, making me pause on the sidewalk. A pink neon sign mounted to the siding read PASTRIES & DREAMS in an oddly familiar font. A few bikes were padlocked to the railing and an open sign in the window turned my feet in the bakery's direction, like my nose had hijacked my body.

I'd slept in my car in a Wal-Mart parking lot on the edge of town and used the bathroom inside the store this morning, changing underwear, brushing my teeth, and working a handful of dry shampoo through my hair before tying it back up in a knot—but I hadn't bought anything to eat. I had snacks and water in the car and even though there was twelve thousand dollars taped under my seat, I wasn't touching that until I reached my destination— wherever that might be.

I'd gotten turned around trying to leave town, though, and ended up in downtown instead of back on the highway. At 7:00 a.m. on a Sunday, the high-rises and commercial buildings and parking garages looked empty and inviting. And I realized, with a slow, unfurling wonder filling my chest, that I didn't have anywhere to be, no schedule to keep, no one tracking my time or decisions. I was free to do anything I wanted. I could say no for any reason or none at all. Every choice was mine and mine alone. I didn't know how long the freedom would last but for this one morning, in a town where no one knew me, it didn't matter. I was unbound.

I parked on a side street and wandered through downtown, passing joggers in sweats and homeless people tucked into corners and sleeping on benches. I followed a squirrel through a cobblestone street, past a playground, and out to the sidewalk where the mouthwatering scent of cinnamon stopped me mid-stride.

Pastries & Dreams. I shouldn't, but before my head could catch up and put a stop to the impulse, I'd already opened the creaky wooden door and stepped into an enclosed porch-turned-dining area. Small bistro tables lined both sides of the room, and two students hunched over steaming cups at the far end of the space.

I moved into the next room lined with bakery cases and a coffee station. No one was behind the counter, but the sound of clattering dishes came from deeper within the house. "Total Eclipse of the Heart" belted on a speaker overhead and a silent TV in the corner played the Colin Firth version of *Pride and Prejudice*, the one Mom and I used to watch while comparing each scene to the book. Mr. Darcy rode a horse across the screen, looking constipated and full of himself, but still pretty hot. I leaned into the nearest bakery case, instantly torn between a maple pecan scone and a giant slice of coffee cake with cinnamon oat crumble piled on top. My stomach growled.

"There are no bad choices."

The voice shot my spine straight and I turned, feeling like I'd been caught doing something wrong. The woman behind the counter wiped down a serving tray and put it away. "I mean in that case there's no bad choices. Outside of it?" She shrugged and winked. "An infinite number."

I swallowed. "Maybe I should just crawl inside and live there."

"I've tried. The headroom is shit. What can I get you?"

The pastry labels didn't have prices on them. Five dollars. I could spend five dollars here, but I wanted coffee, too. "I'm not sure."

"Take your time."

Pulling on gloves, she moved to a sheet of freshly baked cookies and started stacking them in another case. Her bright pink hair swooped over one shoulder in a long, thick braid, with a black silk rose clipped behind her ear. A flour-covered apron was tied over a charcoal wide-necked T-shirt. She wore a silver hoop in one nostril and the kind of winged eyeliner that always smudged and made me look like a natural disaster victim. On her it was impeccable.

A timer went off in the back and she disappeared for a second, giving me time to find the menu board and add up the cost of a small drip and a scone. $6.50 plus tax. The coffee cake was more. I bit my lip and watched Colin Firth ask Jennifer Ehle to dance and murmured the words along to the silent TV as she turned him down cold. "Mr. Darcy is all politeness."

"The best Elizabeth Bennet of all time. I will take no questions on the matter."

"Agreed." I swiveled back to the counter. The baker was setting a tray of muffins topped with chopped walnuts down to cool. "But Matthew Macfadyen is the best Darcy."

"Fuck right out of my store."

I didn't know what surprised me more, that she would throw customers out over fictional men or that she owned this place. She didn't look much older than me.

"He has anxiety. It explains why—"

"It explains why he's not proud, which invalidates the entire premise. You can climb into the case now. You clearly need to make better choices."

Normally I shrank from confrontation, trying to smooth the edges of whatever conflict rose up around me, apologizing, deflecting, agreeing with anything to get out of the situation as soon as possible. But something about this baker, about this place, felt different. Maybe it was the cinnamon, the memories of Sunday mornings baking in the kitchen with Mom while her favorite movies played in the background, her determination to introduce me to Meg Ryan, Julia Roberts, and Audrey Hepburn. Maybe it was the baker's energy, the flour-dusted warmth radiating off her even as she pointed at the bakery case and ordered me to climb inside.

I stepped up to the counter and pulled out my wallet. "You can be proud and anxious at the same time. I'll take a maple scone and a small dark roast."

An hour later, the scone was a core memory and a mess of crumbs on the table. I was on my last sip of coffee, long cold but still biting and delicious. Sunday-morning traffic had picked up considerably. I watched the chaotic influx of university students and hotel guests from across the street, some of them taking orders to go, but most crowding into the tiny porch dining room and snatching up a table as soon as it was available. A couple holding to-go cups and a newspaper pretended not to stare at my empty plate as they loitered by the entrance. I sipped the last dregs from the empty mug, cradling it in my hands, and watched the kitchen until they gave up and left.

I should've let them have my table, but the view was fascinating. I didn't have a phone to scroll or a book to read or a class to study for, and without anything distracting me, I'd spent the entire hour immersed in the bakery and the woman behind the counter.

She didn't have any help, which she mentioned to a few customers who commented on the wait time for their breakfast sandwiches. "My morning person had a medical issue, so it's all me until I can hire someone new. You looking for a job?"

Her smile was quick and sharp and her tone shut down any further bitching before it started.

It was amazing, actually, how well she handled everything on her own, pivoting from the coffee station to the bakery cases to the kitchen with two or three items in her hands at all times, constantly moving and bending and reaching like some complicated dance in time with the opening and closing of the front door.

A group of eight students came in, girls in black and gold sweats with bleary faces, all talking over each other and crowding up to the counter. I couldn't pretend to drink my empty coffee anymore. Reluctantly I got up and skirted the group as I looked for the tub to leave my dirty dishes.

I didn't know where to go after this. I had to find my car, get back on the freeway, and pick a direction. It made sense to keep going west. Mentally, I traced a route on the map, saw mountains rising up to greet me on the horizon, and beyond them, an ocean. Would I stay there? How far did I need to go before it was safe to stop driving?

I almost missed the dish tub because it was completely buried under dirty dishes. There was no room in the tub or the cramped counter space around it to fit anything without playing a dangerous game of Tetris. I glanced at the woman behind the counter, who was still smiling and answering questions but clearly outnumbered by the swarm of students texting, taking pictures of the bakery cases, and debating cold press vs. drip.

"Just leave it anywhere," the woman called to me, but the group of girls blocked her view of the tub. She couldn't see how full it was.

An industrial-size sink was barely visible through a doorway to the kitchen. Before I realized what I was doing, I'd moved around the counter and brought my dishes into the kitchen. The sink was already half-full of pans, but there was room for my small plate and mug.

I ducked back out, but the baker hadn't seemed to notice me. She was ringing up an order. On an impulse, I grabbed the tub and hauled the whole thing back to the kitchen, stacking the dishes neatly in the sink.

I was on my way back to the front when my surroundings hit me. The kitchen was gorgeous in a completely different way from the rest of the converted house. It looked like multiple old rooms had been combined and gutted, making way for a bright and airy space. A massive butcher-block work surface took up the middle of the room, while the walls were lined with commercial fridges, stacked ovens, and two giant stainless-steel mixers. A mini greenhouse stretched in front of a bay window, housing pots of rosemary, mint, chive, and peppers. Jalapeño, it looked like. I took a step closer.

"Uh, hi?"

I whirled around as the baker popped an egg soufflé in the microwave and set a croissant on the butcher block, slicing it neatly in half. The front room had somehow gotten even louder.

"You said to leave the dishes anywhere." But I still felt a flush of heat in my chest and cheeks as I realized I'd violated her business's private space. I wasn't supposed to be here. I shrank away, feeling myself getting smaller, moving into a crash position my body knew like breathing.

"You emptied the dirties?" She glanced from the sink to the tub, which I'd lifted in front of me like a shield. The microwave beeped and she added the egg on top of the lettuce, tomato, and cheese she'd piled on the croissant, barely looking at the food as she did it. Her gaze was somehow cutting and exhausted at the same time.

"I'm sorry. It just looked like—"

"A hundred dollars." She snapped the gloves off and picked up the plate.

"What?"

"I'll give you a hundred dollars if you stay and wash them."

"I—" But she was already gone, disappearing back to the counter and the endless line of customers.

I stood frozen in the kitchen, unsure what had just happened. I should go. The sun was up and I was wasting daylight in a town whose name I couldn't actually remember. But I knew I was still in the Midwest, which wasn't far enough. I needed those mountains at my back. I should find wherever I parked my car and hit the highway, follow the map until it ended, until I was somewhere uncharted and new. A place where they couldn't find me.

I knew all that and still I couldn't make myself leave this room. It was more beautiful than any kitchen I'd been in, with the light flooding in from the window, the thriving plants lining the greenhouse, the smell of sugar and coffee swirling in the air. Like a dream I'd had but couldn't quite remember. I wanted to live right here, in the space where the sunbeams met the butcher block and made it glow.

I took the tub back to the counter, where the line of customers was now out the door, and started collecting the rest of the dirty dishes.

Three hours later, the Sunday-morning rush finally died down into a quiet hum of students studying and scrolling to The Cure's "Just Like Heaven." I'd run the dishwasher twice and washed every pan by hand, drying and stacking them neatly into organizers in the cabinets, and then wiped down the surfaces that were coated in a fine dusting of flour. I was figuring out how to get the mixer attachment and bowl off one of the giant mixers when the baker appeared with a handful of twenties. "Thank you."

As soon as I took the bills, she sagged against the refrigerator, like the money had been the last thing holding her upright. Pressing the heels of her hands to her temples, she rolled her neck out and groaned. "Cancer."

Was she asking about my sign? I pocketed the money, abandoning the mixer since apparently my shift was over.

"My morning help came down with a nasty case of ovarian cancer." She opened her eyes, staring sightlessly through the bay window into the trees in the backyard. "It was so sudden. One day she was hauling trays and complaining about her cable company, and the next . . . they're giving her four months max. Your whole life gone in a blink. Can you imagine?"

"Yeah."

She turned, scanning me with a piercing gaze. I looked away. "Well, thanks. I gotta go."

"Can you bake?"

I stopped mid-exit, but didn't dare turn around to face her. She was offering me a job. I could feel it and a huge part of me leapt at the idea of being in this gorgeous space every morning, spending my days creating edible magic. But I couldn't. Could I?

"I don't live here. I was just passing through."

"To where?"

I shook my head.

"Listen, the kitchen looks amazing. Better than it has in months. I can't find anyone in this entire city who wants to start work at 4:00 a.m., and my mental health literally cannot take any more of this. I dreamed I was drowning in a vat of flour last night and when I woke up it didn't feel any different, you know? I love this place, but it's swallowing me whole. I don't know what to do."

"Eat the whale."

The words slipped out before I even knew I was speaking. The baker frowned at me, looking confused, until the front door opened. She groaned and pushed herself off the refrigerator. "If you're still in town tomorrow, you know where you can make some money, okay?"

I nodded. My heart was pounding, like I'd just given myself away.

She paused at the doorway. "I'm Blake."

Panic crawled up my chest as I realized she was waiting for me to tell her my name. I swallowed and looked past her at the TV.

Say something. Say anything except your actual name. The silence drew out uncomfortably long, until the customer at the counter started talking, drawing Blake's attention.

I headed for the back door and threw a weird wave over my shoulder.

"Darcy."

Max

"Max. No."

Twenty thousand dollars sat on the desk between us. I'd counted it.

I'd texted Jonah to stop into the office after his assignment. By the time he got here it was after ten o'clock and the other businesses in the strip mall had closed up shop ages ago.

Jonah paced the same track Charlie Ashlock had worn into the floor earlier tonight. His hair fell into his face as he shook his head at things I couldn't see. "You said you weren't going to pull this shit again."

"I know, but we need more paying clients."

"This case sounds like a needle in a haystack."

He didn't know the half of it. I'd given him the basics, but I was still easing him past the fact that I'd broken business Rule #3, mostly by pointing at the big pile of cash.

"We've got the time. You said you got enough footage for the Jensen case."

"Yeah." He pulled a hand through his hair, still pacing. He seemed edgier than he normally did after fieldwork. Which was probably my fault.

"Great. I'll call her on Monday and wrap that one up. And you haven't had any dreams lately."

He didn't disagree and I was doing everything I could to keep my energy light and positive. Jonah picked up a lot from the people nearest to him. In the last twenty years I'd become the poster boy for Good Vibes Only, at least when I needed to.

"What about Nicole?" Jonah asked.

"She's completely happy." Nicole Short was the HR manager of ACT, one of the biggest employers in Iowa City. They administered standardized tests to assess high school students' readiness for college. My wife, Shelley, knew Nicole from book club and had spent countless unpaid hours talking up the agency to her. Six months ago Nicole hired us to perform a background and due diligence check on a single new hire. It was a test, obviously. We killed it, bending over backward to deliver everything she asked for and then some. Nicole was thrilled and ACT quickly became our steadiest income stream. "I had coffee with her the other day. She said they might be on a brief hiring freeze soon. So we'll have even more time for this case."

Jonah grunted. "And you panicked and grabbed for the first shady stack of cash you could find."

"Technically it found us, not the other way around." I scooped up said stack and locked it in our safe. "Let's talk over beer."

Jonah and I spent happy hour in one of two locations: his deck overlooking the Mississippi on the eastern edge of the state, or my backyard fire pit. Since my suburban Coralville neighborhood was five minutes from the office, we generally ended up at my place.

When we got there, Jonah grabbed beers from the garage fridge and headed out back. I stopped inside first. Garrett was already asleep, his lanky fourteen-year-old limbs hanging off his twin bed and every light in the room turned on. I switched off lamps, screens, and devices before heading to our bedroom, where Shelley was rubbing lotion on her legs and reading a book.

I leaned in to kiss her. "He barely fits on that bed anymore."

She made a noise of agreement. "I saw a full-size frame on Facebook Marketplace the other day. Just needed some paint."

"And a mattress."

"Which would be three hundred dollars, delivered, but I'm waiting for an end-of-season sale." She smiled at me. "How did the new client meeting go?"

Nightly check-in time. Before I left the force, things were rough. It was early-pandemic. I'd been investigating a case that spiraled out of control and almost got me killed in the process. Again. Shelley had reached her limit with me and I got it. I didn't just need a new start in my career. Our marriage needed it, too. So, for the past year and a half, we'd been seeing a therapist on Zoom and this was one of her suggestions. Checking in with each other every night. Taking time to share what was important. Being honest. And honestly? I sucked at it.

"The meeting was interesting. Jonah's out back. We're going to talk it over."

"So you took the client without asking him."

I sighed. Calling me on my bullshit was one of my wife's superpowers.

"He gave us twenty thousand dollars, Shel."

Shelley whistled. "Damn. Good call."

"But it's complicated."

"You'll figure it out." She rubbed my arm. "And Garrett needs a new bed."

Shelley's day at school was fine. She showed me a picture of one of her student's final exams with the D+ circled and a comment underneath that read: *I studied this time so I think I should get at least a B.*

Points for effort. That was the question all around today.

I headed out back where Jonah already had a fire going. It was probably unnecessary in early June, where the days were breezy and already edging toward hot, but I preferred a fire to the glare of the porch light any day. Garrett's baseball equipment had been tossed in a heap on the grass, nearly squashing Shelley's lilies. Behind the snaps and pops of the fire, frogs called to each other in the distance. Spring was giving way to summer in Iowa.

"Shelley says hi."

Jonah tipped his beer in reply and added another log to the fire. I dropped into an Adirondack chair and cracked open the can sitting on its arm.

"Hear me out on this."

"I heard the pitch already." Jonah sat down across from me. "It's your turn to listen."

I nodded.

"We're partners in this. We've always been partners. But you're trying to pull seventy percent of the weight. You pay the bills and send the invoices and file the taxes. You meet with the clients. You do all the talking. And I know you're doing it because you think I can't."

"I don't think you can't."

"Shut up. I'm still talking."

I nodded again and he stared at the fire. It took a lot of will-power not to point out or think too hard about his lack of talking. He shook his head, having conversations I couldn't hear, and shoved the hair out of his face before leaning forward.

"I knew you would do this, Max. I knew going in that it would be like this. And I was fine with it for a while, because you're better at all this stuff. You're better at life than I am."

"It helps to have a really thick skull," I cut in.

"I want to change. I want this to be a real partnership. Fifty-fifty all the way. I don't know if I can do that, but I need to try. To find out if it's possible."

"I shouldn't have taken the client without talking to you."

"No, you fucking shouldn't have."

"Fifty-fifty." I toasted him across the flames, trying to project confidence with absolutely no idea what an equal partnership with Jonah would look like. I took on everything I could carry, in every situation. It's how I was built. Nightly check-ins and compromises and handing responsibility off to someone who could barely shoul-der the load he already carried went against my entire identity. We'd never talked about the work we each did for the business before, but I'd known Jonah long enough to know he'd been thinking about it for a while. That it bothered him. And he wouldn't have brought it up if he didn't need things to change.

So, all right, we were going to try. Fifty-fifty, whatever that meant.

Jonah slumped back in the chair, like the speech had cost all his energy, and took a long drink. "So we don't know her name. Sounds like one of our cases."

It really did. Usually, when Jonah dreamed about someone, we picked as many details as possible out of his head and compared them to active missing persons reports. Once we had a match, all the legal and demographic information came with it. The person's background—their life up to that point—was there for us to use. We didn't have any of that with Charlie Ashlock's girlfriend.

"He never knew her last name. Asked her once, and she said it wasn't important. Her first name—he's pretty sure—is Kate."

Jonah groaned. "Bills. Credit cards. Driver's license. He never saw any of that?"

"Nope. And she paid for everything in cash."

Jonah took a swig of beer. "They have that in common."

"She was flying way under the radar. She'd only been in town a few months according to him, rented a room in Iowa City, started dating him, and then vanished."

"What makes him sure about the name?"

"She went somewhere a few weeks ago. Gone the whole day, which was out of her routine. Apparently most days she either worked or spent with him. Didn't tell him where she was going. When she came back, he noticed a box of Milk Duds in her bag. It had a heart drawn on it with the word Kate inside the heart."

Jonah drained his beer and chucked the can onto the grass. "Our source is stale caramel?"

"He said she kept the box for a few days, even though it was empty. Unlike her to keep trash around."

"Does he still have anything of hers?"

"Unclear."

Jonah nodded, staring at the flames. "Then we make a house call."

Jonah

Charlie Ashlock's house was about what you'd expect from a thirty-something single guy on a hobby farm in central Iowa. The drive-way was dirt and potholes, the lawn overgrown, and the side of the house looked like a landfill specializing in broken lawn furniture. I parked my Lancer Evolution, a bright blue rally spec car with racing harnesses and a rear fin, next to Charlie's rusted Chevy pickup and killed the engine.

A row of pines created a windbreak from the road, and a few outbuildings were scattered behind the garage. None looked in use. I didn't see any animals or farm equipment, no obnoxious ATV collection or any other reason he'd be living out here by himself. It was a half hour from Iowa City. The only signs of life for the last ten miles were an animal sanctuary and a cluster of wind turbines on the horizon.

"Pretty isolated." Max echoed my thoughts.

The cloud of dust the Evolution had kicked up was still settling as we walked across the weedy yard to the house.

"You okay?" Max asked.

"Fifty-fifty, remember?"

"I know. You just seemed out of it on the way here." Max knocked on the door and stood back. "A dream?"

Hardly. I'd barely slept last night. Normally, living Max's insomniac life would be a reprieve. No terror or pain leaking into my mind from the lost people of the world, their silent, displaced screams shaking me awake without knowing who or where I was. I wouldn't have to spend the morning huddled over my recorded sleep talking, sweating and nauseous as I hunted for clues to bring the lost people back. To find them.

Instead, I'd spent most of last night tossing and turning in bed, wrecking the sheets before giving up and pacing the house in the dark.

Because Eve and I were dating.

Eve wanted to date *me*.

The rotting drainpipes, the people I couldn't save, they all sat on the sidelines eating popcorn while the idea of the two of us together, for real, made my brain explode. I couldn't sit still, couldn't focus. I'd spent more than two years telling myself we were just friends, that she felt close to me because of all we'd been through together, and there was no chance in any reality that someone like Eve would want someone like me. Yet somehow she did.

I barely noticed the road on the way here, let alone Max. I pictured her sleeping off the jet lag and wondered how soon I could text her this morning, what the rules were, and what I could say without scaring her off before we'd even started.

There was no getting into any of that now, because Charlie Ashlock opened the door to his house looking like shit and feeling—from the punch of nerves and misery—a hundred times worse. I could relate.

He invited us in and Max took the lead, introducing me and explaining we were looking for any clues to Kate's actual identity.

"I told you she didn't keep much stuff here." He ran a hand over his beard and pointed somewhere toward the back of the house. "I mean, you can look around, but you should check her place in Iowa City."

"We will," I said, moving through the living room, careful not to touch anything. "But this was the last place she was seen." The last place any traces of her energy might still be lingering.

Charlie gave us a tour of the house, which didn't take long. Two bedrooms, a bathroom, a living room, and an eat-in kitchen straight out of the seventies. There was garbage everywhere. Beer cans, snack wrappers, piles of clothes, a TV remote in the toothbrush cup in the bathroom. Charlie Ashlock wasn't fine.

The tour ended in the main bedroom, where a mangle of blankets and pillows reminded me of my own barely-slept-in bed.

"Is any of this hers?" I nodded at the closets and Charlie brought over a small, gray duffel bag.

"This is her overnight bag."

I braced myself. Objects carried impressions of the people who collected them. Not always, and not usually in any helpful way when it came to finding people, but Max liked to be thorough. He wanted as much information as possible, claiming you never knew what could be important.

Kate's duffel bag had a dull hum, a well-used and comfortably faded feeling. She'd owned it a while. A pair of jeans with fifty dollars in the pocket and a few shirts were tossed inside, unfolded. A toiletries bag held the basics—toothbrush, lotion, some mascara, and an almost-empty lip gloss. She liked the lip gloss. The feeling struck me as I unscrewed the cap and held up the applicator. It was brighter than she'd worn before. A happy pink. Maybe she could be brighter here, too.

"What is it?"

I started, realizing Charlie and Max were both watching me stare at the lip gloss. I stuffed it away. "She never left this bag behind before, did she?"

"No. She always took it with her when she went back to the city."

Charlie's anxiety spiked. The walls of the bedroom started closing in around me, making it hard to breathe. Max immediately took over and suggested looking around outside. Charlie followed us to the door, but got even more panicky in the front yard.

"Which way did she run?" I leaned against the trunk of a giant oak tree and pretended to be interested in the road, trying to untangle myself from Charlie's erratic stabs of panic and paranoia.

"I don't know. I mean, she usually went by herself before I woke up."

"Did you ever take walks together?"

"Yeah, a few times."

Max sent him inside to get his phone so he could show us their walking route on a map. Then he leaned on the other side of the trunk. "You holding up?"

"He's falling apart. He doesn't want us here."

Max watched Charlie disappear into the house, giving him a cop's once-over that looked for weapons and weaknesses. "I'm not getting the desperate lover vibe either. He was different last night."

"He's hiding something."

"Related to Kate?"

"I can't tell."

"What did you get from the bag?"

I glanced at Max. He already knew the answer, but he needed to hear the confirmation out loud.

"She wouldn't have left without it."

Charlie showed us the route he'd walked with Kate, a circuit that started on the road and cut through two fields and along a few other properties. It looked about two miles, a decent jog for someone who didn't know the area well.

"And you didn't hear her leave that morning?"

"No." He shoved his phone away, turning to the driveway and the cars parked there as if for help. "But I sleep pretty hard."

"What makes you think she went for a run before she left that morning?"

"Her running clothes were gone, and the shoes she ran in. Everything else is still here."

I pictured it. The sweaty woman returning to the yard. Going straight to her car instead of the house. Not showering. Not grabbing her overnight bag, her money, or her favorite lip gloss.

"Wouldn't she have come into the house to get her keys?"

He shook his head. "She always kept her keys with her. She had pepper spray on them, and an airhorn."

"She needed that out here?" Max glanced around the horizon, clocking the total absence of threats. "Were there any problems with neighbors? Anyone she didn't feel comfortable with?"

"She didn't know anyone here. Except—" Charlie's energy stuttered with a sudden memory.

"Except who?"

"No one." Charlie dodged, avoiding eye contact.

There were three houses along the route, tops. It wouldn't be hard to talk to everyone who might have seen her that day, and find out whether she'd had contact with any of them. I flashed a glance at Max, letting him know I was on it, and he nodded before shifting tactics.

"Where do you think Kate would go, if she decided to leave?"

Charlie answer was immediate, the most confident thing he'd said all morning. "Somewhere open."

"Open?"

"She needed big spaces. Fresh air, sunlight. She always hovered near the door in any room. When she stayed over, she had to sleep with all the windows open and the shades up in the bedroom every night. Even if it was pouring rain or cold as hell. One time—" He cut off, panic rising as he choked on whatever memory had bubbled up.

Max's attention sharpened, but his face remained cop-placid as he switched topics again. "Did she ever talk about other towns she'd been or places she wanted to visit?"

Charlie shook his head. "It was only ever today. Not the past. Not the future. Just *now*." He backed away from us, stumbling over exposed tree roots into the sunlight beyond the shade of the branches. I could feel his heart pounding, the heat of light baking his clammy face. He felt sick, and an answering wave of bile swelled in my stomach.

"She told me, right at the beginning, that it wouldn't work. That she couldn't commit to a long-term relationship." The wind whispered in the oak leaves above me, daring me to look at the sky. I slumped against the trunk a little more, losing purchase in the bare dirt. Charlie swallowed and looked right through me, his eyes distilled into bleak shadows in his head.

"She never got it. I could never make her understand. I wasn't picking out wedding rings or planning our future. All I wanted was her."

"Well, this just got a lot more complicated." Max finished jotting notes as we hit the highway and I dropped it to ninety, cutting off a freight truck and darting into the left lane. Speed was a balm. It washed out my head, obliterating the thoughts and emotions that seeped in and swamped me, emptying it of everything except adrenaline and asphalt. I swerved around a Dodge Ram to open road, not a car in sight ahead of us, and edged toward a hundred.

Max flipped his notebook closed. "The way he tells it, she was half out the door their entire relationship. It makes sense that she would leave without any good-bye."

"Not without her bag."

Max grunted, oblivious to the landscape blurring around us. "But she did. Her car is gone and she left the bag behind."

After another mile I eased back on the gas. My heart rate evened out and the nausea in my gut receded. I could breathe again.

"Better?" Max asked.

I nodded. "Let's go through scenarios."

Fifty-fifty. I was holding up my end.

The first, most obvious, option was that Kate had left. She'd gotten tired of *nows* with Charlie and headed for the next town to live her cash-only existence under a brand-new pseudonym. And for whatever reason, she'd left some things behind.

The second option was that she hadn't left voluntarily. Someone or something had scared her into leaving, and she hadn't had the time or opportunity to take her things with her.

The third option, Max pointed out, was that she hadn't left at all.

"You think Charlie could've killed her?" I asked.

"Yesterday I would've said no, but today? He didn't want us on that property. I've never seen anyone sweat that much outside an interrogation room."

"Why hire us then? Why drop twenty grand on a PI if he killed his girlfriend and ditched her car to make it look like she split?"

"Maybe he wants to seem like he's trying to find her. To create a narrative."

"For who?"

"Law enforcement, if a case gets opened or a body turns up."

"Go to that much trouble and forget to get rid of her possessions? It doesn't add up, Max."

"There was something off when he talked about her. Did you notice the past tense? 'All I wanted was her.' Like he knows she doesn't exist anymore."

People thought I was the dark one, with my horror show dreams and antisocial personality. They never noticed that under his Joe Protector facade, Max Summerlin was always calculating the odds of someone stabbing their grandmother.

I focused on the farm behind us. Now that I had some distance, I could let Charlie's energy back in and sift through it for clues.

"He's a mess. Emotional chaos. Panic, fear, but genuine grief, too. He's broken without her."

"Could be regret over what he did."

"You're one sunshiny motherfucker, you know that?"

"Yeah, yeah. But after today?" Max made another note. "Charlie Ashlock is officially on the suspect list."

Darcy

"'Every now and then I get a little bit lonely and you're never coming round.'"

"Turn around." I nudged Blake out of the way to get to the ovens and popped in a tray of honey scones. She didn't miss a beat.

"'Every now and then I get a little bit tired.'"

"'Of listening to the sound of my tears.'" I chimed in, closing the oven.

Blake sang into a clean whisk, her pink braid tucked in front of one shoulder, a Molly Ringwald T-shirt hanging off the other. Her hands were dusted white with flour, which flew off her in clouds as she slunk around the butcher block. After two weeks of working at Pastries & Dreams, I had "Total Eclipse of the Heart"—Blake's favorite song—completely memorized. It always cycled to the top of our playlist, and if she was tired or depressed or on her period she would cue it up as the first song of the day, a 4:00 a.m. power ballad that vibrated the entire kitchen and the two of us in it.

I hadn't meant to come back after that first morning. I really hadn't.

It was the car's fault. I couldn't remember where I'd parked and ended up walking the streets for over an hour while Blake's offer swirled in the back of my head. *If you're still in town tomorrow, you know where you can make some money.*

I didn't need money immediately, but what I had wouldn't last forever. Jobs became tricky when they asked for things like name, birthdate, and social security number. Information that would get entered into databases and could be used to find me. I couldn't risk that. And despite all the times it would've been useful in my life so far, I didn't know how to create an identity from scratch. So I needed to work under the table. Agricultural labor was an option, the kind of jobs undocumented workers filled. I didn't mind the idea of open fields and coworkers who spoke different languages. Fewer questions that way. But Blake had stood in her gorgeous kitchen and handed me a hundred dollars, cash, without any paperwork. I didn't have to fill out a single form. I didn't even have to tell her my real name.

By the time I found my car, I'd decided to stick around town for a day or two. I parked in the Wal-Mart lot again to sleep that night and bought a bag of trail mix to feel better about brushing my teeth in their bathroom. Blake was so happy to see me the next day that she hugged me, right on the back step at four in the morning, mumbling—"This is intrusive. I'm sorry."—even as she hung on. I laughed, caught between returning the hug or pulling away, until she drew back and said, "I'm in a cinnamon roll mood now. Let's make some obnoxiously giant cinnamon rolls."

We made cinnamon rolls and scones and cookies and bars. We made lemon zucchini bread and cheddar jalapeño rolls. Every day,

I told myself I would only come back tomorrow. Just one more day and then I'd hit the road. But the longer I stayed in Blake's kitchen, baking the air into sweetness and singing the sun up every morning, the more real Pastries & Dreams felt and the more distant the idea of the road became. The shadows I'd craved on the edges of the map faded into an abstract future. They would always be there, waiting for me whenever I needed them. And there was no reason for anyone to look for me here, minding the mixers and ovens in a tiny café somewhere in the Midwest.

Almost instantly, Blake became another reason to stay. I'd never had many close friends. We moved around a lot when I was young, and then—when we found a place that seemed more permanent—sleepovers and parties were forbidden. I never lived in the dorms in college, where most undergrads found their crew. I hovered on the edges of any classroom or gathering, gravitating toward the exits even then. Blake wasn't like anyone I'd met before. She was obsessed with cooking shows and the eighties, calling the entire decade her origin story slash spirit animal. She loved the movies, the music, and the whole over-the-top cultural vibe. She talked constantly while we worked, but not in an exhausting way, and the questions she asked never got too personal. On my third day at the café, she demanded I rank my top five John Hughes characters to "see if we're compatible coworkers." I had to think about it for a half hour before deciding:

5. John Bender from *The Breakfast Club* (hot and rebellious)
4. Ferris Bueller from *Ferris Bueller's Day Off* (hot and daring)
3. Jake Ryan from *Sixteen Candles* (hot and sweet, except for the sex trafficking)

2. Allison Reynolds from *The Breakfast Club* (hot and trying not to give a shit)

1. Watts from *Some Kind of Wonderful* (hot and actually not giving a shit)

Blake listened to my entire list and reasoning without making a single comment. When I finished, she took a moment to digest with a level of seriousness that would have made more sense in an existential debate, and said, "Okay, I like where your head's at, but you're wrong for a few reasons."

"How can I be wrong about my own preferences?"

"First, my girl Molly doesn't show up anywhere and you have to be either Team Claire or Team Sam. Second, Watts is an incredible character but John Hughes didn't direct *Some Kind of Wonderful*. It was Howard Deutch, aka Nuanced John Hughes, which also disqualifies Duckie from *Pretty in Pink*."

"I forgot about Duckie."

"I'm going to pretend you didn't say that."

After picking Team Sam—because who could pick spoiled Claire over Sam?—Blake allowed me to stay. And when I made her rank her all-time favorite rom-coms, she correctly included *My Big Fat Greek Wedding* even though it came out in 2002.

Every day after the lunch rush, she handed me another wad of twenties and told me to come back tomorrow. And I did. I explored the town in the afternoons and spent the nights in my car at Wal-Mart. Luckily, on one of my walks I stumbled across a student ID someone had lost by the river and used it to get into the university gym. I'd been showering at the gym ever since, reading discarded paperbacks at the laundromat, and running anonymous searches of news headlines at the library. There was nothing about a missing person, the discovery of a body, or a homicide investigation. The lack of news bought me one more day in Blake's kitchen.

"Where are you staying?" Blake asked when "Total Eclipse of the Heart" was over. My heart started pounding, even though I didn't have anything to hide. I wasn't homeless. My home just happened to be my car. I focused all my attention on the pan of cookies in front of me and said, "South of here."

That was the truth. Wal-Mart was on the south side of town.

Blake shrugged and started singing the chorus of the next song. Sweet dreams are made of these. The subject was over until the end of the lunch rush, when her part-time worker showed up and Blake asked me to come upstairs.

"I live above the store," she explained as we walked up a narrow, dark flight of stairs that made me instantly anxious. It opened to a bright, four-room apartment washed in whites and neons and I breathed a little easier seeing the living room had a sliding glass door that opened to a rickety wooden deck. Two ways out meant I couldn't be trapped, at least not by one person.

Blake opened a door to a room that held a stripped bed, a dresser, and sad-looking twinkle lights half hanging from one wall.

"I sometimes rent this room out, until my last roommate took off with half my jewelry, including my mother's engagement ring."

"Oh god. I'm sorry."

She waved off my sympathies, shrugging her pink braid behind her shoulder. "If you wanted to stick around town, on a semipermanent basis, you could stay here."

For a second I could see it so clearly—cooking dinners together, watching all the movies we could possibly consume, both of us in bed before sundown and waking each other to drag our butts downstairs by four o'clock—and I wanted it. I wanted to be Blake's roommate, to be her friend. I wanted to deserve a friend like her.

"How do you know I won't run off with the rest of your jewelry?"

She laughed, sizing me up, and I saw my own reflection in her eyes. Dishwater blond hair. Pale, sun-starved skin. Forgettable Target clothes. Downcast gaze. No one to worry about, or even remember. No one who would be missed.

"You're not a thief," she told me, leaning against the back of the bright pink couch.

No, I wasn't. I was something else.

"We can knock the rent off your paycheck," she said.

My heart rate immediately kicked up again. The vision I'd had of living here shriveled back into the shadows. "I don't do paperwork. I can't . . . work for you. Not officially." Out of nowhere, tears sprung into my eyes and I walked to the sliding glass door trying not to let her see. It was ridiculous—I'd only known Blake a few weeks. But then again, she was the only person I knew. The only companion in my once again uncharted world. I tried to shrug off the thought. "I should probably move on, anyway. I didn't mean to stay so long."

"Darcy."

I made a questioning noise, hoping it sounded casual and not like my heart was breaking. *Every now and then I get a little bit lonely.* Fucking Bonnie Tyler. I'd never be able to listen to that song again.

Blake stepped up next to me. "I don't know what your plans are or where you need to go. But if paperwork is the only issue, we

can get around that. It wouldn't be the first lie I told my accoun-
tant." A gleam lit her eyes, making her winged eyeliner pop. "We
all have secrets."

Something good sparked in the air between us, an unspoken
agreement to not look too closely at the secrets we both needed to
keep.

So I stayed.

Or, Darcy did.

Max

"Secrets will kill a relationship."

The woman pushed the photos back across the table and I tucked them into a folder that held a flash drive, our final invoice, and a comprehensive report on her husband's infidelity. The pictures Jonah had taken of the guy at the hotel turned out perfectly. Full face, easily identifiable. Thanks to his complete idiocy it was some of the easiest money we'd made yet. Or at least the easiest we'd worked for.

"He doesn't have as many secrets now."

The woman signaled the waiter and ordered a complicated coffee that might or might not have had alcohol in it. She'd never met me at the office, preferring to conduct our check-ins at various five-star restaurants around town. Today she wore a crisp, pale pantsuit and oversized sunglasses that surveyed the restaurant's flowery patio.

"If you need any continuing assistance, we offer asset identification services, too."

She waved a manicured hand. "I handle all our finances. He doesn't own a dollar I don't know about."

"I'm sorry he's put you in this situation."

The waiter set a mug in front of her and she stared at the froth swirled into a flower design. This place loved flowers. The folder with its incriminating photos sat next to it, closed. "Are you married, Mr. Summerlin?"

"Yes."

"It's funny, isn't it? You can't remember how anything started. It all becomes a series of moments, petty grievances and stupid fights, silence that lasts for days, until you don't know who stopped talking first. Who turned away quicker. And you stop recognizing yourself. You don't know where the coldness has come from, and the words coming out of your mouth don't sound like yours. You slip further and further inside yourself, like a voyeur to a life you can't stop from happening. Until it's too late to change it."

Tears slipped underneath the sunglasses. She didn't touch the coffee, didn't lift her head. I awkwardly offered her a napkin, wishing I'd ended this meeting five minutes ago.

"You changed it now. You're changing your own life, finding a new way forward." I hoped it sounded like something our therapist would say. This wasn't my territory. Jonah was the one who understood feelings, who could see beneath the surface of things.

She ignored the offered napkin and downed her coffee like a shot before pulling out a checkbook. "Do you keep secrets from your partner, Mr. Summerlin?"

I fumbled, unsure how to respond. With a flourish, she ripped the check out and pushed it across the table. The zeros at the end of the number distracted me from the conversation at hand.

"Of course you do. We all do. But trust me, they're going to find out eventually. It's up to you how they do. And that's the key. That's how they'll know what to do about your secrets."

* * *

The client's parting words stayed with me all afternoon as I typed variations of 'Kate' into the Tracers database. Catherine. Kathryn. Katrina. Katie. Katelyn. Assuming it even was her first name. Could we trust the source? A name scrawled on a Milk Duds box wasn't the least reliable piece of information I'd ever worked off of, but it was damn close.

The missing woman never told Charlie her name was Kate. She hadn't given up that secret. But when he found it on a box of candy he'd immediately recognized it as truth. Would he have felt the same way if the information came from her? Would she have stayed with him, if she could've trusted him with her identity?

Jonah worked on the other side of the room, depositing the client's check and going through our monthly expenses looking like someone was forcing warm keg beer down his throat.

"Kathleen?" he suggested. I typed it in. Zero hits.

"Maybe we need to widen the geographical area." I expanded the search area and dates. We'd decided not to start looking for where she'd gone, but where she'd come from, tracing her movements backward to find her actual identity. There was also a stronger possibility that a missing person's case had been opened in her hometown, and although we'd promised not to involve the police in our investigation, we had no problem pulling as much information from them as we could.

Her license plates were from Illinois, according to Charlie, although he couldn't remember the actual plate number. He thought there might have been a three in it. So helpful. We'd been running under the assumption that she was from Illinois, but maybe she'd just picked up the car there. Her accent, according to Charlie, was as neutral as a native Iowan, which placed her original home somewhere in the lower Midwest. "I'm going to check Indiana. Maybe Ohio. Let's assume she picked up the car on her way west."

"Check Catriona, too."

"You sensed it?"

"No, Google says it's a variation of Kate."

Expanding the search yielded more hits under various names. I eliminated some based on age, others on ethnic identity. By the end of the session, I had two possible Kates who'd disappeared in the last three years and looked enough like the photo Charlie had shown me that I texted their pictures to him. I didn't see a huge resemblance in either one, but wanted to show Charlie we were working, earning the brick of cash I'd deposited at the bank earlier today.

Then I turned my searches on him.

Charlie Ashlock was a much easier target to investigate. A lifelong Iowan, he'd graduated high school in Cedar Rapids, got an associate's degree in computer science, and worked a variety of jobs, never staying anywhere longer than a few years. He'd bought the hobby farm five years ago. A lot of mildly late payments on his credit report, no arrests, no marriages. He had a Facebook page, but the only posts were from his mother tagging him in random memes and old photos of him and his siblings. A bigger kid even then, Charlie hung at the back of the pictures, letting his brother and sister pull faces and absorb the camera's attention. His profile said he was single but it also said he lived in Cedar Rapids, a home at least ten years out of date.

"Still trying to pin her disappearance on him?"

Jonah dropped the paid-in-full invoice on my desk, scanning the social media page over my shoulder.

I pushed away from the desk, rubbing my eyes. "Nothing violent in his past, at least on paper. The guy's a slacker, coasting through life at the fringes."

"Until she showed up. And changed everything."

"Is that what you got from him?"

Jonah looked queasy and started pacing the office. "Yeah." He picked up a mug and set it down without drinking it. "I don't know."

"Jonah."

He kept pacing, avoiding me.

"Did you have a dream last night?"

He shook his head.

"Then what is it?"

"Nothing." He stopped at the storefront window, looking blankly at the curb outside.

"How's Eve?"

He whipped around, shrugging and making an incoherent noise. Bingo. The investigator in me wanted to press on the crack until it broke wide open. Thank god the friend in me had enough decency to get another cup of coffee and wait out the silence. Another tactic, sure, but a friendlier one.

Eventually, he dropped into one of the client chairs and buried his face in his hands. I stirred cream into my coffee and kept my head as blank as possible. It looked like he had enough on his plate already.

"We've decided to start dating. Officially."

"Congrats, man. That's great."

"It is, but I'm freaking out, Max. When have I ever had a girlfriend?"

"Never."

"Exactly. I have no idea how to do this. Where am I supposed to take her? What do we do on a first date? Does it matter? I told her I'd think of something, and everything I think of is the dumbest, worst—like, what, a restaurant? A hike? A picnic? No, I can't take her on a picnic when her dead husband proposed to her on a picnic. What am I even . . . ?"

He shot out of the chair, back to pacing and running his hands through his hair. I hadn't seen Jonah this bothered in—well, ever. Withdrawn, depressed, anxious, suicidal, sure, but never like he was about to implode with frustrated, incoherent energy. It was, frankly, adorable.

He glared, immediately picking up my mood. "Happy I can amuse you."

"Okay, for the record," I tried to keep the smile off my face, "Shelley thinks you've been sleeping together for at least a year."

"I've never even kissed her."

"Why not?" It was obvious to literally everyone who looked at them that they made sense. Opposites attract. Maybe a scientist and a psychic were more opposite than usual, but the principle held up. And Jonah had been gone on her since the day they met.

"Because I'm barely functional. I sleep in bathtubs. I need enough medicine to tranquilize a horse in order to get through a regular day. And beyond that, I can't be in the same room as her without sensing every idea and feeling in her head. I'm a mental stalker. There's no restraining order for that, Max. No consent on either side. If we do this, she'll have no personal life, no boundaries."

"Do you hear me complaining?"

"That's different."

"How?" I pushed back in my chair, sipping coffee. "We've been friends for what, twenty-some years? And we lived together for the first five. The only time it ever got weird with you in my head was when I had a girl over."

"That's why I left the apartment whenever you brought someone home."

"Exactly." I remembered the first time it happened, making out on the couch with some co-ed and startling apart when Jonah stalked out of his bedroom and straight through the front door. The girl didn't understand why I started laughing, got mad when I wouldn't explain it, and left a few minutes later.

"You knew when I needed space and you always gave it to me. You'll do the same for Eve."

He dropped into his chair again, spent. I didn't wonder. The mental gymnastics he'd been doing looked exhausting.

"Look." I set the coffee down and leaned forward. "I'm lucky to have a partner who already knows what I'm thinking. It's a lot less work." My life would be a hell of a lot easier if Shelley could read minds, too. No more communication exercises or nightly check-ins. "Eve's already been in your life for what, two years? She's not an idiot. She knows exactly what she's signing up for."

"Wait." Something occurred to me. "Is this why you wanted to take on more work?"

He sighed and I knew I'd nailed it.

"I thought if I could handle more here . . ." He pulled out the notes I'd taken on Kate's movements and her life in Iowa City, staring at the paper like the missing woman would appear between the scrawled details. "Tomorrow morning I'm going back to Charlie's place. I'll run the route she might've taken on her last morning, see if I can interview any neighbors."

I picked up my coffee and refreshed my search engine. "Good. I'll go to her work and talk to her boss. See if I can dig up anything there."

We dove back into our own rabbit holes for a while. I tried more variations of Kate, checked more years, more states. Nothing popped. It wasn't until we were locking up the office for the day that Jonah asked.

"You honestly think I can do this? That I can be in a relationship?"

I wanted to say yes, to clap him on the back and tell him of course he could. After all, if I'd managed to keep a marriage mostly together for fifteen-plus years, who the hell couldn't? But Jonah had never let a single person into his life further than he'd let me. He'd have to change a lot of things to make room for Eve. And even if he could do that, I still knew better than anyone, his wasn't the easiest life to witness.

The worst part of having a psychic best friend was being unable to bullshit him. Reading all the hesitation in my head, he nodded and went to his car. "I'll check in tomorrow after the farm."

"Jonah."

He shot me a wave and disappeared into his car.

* * *

It haunted me the whole way home.

Could a person ever really change? Could Jonah? Could I?

That was the question, the central problem I'd revolved around for the past year and a half. I stared it in the face in therapy, at the office, at the dinner table, and in bed at night, wondering if it was even possible. Can you rewire a forty-year-old brain? Can you unlearn instincts and habits you've built over a lifetime until they're second nature? I was used to taking charge, being the provider, the authority, the buffer who stood between the people I loved and the world. I knew how to do that. I knew who I was when I did.

This new Max—business owner, private investigator, collaborative partner—felt like someone I was impersonating. Imposter syndrome, the therapist called it. I was fumbling through a performance of my own life.

Could I change?

I was the guy who asked the questions, not the one who had the answers. But I needed this one to be yes. I needed to know this new life could work. I was doing the nightly check-ins with Shelley. And yeah, I'd taken a possibly shady client without talking to Jonah first, but I came clean quick and we were investigating this together, all the way.

I pulled into the driveway with conviction settling in my gut as solidly as last year's leaves clogged dirt and debris into the rain gutters overhead.

If Jonah had the balls to change his life, so did I.

Jonah

Fields met the horizon in every direction. The newly planted corn shimmered in the sun, stalks still young enough that the dark tilled earth was visible between the rows. It was a pattern, hypnotizing us as we jogged along the edge—green, brown, green, brown, with the flawless blue sky arching overhead—a world distilled into color, breath, and pungent earth.

It was beautiful. I wanted to die.

"Jesus." I stumbled, bending in half to brace my hands on my legs. My lungs felt like burning pulp.

Eve ran a few paces ahead, then circled back, grinning. She wasn't even out of breath. The only concession she'd made to this torture was unzipping her running jacket, baring her stomach beneath a shiny sports bra. If I wasn't already dying, her clothing choices could've done the job.

"Don't," I said as she approached. "I don't want to hear about a single study right now." The benefits of running could go fuck themselves.

When I called Eve on my way home last night, I'd just wanted to hear her voice and find out how her day went. She didn't have any more summer classes to teach, and the Australia trip research was winding down. I still hadn't figured out what to do for our official first date. I was debating between dinner on *Joan*—Eve's high-tech weather plane—or ice skating at Coral Ridge. When I mentioned the new case and how I'd be retracing Kate's jogging route this morning, Eve invited herself along. It was an excellent opportunity, she reasoned, to try running as a form of therapy. I agreed and she threw my heart into my throat by saying, "Perfect. It's a date."

Maybe I hadn't pictured dying on our first date, but investigating a missing person felt undeniably on-brand for us.

She slipped into step next to me as we walked to the edge of the field, where a county highway bisected the world. The sky stretched huge and unbroken over us, giving Eve the unobstructed views she always craved, the ability to see what was coming. Hands on her hips, she swiveled in each direction.

"Which way did they go from here?"

"East," I waved, pathetically grateful that it was slightly downhill with the wind at our backs. We were taking the route Charlie had shown us. It started out on the street and cut through two fields to the road we'd come out on now. A mile or so east of here was a creek that wound back to the edge of Charlie's property. I could see two houses from here, which meant two houses could see us and might've seen Kate if she jogged this way on the morning of her disappearance.

We found the first homeowner in his barn, half buried in the motor of a tractor. He didn't recognize Kate's picture. Max had cropped a selfie of her and Charlie to show just her. She was slightly out of focus, facing the camera with a reluctant smile.

"Seen a woman jogging out this way a time or two. Didn't recognize her." He wiped his face with a handkerchief and asked for an impact wrench. I handed it to him. He was telling the truth. More concerned with the motor than the missing woman, but honest.

"Any chance you saw her two weeks ago? June 7?"

"Don't know as I did."

Eve stepped forward. "It was an especially windy morning. Twenty-five-mile-an-hour gusts. You might've been worried about crop abrasion."

It clicked for him and he smiled, bouncing the impact wrench in Eve's direction. "Sure, I remember. Walked the property to see how the fields were faring." He paused, thinking. "Seems I did see her out that day. T-shirt looked like a sail in the wind, ponytail getting blown all over. I waved to her, but she didn't see me."

He confirmed the route and her direction matched the one we were retracing, causing a hum of satisfaction to emanate from Eve. We were on the right track.

We left the farmer to his engine and headed toward the other property, falling silent. The sun baked the strip of pavement, unseasonably warm for June, and the wind made the young leaves of the planted fields rustle, whispering around us. Eve's energy shifted into a more solemn, questioning tone.

"Is it hard?"

I glanced at her profile. "Maybe. Be more specific."

"Walking into a barn with a picture of a missing woman."

I'd met Eve while searching for my niece, Celina. I'd dreamed about her bound and bleeding in a barn and had driven myself to the brink of sanity searching every barn in the state trying to find her. In the end, she wasn't in any of them, at least not by the time we found out what happened to her.

"Yes and no." There were certain triggers. It had taken months of seeing the Celina Investigations sign on the office door before I could breathe normally reading it. The right pitch of a squeaky barn door, a voice that sounded like Celina, gunshots. Any of it could send me spiraling into a panic attack or drifting into an ocean of sucking grief. It helped, though, to remember other things. Her sweaty childhood hand slotted in mine, the convictions of the players in the drug cartel she helped destroy, the bald shock and rage on her murderer's face in the second before he died. I took comfort where I could.

"I've been doing some version of this since I was twenty years old. It's familiar, the only thing I know. And it's easier with Kate, because—"

"—you haven't dreamed about her."

I nodded as we turned into the gravel driveway of the other property. It did make it easier, not being haunted by the missing person, not feeling their desperation or fear tainting every interview, shredding the edges of every clue, stretching each step in the case as taut as a wire. But this time I almost wished I could dream about her. Kate—the woman with half a name, no family, friends, or connections, who'd trod through life so deliberately lightly she hadn't left a single footstep behind. The dreams at least gave Max and me places to start looking. With Kate, we had an evasive, broken ex-boyfriend and a Milk Duds box.

I looked behind us at the road, the last confirmed place Kate—or whoever she was—had been seen. "Would you go for a casual morning jog before you abandoned your life?"

Eve considered the question and the buzz of her analysis was as comforting as white noise. I drifted closer.

"I might," she decided. "It's good for your circulation, especially if you're planning to be sedentary for an extended period, such as driving a long distance."

"It just seems—"

"Mundane," she finished.

"I was going to say hellish."

"No, you weren't." She laughed and moved into step with me, shoulder to shoulder, the backs of our hands brushing each other as we crossed the weedy front yard. There was no sidewalk, just a path of worn dirt through the dandelions and crabgrass. We hadn't even gotten to the cracked concrete slab in front of the house before the screen door banged open into the siding.

"I'm not buying any."

A white guy, late seventies or early eighties, with a face that could double as a russet potato, barred the entrance to the house. He wore a bathrobe and sweatpants. A TV remote stuck out of his pocket. Eve stopped walking and a twinge of unease pinged through her. She didn't show it, though. All she gave away was a calm, professional smile. "We're not selling anything."

"What do you want?"

I showed him the picture and explained our visit. He barely looked at the photo, but he didn't have to. His reaction was visceral as it echoed through me. Recognition, anger, a hint of greasy fear: he knew who Kate was.

"Did you see her that morning?"

"No." He started to shut the door.

I stepped forward, bracing against the wave of toxicity spewing out of this guy. "Did you ever talk to her when she was out on a morning run?"

Yes. The unspoken answer came instantly, making the anger inside him swell.

"No." He slammed the door in my face and locked it.

Eve already had her phone out and was photographing everything from the house to the tilting outbuildings to the view of the road. From this vantage point, russet man would've been able to see Kate coming as she cut through the field. He would've had plenty of time to intercept her if he had a mind to.

And he had.

"Put it away."

Eve swiveled back to the property. "But I haven't gotten—"

"He's watching."

She didn't ask how I knew, didn't demand her usual reams of evidence when I said something that couldn't be observed by normal people. She turned toward the road before startling into me with a jolt of surprise. I steadied her and followed her gaze to a small trailer off to the side of the house. A face peered out from a dirty window. Long, blond hair, round cheeks, pale eyes that followed our every move. But it wasn't the face that sent a current of fear coursing through Eve and bleeding into me. It was the shotgun barrel the girl aimed through the window.

Darcy

The trees painted black spiderweb shadows on the bay window as we shuffled around each other in the bright work lights of the kitchen, hitting the high notes of "Total Eclipse of the Heart" while the world beyond the shadows still slept. I beamed, singing with my entire half-awake, raspy-lunged being. It was almost impossible to believe I used to work in a drab cubicle, jumping every time the phone rang and listening to coworkers who were decades older than me complain about their spouses, their joints, their raises. I dreaded being there as much as I dreaded driving there and home, looking over my shoulder at every noise, checking the rearview mirror like a nervous tic I couldn't shake. Every hour of the day felt like a bargain between the bad and the worse, and I couldn't imagine any other options. I didn't know my life could be anything different, that it could be something beautiful.

Pastries & Dreams was the best job I'd ever had. The store was open Tuesday through Sunday, and Blake told me I only had to work five days a week, but I didn't have anything else to do and it felt wrong sleeping in while Blake worked downstairs. A few part-time workers came in to handle the counter in the afternoons, but other than that Blake ran the whole place. I learned everything I could to help her and make myself worth her unfounded faith in me. She paid me cash weekly and I used most of it on groceries or items for the apartment. The twelve thousand dollars I'd brought from my old life sat untouched in a safe deposit box, opened with the same student ID I'd found, in a town thirty minutes down the road. It would be there when I needed it.

Blake was scooping cookie dough and I'd started the first coffeepot of the day when a pounding at the back door made me splash water all over the coffeemaker and down my apron. My heart rate skyrocketed.

"Can you get that?" Blake shouted over the music.

I nodded, but it was hard to make my feet move. No one had ever come to the kitchen door. It led out to a small fenced backyard with only a few lounge chairs and a grill on the cement patio. Deliveries always came through the front and always during business hours.

Drying my hands, I went to the door and opened it. A man stood on the other side, fist raised. We both jumped when we saw each other.

"Sorry." He stuffed his fist into the pocket of his flannel. "Sometimes Blake doesn't hear the door over the music."

"Take on Me" by a-ha wailed behind me, spilling onto the patio where the tree branch shadows rustled in the wind. The guy looked like a bear, tall and thick with a full beard and brown hair curling over his ears. I didn't move, didn't say anything until Blake shouted, "Well, look who it is."

I retreated to the abandoned coffeepot in the sink.

"That's far enough. This is a clean kitchen, dickwad." Blake kept scooping while side-eyeing the guy, who followed her instructions and leaned against the door. "You haven't responded to a single text I've sent you in the last two weeks."

"I've been busy."

"Bullshit."

"Blake has control issues," the guy said to me. "If you've worked here for over an hour, you probably already knew that."

"Chooch has communication issues. He thinks texts are just for reading."

"The *Home Alone* tweets were funny." He grinned and dropped a backpack next to the greenhouse, leaning down to untangle a cluster of cilantro stalks from the basil. The gentle movement from such a giant, burly guy made me pause, full coffeepot in hand.

"But *Home Alone* was from the nineties." I spoke up, as if Macaulay Culkin was the source of all my confusion in this moment.

He laughed, plucking a yellow leaf from one of the plants. "You do know Blake, huh?"

Blake slid pans full of cookie dough into one of the ovens. "This is my new roommate and coworker, Darcy. Darcy, meet Chooch."

"Charlie," the guy corrected, but quieter, as though he was less sure of his own name than of *Home Alone* tweets. He smiled at me, flashing white teeth in his mass of beard before quickly looking away.

"If you stick around, you'll see Chooch every few months. He's got a hobby farm south of town."

Blake was close enough that I could ask under my breath without Charlie overhearing. "Are you two together?"

The laughter that shot out of her was so loud it caused ear damage. Her pink braid swung toward the floor as she doubled over against the butcher block.

"What?" Charlie asked.

She didn't answer and I felt myself blushing, even though I didn't know why. Washing her hands, Blake picked up the backpack Charlie had dropped on the floor and took it to the stairs that led up to the apartment. He didn't follow her.

"He's my idiot brother," she managed between giggles.

"Oh." I could feel even more blood rushing to my face. "Hi."

He nodded at me, returning the greeting. As soon as Blake disappeared upstairs with the backpack it felt suddenly quiet in the kitchen, despite the music.

"How's it going so far?" He asked in the same quiet way he'd said his name.

I left without answering.

Charlie came back a week later with another backpack and he and Blake went through the same ritual—insulting each other with old familiar affection before Blake took the bag and disappeared with it. I stocked the bakery case, filled the coffeepots, and dusted the counter, staying in the front room until he was gone.

I didn't know what was in the backpacks and I didn't ask. Blake was entitled to her secrets as much as I was entitled to mine. She'd never asked about my life before Iowa City, never made me come up with stories that I'd have to keep track of later. Blake knew there was an uncrossable line in our friendship, a dark space that, if she tried to breach it, could swallow Darcy as though she'd never existed.

Once, when she served us both the unsellable ends of a loaf of banana bread, I took a bite and said without thinking, "It tastes just like my mom's."

"Half butter and half shortening. That's the secret." Blake stuffed a piece in her mouth and chewed, glancing at me. "Is that what she did?"

It was hard to swallow. The bite seemed to swell in my mouth. I could smell the burnt crumbs and coffee in my mom's cramped kitchen, hear the whirr of her wheezy refrigerator that the landlord said was fine, and see the locks on the front door, the two that came with the apartment and the special one she'd ordered online, with its shiny metal and promises of safety.

For a second I could see the exact contour of her slight neck and shoulders, the way they curved more the older she got. She denied it whenever I pointed it out, but I saw the weight of everything that pressed on her small frame. The way her hands shook when she set the banana bread on the cooling rack. I read once that fetal cells stayed in a mother's body after a child was born and the reverse was true, too: a mother's cells lived in her child's blood and tissue for decades. Maybe that's why it felt like I'd been transported directly into her kitchen, why she was so clearly imprinted in my head. We carried each other inside us.

Tears clogged my throat and I forgot what Blake had asked. I nodded, trying to swallow the knot, to bring myself back into the present. This was exactly the life my mom had wanted for me. But it was a life without her, a life where she only existed as stray cells wandering unmoored through my blood.

* * *

Movie night became a Sunday tradition, the one night of the week we could stay up late without worrying about turning the ovens on at 4:00 a.m. We rotated through eighties films and rom-coms, with a giant tub of popcorn between us on the couch as we debated the best characters and which parts of our favorite films stood the test of time. Charlie started joining us, too. He was a strange but not completely unwelcome addition, since he brought beer and boxed theater candy. Last week I'd let slip that Milk Duds were my favorite and tonight he set a box of them casually in front of my spot before we all settled in.

The three of us sprawled on the pink couch in a pile of blankets and pillows, passing snacks and watching *Say Anything*, but my head wasn't contemplating Lloyd Dobler as much as the tasting notes of Milk Duds and how I might be able to reimagine them for the bakery.

"What about a dark chocolate muffin with a salted caramel drizzle? Maybe with an espresso base to balance the sweetness?"

Blake shushed me and shoved the popcorn into my lap. "It's almost the best part." Her whole body exhaled as the iconic shot came on-screen—Lloyd standing outside Diane Court's house, blasting Peter Gabriel's "In Your Eyes" with a massive boombox held over his head.

"That's stalking," Charlie said through a mouthful of Raisinets.

"Shut up. It's romantic."

"You're telling me you wouldn't call the police if your exboyfriend stood on your property playing your sex soundtrack on repeat in the middle of the night? Look, she can't even sleep because of that asshole." Charlie threw a Raisinet at the screen.

"He's not standing on her property. He's in the street."

"Disturbing the neighbors."

The two of them bickered for the next two scenes. I half listened while thinking about muffin recipes, until Blake demanded I take a side. It wasn't the first time I'd had to choose a sibling and I'd always come through for Team Blake. This time, though, it was harder to see her point.

"It . . . could be sweet." I hedged, even though the idea of someone tracking me down and standing outside my window made me put the popcorn back on the coffee table.

"It's emotional abuse," Charlie said, and his deadpan tone made me snort. I swallowed the laugh, scrambling to back Blake up.

"It's a grand gesture," I said. "The hero has to do something out of their comfort zone to win their love. Grand gestures are a pillar of the romance genre. The entire trope was probably built around that exact scene."

"See?" Blake elbowed Charlie, looking smug. "The grand gesture."

As she leaned into her pillow to watch the ending, Charlie and I looked at each other across her back. Even though I'd gotten used to seeing him, something about his presence made me feel unbalanced. Maybe it was his size, the way he filled a doorway or took up half the couch. Maybe it was how most of his face was obscured by his beard and shaggy hair. He could have been intimidating or straight-up scary if he wanted to be, but he never came off that way. He deflected attention, deadpanning or shrugging off direct questions, and even seemed to dissociate from his constant arguments with Blake, as if baiting her was as familiar and unremarkable to him as breathing. And his eyes. His eyes were the softest brown I'd ever seen and they'd never gotten angry. Not once. The first time I met him I thought of a bear. Now I thought of a teddy bear. A sort of sweet, sexy teddy bear.

Blake talked over the movie, pointing things out that neither of us paid attention to. Charlie was still looking at me, shaking his head slightly at my defense of Blake, but on the verge of smiling, too.

Emotional abuse, he mouthed.

Grand gesture, I mouthed back, feeling an answering smile spreading across my face.

Later that night, Blake was brushing her teeth and I was washing dishes when a noise outside brought us both to the living room.

"Do you hear—?" Blake cut off as the noise registered and her face transformed from confused to murderous. She marched to the sliding glass door and pulled it open.

Charlie stood in the yard, holding an iPad above his head that blasted the Police's "Every Breath You Take" into the night. As Sting sang, "Every move you make, I'll be watching you," he slowly pointed two fingers at his eyes followed by one finger up at Blake.

"You're an asshole!" she screamed, spitting toothpaste at him before stomping back inside.

"Exactly!" he shouted back, swinging the iPad down and stopping the music as his gaze shifted to me. In the sudden quiet, his voice dropped to a huskier pitch. "Right?"

Heat flooded through me, catching me off guard. I'd known something was there, but I wasn't prepared for the force of the sudden knowledge zinging through my body. God, I was attracted to Charlie.

It felt dangerous to agree with him and impossible not to. He stood underneath the balcony, staring up with those chocolate eyes, the iPad dwarfed in his giant, gentle hand. The silence stretched out and it was only when Blake came back with a pitcher of water, dumping it over the balcony, that I forced a laugh and ran back into the safety of my newfound home.

Max

"How much of this was already here?"

I walked through Kate's room, looking for anything useful, while her roommate/boss watched me from the doorway.

"All the furniture is mine. That poster, too." Blake Ashlock, the neon-haired millennial baker, pointed to the only print on the wall—a framed Twisted Sister poster that looked twice as old as her. "Darcy bought the curtains."

The fabric was sheer and mint green, letting light flood in. The room looked lived in, relatively neat but not fastidious. A few pieces of clothing littered the floor near a plastic laundry hamper. The bed was made but rumpled, with a pair of pajamas loosely folded on top of the blanket. The only photograph in the entire space was a Polaroid propped next to a bedside lamp, showing Blake and Charlie with an arm around each other, siblings cheesing into the camera. Charlie looked flushed and happy, a different man than the one I'd first met a few days ago.

"Charlie thinks her real name is Kate."

"Yeah, he told me his incredible Milk Duds theory." She played with the end of her pink braid, eyes darting around the room. "He didn't get the brains of the family."

"Do you think her name is actually Darcy?" I checked under the mattress and bedspring. Nothing.

Blake bit her lip, eyes unfocusing as they turned watery. After a long pause, she shook her head. "She's Darcy to me. That's how she identified, who she wanted to be. And I know her, no matter what her birth certificate or driver's license says. It doesn't matter what her legal name is."

Except it did, if we ever wanted to find her.

Kate/Darcy/Whoever She Was's room wasn't giving up much in terms of clues. She'd left library books stacked on the nightstand, all of her clothes as far as Blake could tell were hung in the closet and folded in the drawers, and several lotions, sprays, and other women's bathroom stuff were lined up on top of the dresser. It didn't appear like she'd gone anywhere, or at least not anywhere she'd planned on. It looked, on its surface, like a lot of the homes I'd visited while investigating cases on the ICPD. I'd been in too many bedrooms like this, where a victim's stuff was comfortably scattered, just another regular day until something happened to take them away from the place they belonged.

I wished Jonah were here. Our mystery woman had left no hard evidence, no clues someone like me could follow to figure out who she'd been or where she'd gone. At the very least, Jonah would've been able to sense more about her than just a life interrupted.

Giving up on the bedroom, I followed Blake to the apartment's kitchen. She took a bowl out of the dish dryer, opened a cupboard, and stood there, one hand on the handle, the other gripping the bowl as she stared blindly across her living room. She was maybe thirty, young to own the bakery downstairs, but it must've been doing well judging by the quality of the furnishings, the giant TV, and the tech lying around the apartment. The brands of the appliances on the counter looked French or Italian and several notches above the GE specials Shelley and I picked up at Lowe's. I leaned against the other side of the peninsula.

"What did K—Darcy like to do? How did she spend her time?"

Blake startled, shutting the cupboard. "She loved to bake. She loved being in the kitchen. I don't think she ever asked for a day off." Blake hugged the bowl to her stomach.

"And when she wasn't working?"

Blake shrugged. "She took walks all over town. She liked being outside. Even on movie nights she always opened all the windows. And Charlie. She loved Charlie." Her eyes filled and she cut off, looking down at the empty bowl. "He's hopeless, but a sweetheart, you know? Total mush. And he's never been with anyone who got him, someone who didn't want to change him into something else. I was shook when they first got together, but then it was like—I don't know, like puzzle pieces. They just fit. And they made each other fit."

I asked about any arguments, any trouble in the relationship, but Blake shut that down.

"Never. Neither of them were fighters. Except . . ." A look came over her face as she trailed off.

"What?"

"One time Darcy thought someone broke into the bakery after hours and went to confront them." Blake glanced at the kitchen counter. "She took a knife. She looked terrified, ghost white, but she went anyway. Knife first. I wouldn't have thought she had it in her."

"Was there an intruder?"

"No, it was—no."

"Did she ever talk about her life before she came here? Places she'd lived? Family or friends?"

Blake shook her head. "She mentioned her mom a few times, mostly about recipes she'd made. No names or places or anything." Blake paused, thinking. "It seemed like she missed her mom a lot."

"Did you get the impression her mother was dead?"

"I don't know."

I tried a few more avenues, but Blake couldn't recall any other mentions of Kate's family or friends. Just a mom. Maybe that was all the family she had, or at least all the family she cared to remember.

I paced the rest of the living space, looking for any signs of Kate in the retro neon, jungle of plants, and wall of DVDs. "Did she own anything that seemed special to her? Like it might have significance to where she came from?"

Blake didn't hesitate. She discarded the bowl and ran downstairs. I followed, but a text from Jonah made me pause on the stairs.

Strange neighbor on the running route. He knew Kate, wouldn't admit it.

What did you get from him? I texted back.

Anger. Fear. He felt threatened by us. According to property tax records, his name is Silas Hepworth. There was someone else on the property, too. Watched us while holding a shotgun.

Hepworth have any priors?

TBD.

Blake waited impatiently at the bottom of the stairs, a kitchen tool in her hands. I put the phone away and joined her. "Does the name Silas Hepworth mean anything to you?"

"No."

"Did Darcy ever mention running into someone when she went for jogs at Charlie's place?"

Another negative. I broadened the question.

"Did she feel uncomfortable around anyone at the bakery or in town?"

Blake glanced through an open doorway to the front of the store, where a line of customers waited for their coffee and pastries. She leaned against the butcher-block work surface in the center of the kitchen.

"Yeah."

"Who?" My attention sharpened.

"Everyone. Everyone except me and Charlie. She never wanted to work the front counter, hated talking to people. She was just shy. An Allison."

"A what?"

"Allison from *The Breakfast Club*. She's shy, but she wants to belong because she's never belonged anywhere before. I think Darcy was dealing with some past trauma, too, just not parents who ignored her like Allison's. But she wanted to belong to us. An Allison, you know?"

The only thing I understood was that it was some kind of metaphor and I didn't have to add another alias to the case file.

"Here." Blake thrust the thing she was holding at me. It was a flat stainless-steel rectangle with a rubber handle along one of the long edges. The opposite edge ended in a single, sharp line that glinted in the work lights of the kitchen.

"A . . ."

"Dough cutter." She supplied. "You asked if she owned anything that seemed to have significance."

76

I ran a finger along the cutting edge. It was duller than a knife, sharper than a mail opener. "This was special to her?"

"She brought it to the kitchen in probably the first week she started working here and she always used it, even though I've got commercial-grade cutters that are way more efficient. That's for home use. But Darcy always reached for this one. Once I saw her put it into an apron pocket when she was scooping cookies. Totally unnecessary for the job but maybe it was like an emotional support animal, you know?"

Or like she wanted to hide it. Keeping it close for another reason. Pulling the case notebook out of my pocket, I tested the cutter on a few pages. They sliced away with little force. The dough cutter, whatever it meant to her, could fucking cut.

Blake braced against the butcher block, her face falling into quiet, somber lines. "Do you think you'll be able to find her?"

With no name, a complete lack of physical or electronic trails, a mystery kitchen tool, and an angry neighbor as our only possible lead?

"It might depend on whether she wants to be found."

Jonah

It was getting late. The sky outside the Celina Investigations storefront had softened into a hazy overcast. The parking lot was empty except for Max's and my cars, and the businesses on either side of us had fallen quiet. I loved this time of day, when people retreated to their homes, sealing the chaos of their minds away into the night. I had hours before sleep and whatever nightmares would come with it, hours to enjoy the relative quiet with only Max's brain for company.

"Go." Max threw a stained tennis ball at me, which had shown up at the office months ago and weirdly become our talking stick during these sessions. We were in the storage room, a dark rectangle of a space with a bathroom on one side and clunking pipes snaking overhead. Three rolling white boards stood against the wall, procured by Shelley during a purge at her school. We'd repurposed them from geometry lessons to investigation boards, a place for me to keep notes, maps, pictures, leads, and random thoughts on our more complicated cases. Max called them my shrines; he preferred his mini notebooks and computer, but I'd always needed to make cases more tangible. Seeing a missing person's face outside my head, taped to a wall or whiteboard, calmed me in a way I couldn't completely explain. It made them real. It made them part of a world outside my nightmares.

Not that I'd dreamed about Kate, but somehow that made her even harder to manifest. The woman with no identity, no past, and maybe no future. I tapped the tennis ball on the blown-up picture of her cuddled into Charlie's side on his living room couch, which was the central image on the current shrine.

"I'm not getting any vibes that she left voluntarily."

Max sat backwards on a folding chair, drinking a beer as he stared at the board. "Okay, I agree, but why?"

"She took nothing with her. Her overnight bag is still at Charlie's house. She left everything in her apartment, including her suitcase and her toothbrush. If she did disappear on her own, at the very least, it wasn't planned." I tapped the photos of her abandoned stuff and tossed the ball back to Max.

"Don't forget the dough cutter." Max snorted.

I walked over to it and picked it up like a hot coal. We'd googled the thing already and watched how it sliced balls of dough into smaller balls of dough, scraped surfaces, and smoothed cakes. None of those functions prepared me for the shot of heat and emotion singing off the metal when I first handled it.

"It's important." I closed my eyes and tried to feel through the tangle of impressions. Deep breaths. Yoga breaths. "It's the most personal thing she owns. A piece of her past. There's a lot here. Trauma. Reclamation. Severance. Love." Max's skepticism wove through the energy of the dough cutter. "Yeah, all of that. Fuck you."

"How?" He stared at the tool, which I put as far away from my chair as it would go. "How can something so random have that much emotion associated with it? What does it mean?"

He threw the ball back at me. I took it to the board and started writing. "She knows how to bake. She learned that somewhere. The dough cutter might've come from a kitchen she used to work at. It could symbolize anything or anyone from that time and place—a mentor or boss. Maybe something that happened to her there."

"We could call bakeries around the Midwest, see if anyone matching her description used to work there."

"Let's start with independent ones. Mom-and-pop places. I don't get the feeling she'd be making cakes at Hy-Vee."

Max nodded as I added an arrow and action item to the board.

"I wonder if you could slit a throat with that thing." He took another swig of beer.

"Jesus."

"What? You said trauma and severance. Maybe she severed an artery with it."

"And uses her murder weapon at work every day?"

"Blake said she seemed protective of it. Kept it close to her." Max got up and tossed his beer can in the recycling, stretching and grunting as he cracked his back like gunshots. There was no stutter in the energy, no jolt of nerve pain shooting through him. After almost three years, his shoulder had finally healed. Max turned and caught me staring. "What?"

I shook my head and turned back to the board.

"I wish you would've been at the bakery and gotten a read on Charlie's sister."

"You think she's hiding something?"

"I can't tell. Everything she said about Kate seemed so . . ."

"Generic." I picked the word out of his head.

"Yeah." Max shrugged on his coat. "Kate liked movies, walking, and fresh air. Mind-blowing. Oh, and she liked Charlie, too."

"Don't forget the dough cutter."

"Christ, I need a drink."

"You just had one."

Max paused at the door. "You coming over for dinner?"

Having dinner at Max's house with his wife and kid wasn't something that happened much before the pandemic. Shelley and I had never gotten along, and I didn't blame her for keeping her husband's unhinged friend at arm's length. When Max went off the rails on his last case as an ICPD investigator, though, Shelley and I had found common ground as two people who loved this dipshit, in spite of his thick skull and savior complex. I had dinner with them now almost more than I ate alone.

"I can't. I'm cooking for Earl tonight."

"And Eve?" Max grinned.

"No, she's having dinner with some colleagues and her new PhD student." Chris. They were going to be discussing his "brilliant" research from Australia.

Max pulled out his keys and opened the back door. "Already jealous, huh?"

"Good night, Max."

Retired farmers were seriously underrated investigators; they had a lot of time on their hands and an ingrained need to fill it. Earl had been in a wheelchair since I'd met him and he communicated mostly by text, but none of that kept him from googling with the best of them. After I got to the house and filled him in on Kate's case, he started compiling a list of independent bakeries in Iowa and Illinois while I made dinner.

Eve had left ingredients and a recipe for jerk tofu bowls with plantains and quinoa. She made or picked up mostly vegan dishes in light of Earl's condition, citing all the evidence in favor of low salt, low sugar, plant-based diets for stroke survivors. Earl put up with it, but he'd been the happiest I'd ever seen him when I brought steaks over a few times while Eve was in Australia. Tonight, we had bloody ribeyes with onions and baked potatoes that we drowned in butter, sour cream, and bacon. I opened all the windows, hoping most of the meat smell would air out before she got home.

It felt right being here, sitting side by side as we licked our plates clean and mapped possible prior bakery jobs for a missing woman. If Eve were home, she'd be arguing with Earl over the benefits of tofu, her hair glinting off the pendant lights, her eyes sparking with love and logic and the challenge of getting her meat-and-potatoes father-in-law to admit he liked curdled soy milk.

It's functionally the same process as cheese-making, she would say.

Cheese doesn't taste like soggy cardboard, Earl would jab out on his iPad.

And I would let them bicker, listening to the affection weaving in and out of their heads as I cleared the table. We'd bubbled over the pandemic and I knew where all the dishes went and which utensils Earl could use with the least amount of problems. I knew the looks Eve would shoot me behind Earl's back, the grunts Earl would send in my direction when he knew he was losing the fight.

Everyone lost their fights with Eve. She won every debate because she was smarter than all of us and she saw our points coming days and weeks ahead of time. She'd been trained to dissect storms long before they crested the horizon.

After we finished the list and dinner, I lingered longer than I should have. Eve didn't say when she'd be home and I resisted the urge to text her. Earl was watching the news and playing Candy Crush, perfectly content on his own. There was no reason for me to stay. Except that I wanted to see her.

Our date this morning had ended when I'd dropped Eve off with a stitch in my side and covered in dried sweat. Any thought of kissing her had evaporated during an intense discussion of the woman holding a gun on Charlie's neighbor's property and a debate over the difference between explicit and implied threats. And for the rest of the day my brain had been on a loop, watching her climb out of the car again and again. I'd see her soon. I knew that, rationally. But my body wasn't in a place of logic.

A thwack brought me back to reality. Earl hit the couch again, inviting me to sit down and join him.

Eve hadn't told Earl that we were dating yet, and I understood her hesitation. Earl was her father-in-law. They were bound together through a dead man whose picture still hung on a few walls in this house. Eve and I being together wouldn't only change our relationship; it could change things between them, too. If she got home and both of us were sitting here, it might be awkward for her.

"I should go." I picked up the list of bakeries and clapped Earl on the shoulder. Satisfaction and gruff affection emanated through him. "Thanks for the legwork."

Thanks for dinner, Earl typed. **You can throw the tofu in the trash on your way out.**

"Nice try. I'm not taking the heat for that."

I drove around the city for a while, staying well clear of the restaurant Eve and her colleagues were at, and made myself think about bakeries instead. Pastries & Dreams sat on a side street in the shadow of the ped mall, an old converted house with gables and a wide porch. The sign in the window said closed, but as I drove past, covered windows glowed with light in the back of the bakery.

I parked and paced up the block, inhaling sweet explosions of lilac bushes crowding the sidewalk, the faint stink of a dumpster due for pickup, and the sharpness of cut grass from an apartment building lawn. The city had quieted, as it always did, after graduation and the exodus of the undergrads. Even the noise of the bars on the ped mall was muted, letting the quiet of the early summer night steal over the city. I breathed deep, centering myself in the here and now, in the case I needed to solve to prove I could. I could be part of a world outside my nightmares, the world where Eve lived.

Security cameras were mounted on the front door and along the narrow, overgrown sidewalk to the backyard. I skirted the house and tried the gate to the backyard, which was locked. The fence was privacy height, too tall to climb. I could've knocked on the front door, but something told me not to, to keep moving to the other side of the house, where a path had been worn toward the gap of a loose board in the fence.

I squeezed through and crept into the backyard, where motion-activated security lights immediately flooded the grass with me standing in a black trench coat, hair obscuring most of my face. The blinds on the bay window were yanked up, revealing two people inside. The woman screamed when she saw me. And through the wood and glass and the stutter of shock piercing the night, I understood what was really happening at Pastries & Dreams.

Darcy

I woke up in the middle of the night to a faint banging noise, the sound of a door closing, maybe, or a window hitting the frame. I ran to the living room, searching the entrances, looking for the source of the intrusion, but there was nothing. The door to the deck was latched with the pole of wood notched firmly in the sliding glass frame. The windows were empty of everything except shadows and the door to the stairs was closed, too.

"Blake?" As I moved to her bedroom door, another bang stopped me cold. It came from downstairs. Knocking quietly, I pushed open Blake's door. Her bed was empty. Maybe she was the one making noise downstairs, but she'd also gone out last night with a guy and I hadn't heard her come home.

Slipping to the apartment kitchen, I pulled a carving knife out of the block and crept to the stairs. My heart knocked against my ribcage. If I had to use the knife, it wouldn't be the first time I'd attacked someone. I guess some things didn't get easier with practice. Shifting my grip on the handle, I paused at the bottom of the stairs. Voices drifted from the other side of the door as metal scraped against metal. Someone was definitely here. I couldn't run or hide, not if Blake's business was in danger. Taking a deep breath, I shoved open the door and sprang into the bakery kitchen, making both of the people standing next to the stove jump in surprise.

Blake and Charlie.

Blake dropped the pan she was holding with a crash. Charlie tried to lunge in front of her, slipped on the pan and fell into his sister, sending them both to the floor. I stood frozen, knife raised, in complete shock.

"What. The fuck!" came Blake's voice from somewhere behind the butcher-block counter.

"I thought someone broke in," I whispered. It felt like all the air had been knocked out of me. With the adrenaline fading, I felt weak. Trays of silicone molds filled with tiny gummy doughnuts wavered in front of my eyes.

Suddenly, Blake was right in front of me. She was talking, but I couldn't hear what she said.

"What are you making?" I asked eventually, trying to breathe.

She looked at her brother, who stood behind her and wore a bright pink apron over his flannel. He glanced at me before nodding to Blake.

"Chooch is a farmer, and his best crop is . . ."

"Gelatin?" I blinked the silicone molds back into focus. The whole counter was covered in them, and I noticed for the first time that all the window blinds were closed. I stuffed down the feeling of being trapped and tried to concentrate on what Blake was saying.

"Weed." She smiled. "Chooch grows some pretty fine pot, and I help him turn it into some pretty spectacular edibles."

"Oh."

It made sense now, the closed blinds, the middle-of-the-night cooking. Marijuana was still illegal in Iowa, which was probably why they had to do this at 3:00 a.m. on the day the bakery wasn't open. The pungent tang to the air—a bitterness riding underneath the smell of liquified sugar—would clear out long before the next customers came through the door. That must've been what was in the backpacks they exchanged. Weed, edibles, cash.

"Are you freaked out? You look freaked out." Blake seemed worried as she loaded trays into the fridge.

"I'm not."

"I would've told you before, but . . . "

"No, you don't have to tell me anything." We'd only known each other a month. She didn't owe me details about her life. And the less she told me, the less I would feel pressured to share with her. I shifted the knife awkwardly and started moving to the stairs. "I'll let you finish."

Blake grabbed me by the shoulders. Her wide, makeup-less eyes peered deep into mine. "Are you one hundred percent sure you're okay? Because—"

"Blake." Charlie pried her hands off me. "Back off."

"Oh, right. Sorry. I can get a little—"

"You can get a lot," Charlie cut in.

"Shut up." Blake elbowed him in the side. "Darcy's the best thing that's happened to the bakery and I don't want your shit scaring her off." She turned back to me, not grabbing me this time but it looked like she was half a second away. She shifted her weight between her feet nervously. "Are you okay with this?"

The knife felt suddenly slippery in my hand, like I would drop it or cut someone. Blake's words bounced around in my head, not finding anywhere to settle. *Darcy's the best thing that's happened to the bakery.* My heartbeat picked up again, not because I was scared of a break-in or worse, that someone had found me here. My pulse beat faster this time because my answer actually mattered.

I smiled at Blake and clutched the knife harder.

"Do you need any help?"

Edibles were a whole new subgenre of cooking. I'd only smoked pot a few times, when I briefly dated a boy in high school who always seemed to have a joint in his pocket. He said it would help me relax, but he was wrong, just like he was wrong about the musical significance of Bon Iver. Weed made me feel like I was underwater, my limbs weighted down while a giant air bubble was trapped inside my chest. I got paranoid, convinced my stepfather would somehow burst into the boy's parents' basement and I'd be too high to get away. Stoner boy said I had issues. I broke up with him a few days later.

I'd never tried edibles. I'd heard of pot brownies and I knew dispensaries carried gummy products, but in a vague, distant way, trivia that would never touch my life. And it wouldn't have, not my old life, not the person I used to be. But I was Darcy now. Darcy started her days with rock ballads and dancing. She made baked goods that smelled like heaven and worked in a sun-drenched space without computers or copy machines or bosses who spoke in monotone acronyms. Darcy had friends and a home here. She was needed, valued. And the longer I stayed Darcy, the more real it all felt.

A few days later, Blake and I drove a batch of edibles out to Charlie's farm.

"You never wear dresses." Blake commented as we left the city.

I smoothed a hand over the paisley skirt of a wrap dress. "I found it at Ragstock for six dollars."

It wasn't like anything I'd worn before. I'd dressed in baggy, dark-colored clothes in my other life and grabbed whatever was comfortable for the bakery, but when I'd browsed the racks the other day this dress had caught my eye. It was buttery soft and hugged my hips in rose and brown swirls. Instantly I could picture a woman wearing it with boots, her hair in loose waves. And I knew—it was Darcy. The woman I pictured was me.

"It looks great on you." Blake side-eyed me in the car, not saying anything else about my makeover.

When we got to the farm, Charlie sat on the front porch of a rambler that looked like it had seen better days. Paint peeled off the window shutters and debris was clogged in the gutters. A few flower beds grew weeds in the front yard, but the lawn was freshly mowed and a brass wind chime hung next to the front door, sending low, lazy notes across the yard.

We brought the edibles inside and set the plastic tubs on a kitchen table crowded with books and newspapers. The smell of coffee hung in the air. Blake started in on Charlie about the peeling siding when she was interrupted mid-shade by a text from someone she'd been messaging on Tinder.

A slow smile lit up her face as she read. She was already typing back as she slipped out the front door, calling behind her. "To be continued. This could take a while."

Charlie and I faced each other, making eye contact before looking away.

"Do you want these somewhere else?"

"What?" He seemed distracted by my dress and it took a second for him to remember the existence of the tubs of edibles on the table. "No, don't worry about it."

There was another awkward silence as I tried not to stare at his mouth. Outside, Blake wandered into the yard and sat on a tire swing hanging from a tree, aggressively texting and grinning at her phone.

"Do you live here alone?" It seemed like a safe enough question. I never asked Blake or Charlie anything too personal, but I was standing in his house, trying to think of anything to say that wasn't *Can we please make out now?*

"Yeah. I had a roommate for a while, but he moved to Milwaukee." He shrugged, and one corner of his mouth lifted. "I like a lot of space."

"Me too," I agreed even as I stepped toward him, closing the space between us. Suddenly we were both smiling. The air in the kitchen felt warm and taut. I wondered if he could see my heart beating through the fabric of the dress.

He asked if I wanted a tour of the grow room. I had zero feelings about seeing it, but it gave us something to do. A reason for Charlie to touch my back lightly and steer me toward the front door. And Charlie seemed eager to talk about it as he led me around the house.

"It's insane that Iowa is still policing marijuana. Most of the cities don't give a shit, but out here some departments still hunt growers. And there's the DEA. You can't grow in a field because of drones."

"Do you use a barn then?" He had outbuildings on the property, a medium-sized barn and a handful of smaller sheds and garages.

Charlie shook his head, stopping by a cellar door on the back side of the house. "They can find grow sites in barns using infrared. That's why I keep it under the house."

He opened the horizontal door and gestured for me to go first. Something clenched in my chest at the sight of the door opening into the ground, the stairs that led down into darkness. It was fine, though. I was fine. I was Darcy. I took a deep breath and tried to shake out the uneasiness in my chest, flashing a tight smile at Charlie as I passed him and started walking down.

The stairway was narrow with a low ceiling and roughed-in walls that bled dirt and cobwebs. A tarp hung at the bottom of the stairs, curtaining the refracted light from the room beyond it. I stared at the light, clinging to it as my heart kicked into high gear. Two minutes. I could do this for two minutes; a quick walk around and then back out. I just had to keep breathing.

Charlie pulled back the curtain to reveal rows of pot plants baking in the artificial light. He gestured for me to go first and I stumbled ahead, trying to look like I was paying attention while scanning the far edges of the room for any windows or other ways out. There were none.

"—why LEDs really help. They don't draw enough electricity to ping any radars." He kept talking, and I tried to focus on what he was saying, but the more he talked the less sense any of it made. All I could hear above my racing pulse and breathing was white noise. We got to the end of the row, which dead-ended into cinderblock. I turned around, but Charlie's massive shadow took up the whole space. I couldn't get around him, couldn't get outside. The stairs beyond the tarp had disappeared. The sky and sun were gone; I'd been swallowed by this room. My back hit the wall as Charlie's voice rose. It wasn't him anymore. The voice changed, became sharp and angry. The silhouette grew bigger. A hand raised and I flinched. My knees started to give out.

"No, don't. Please." I couldn't breathe. Hands—impossible hands, how were these hands here, now?—caught my arms and I fought against them. I couldn't let them grab me. I wouldn't, not ever again. The world I'd created, the world where Darcy existed, melted away until there was only panic and sweat and screaming. My stomach heaved. The lights dimmed. I lunged sideways and felt a crash. Something hit my head and I curled up, trying to become as small as possible, contracting everything I was around my frantic, spasming lungs.

There was nothing.

Black.

Quiet.

And then, light.

I opened my eyes to blades of grass eclipsing the robin's egg blue of the sky.

"Breathe, Darcy. Just breathe."

The voice came from somewhere above me. A large hand gently rubbed up and down my back. I tried breathing, found I could, and without thinking began to inhale in time to the movement on my back.

After a minute the pieces of what happened in the grow room started coming back to me and I pushed myself upright, sitting with my knees drawn up tight in a patch of grass in Charlie's backyard, a few feet away from the cellar door.

Charlie sat across from me and my back grew suddenly cold where his hand had been. I was covered in sweat and shivering, despite the warmth of the sun.

"What do you need? Water? A blanket?"

I shook my head, afraid to look at him. The back of my head throbbed and I flashed back to something crashing in the grow room. "Did I break your greenhouse?"

He waved the question away. "A plant or two. Don't worry about it. But the light—" He scooted marginally closer, cautiously examining my hair. "I think it hit you. Are you okay? Do you want an aspirin or something?"

My stomach pitched at the idea of putting anything in it. "No. I just—" I broke off as a tremor ripped through my body, making me shake all over. "Could you maybe put your arm around me? Just for a second. I'm so cold."

He did immediately, sitting next to me and pulling me in toward his chest. I closed my eyes and listened to his breathing, the steady thump of his heart. We didn't talk. He didn't press me with questions about what happened or why. He didn't make me feel like I needed to get up and pretend I was okay, like none of it happened, like I had to be Darcy in my new dress. I could just be. I could just breathe in the grass and clover and sunshine and the warm, clean smell of him against my temple. Just be here, and not alone. His hand wrapped around my entire shoulder, his touch light but overwhelming in the amount of comfort it offered. I felt safe, truly safe, for maybe the first time that I could remember. I never wanted to move from this spot.

Gradually, my heartbeat evened out and the cold sweat soaking my Ragstock dress dried in the sun. I lifted my head, reluctant to break away from him even though I should. Blake could pop around the corner any second, and I wasn't ready for the amount of questions, demands, and general chaos that would ensue if she found us together on the grass.

"Thanks," I offered, scooting away and sitting cross-legged. "I'm . . . claustrophobic."

It was true, but the shade of truth that described the ocean as wet. I couldn't tell him anything more, and he didn't seem to expect me to. He looked at the open cellar door and shook his head.

"You should have told me. I wouldn't have made you go down there."

"I know. I thought it would be okay for a minute. Exposure therapy, or something like that." I gave him a shaky smile. "I'll help you clean up, or pay for whatever I broke."

"You've already paid for it by helping Blake and me." His warm brown eyes found mine. "You don't have to, you know. I don't want you to feel obligated because you work at the bakery."

"That's not it."

One of his hands was braced in the grass. In the cellar, I'd thought his hands were someone else's. Hands that closed like vices, that could find you anywhere, no matter how small or quick you tried to be. But those hands were gone now, forever. I'd buried them. I'd covered them with dirt and branches and leaves and walked away, praying that the worms would find them and feast.

Charlie's hands were nothing like my stepfather's. Charlie's hands were bear paws, massive and adorable and alive. I reached over and slipped my fingers under his palm, holding on to the warmth and strength. It felt like my entire life rested on the edge of a knife, and everything that came before was on the other side of the blade, ready to finally be cut away.

"I've never had friends like you and Blake before."

"Bickering siblings in arrested development?"

I huffed out a laugh that felt impossible ten minutes ago. "It's not easy for me to get to know people. It feels safer sometimes— being alone. Keeping space between me and everyone else."

"I get that." Charlie glanced toward the horizon where the fields rolled into the sky.

"But it's different with you and Blake. I want to hang out with you and help you and be part of your lives. I guess that's what friend- ship is?" It had only taken me twenty-four years to figure that out. Twenty-four years, a murder, a fake identity, and a new life. And all of that had somehow brought me exactly here, sitting in the grass with Charlie on the edge of an endless spring field.

His fingers curled around mine and squeezed, sending warmth through my entire body. When his mouthed curved up, lifting his beard into a shape I already knew so well, my heart picked up again, but in a way I'd never thought I would feel in any version of my life.

"Friends." He nodded and lifted my hand out of the grass, looking at them linked together. "You know, sometimes friends go out with each other. If they both want to."

His gaze traveled up my arm to my face. I smiled, tilting my head. "That's good, because I was thinking of asking Blake out."

He shook his head and the grin turned lopsided. "Makes sense we'd start fighting over you, too."

I pulled his hand up and held it in both of mine before press- ing it to my lips. He shifted, cupping my jaw and lacing his fingers through the hair behind my ear. Then Blake's voice made me jump.

"Well, shit." She looked at the two of us in the grass, hands on her hips, eyes narrowed, pink hair rippling in the breeze. "Here we go."

Max

"So, this is what you were hiding when we came out to your house."

I stood in the kitchen of Pastries & Dreams at ten o'clock at night, bellied up to the butcher-block worktable next to Jonah and across from a very guilty-looking Charlie and Blake Ashlock.

Jonah called just as I'd finished cleaning up dinner and Shelley was prying the screens from Garrett's hands to send him to bed. When Jonah explained the situation, I wasted no time driving to the bakery.

In front of us, a dozen pans held hundreds of brownies and bars, alongside molds of gummy-looking candy in every color of the rainbow. It was, apparently, the secondary business of Pastries & Dreams and a lucrative one at that.

"I wanted to tell you, but Blake said not to." Charlie glanced at his sister, who glared at him.

"Your website bio says former cop." Blake tossed her braid over her shoulder and started loading the gummy trays into a commercial refrigerator. "And for bullshit red-state reasons, this is somehow a crime. So are you going to report us? Do you have some ex-cop code of honor obligating you to blow up my entire life's work?"

"He's not going to shut down the bakery," Charlie said, but Blake whirled on him, visibly cowing the brother who was twice her size.

"This is your fault." She jabbed a tray into his chest. "You and Josh Grohl getting high every day during the summer after tenth grade, sitting out in the barn and inviting me to join you."

"You could've said no."

"To piercing blue eyes and a leather jacket? He was basically a young Rob Lowe," she explained before turning back on her brother. "You coerced me with a young Rob Lowe. I never even got to make out with him and now I'm going to lose everything."

"I think he's in prison now if that helps," Charlie mumbled.

The look Blake leveled on her brother could've shattered glass. I'd bet a thousand bucks Jonah could literally feel the guy's testicles shriveling. Clearing my throat, I held up both hands.

"Let me stop you there. You've hired our firm to investigate Kate's disappearance. We're working for your benefit and your interests. We're not obligated to report any criminal activity that we uncover during the course of our investigation."

"But you could," Blake said, slamming the refrigerator door.

"We could," Jonah agreed. He'd been silent for most of the conversation so far, gripping the edge of the butcher-block as he rode the cyclone of emotions thrashing around this room. It took visible effort for him to speak. "But reporting our own clients to the police isn't exactly great for business."

"You won't turn us in?" Charlie asked, careful not to make eye contact with his sister.

"Why don't you start from the beginning?" I gestured to the front of the café so Jonah could sit down. "What exactly are we talking about here?"

Over fresh coffee and leftover cinnamon bread, we found out that Pastries & Dreams had more than one original dream. After Josh "Rob Lowe" Grohl brought a batch of terrible pot brownies to the Ashlock family farm, Blake became determined to bake a better batch.

"Not because I wanted to make out with him." Glancing at her brother. "Okay, not only because of that."

Blake had always been a foodie and a perfectionist in the kitchen. She spent years experimenting to find the exact balance of THC and other ingredients, to hide the pungent taste of the weed inside an envelope of dark cocoa, fat, and sugar. After that hill was conquered, she moved on to other edibles: cookies, bars, and the current favorite in most dispensaries—gummies. Charlie helped by procuring different strains of weed suited to each recipe and as soon as he bought his own place and got the opportunity to farm his own plants, he began in earnest.

He maintained a single, large grow room under his house, which explained why he'd acted so shady when we visited his place. He wasn't keeping Kate's body on the property somewhere, but a thriving marijuana business. It also explained the stacks of cash he'd used to pay for the case. Celina Investigations had unwittingly accepted proceeds from criminal activity. And it was my idea. Awesome.

Jonah glanced at me, reading everything in my head as Charlie and Blake kept talking. He shrugged. I narrowed a look at him. He shook his head, telling me to calm down and get over it.

I turned back to the siblings. Charlie was detailing his products, a topic that—once he got started—made him surprisingly chatty. Some strains, he explained, were sold as is for smoking and others went to his sister. Afterward, Charlie sold the edibles wholesale to dispensaries in Illinois, who didn't ask a lot of questions. They'd been making products after hours and splitting the take since the bakery had opened five years ago. It worked well for both siblings. Charlie got to live largely off the grid and Blake's illegal business kept her legal one flush with cash.

"It was great when Darcy wanted to be paid under the table, honestly, because it meant less cash I had to try to funnel through the business."

"Did she know?" Jonah asked, nodding as he sensed their answer before they even spoke. "What role did she play?"

"None, at first. She just worked in the bakery. She didn't know about any of this until one night . . ." Blake explained the shock of seeing Darcy/Kate on the stairs, holding a knife like she was ready to stab them.

"She looked, I don't know, like a completely different person. She was sweating and shaking. It was almost like she was in shock. We had to say things a few times before she heard us. I thought for a second she was going to attack us."

"Blake," Charlie scolded.

She shrugged. "What, you didn't? It was weird, but then it was over and she offered to help."

"Did any of your inventory go missing when Kate disappeared?"

Charlie seemed taken aback by the question. "No. Kate didn't smoke."

"She could've taken it to sell, not use," Jonah pointed out, but both siblings denied the possibility. Kate wasn't money-oriented. She rarely shopped or went out, and the few things they could remember her buying were nominal and largely for the apartment or Charlie's house: a soap dish for Charlie's bathroom, a popcorn bowl for movie nights.

Blake explained. "Her love language was quality time, one hundred percent. Whenever I saw her alone in the backyard or walking through town she always looked sad, serious, like she was having some unending existential crisis. But when we were working or hanging out, she changed. She bloomed around Charlie too, for some reason." He sighed and Blake hip-checked him from her chair. "She was still quiet and I always knew there was a huge part of her she wouldn't share, but she seemed happy. At ease with us. Quality time, you know?"

I'd been down this road with Shelley and the marriage counselor. Love languages were a means to understanding your partner's needs. Shelley's love language was acts of service, which basically meant I needed to keep the lawn mowed and the furnace running. Thank god her love language wasn't quality time, or we would've been years into a divorce by now. Next to me, Jonah chuckled. The two siblings glanced at each other.

"What about your other customers besides the dispensary, the people you sold weed to?" I asked, making notes. "Any disputes or conflicts recently? Would any of them have a reason to want to hurt you or someone close to you?"

"No." Charlie pushed out of his chair and started pacing the cramped dining room. "I'm not selling meth or fentanyl. It's a pretty chill business."

I could've told him stories from ICPD, the things I'd seen that resulted from a "pretty chill business." Theft, assault, coercion, rape. I guess I'd never seen anyone kidnapped or murdered over weed, but when you put an illegal substance into the public arena, it attracted more criminality, like gravity. I looked out the dining room windows at the empty road where streetlights pooled like oil in dark water.

"Was Silas Hepworth one of your customers?" Jonah asked, bringing my attention back to the conversation.

Charlie came up short. His face turned red and his hands clenched into fists. "How do you know Silas?"

Jonah explained his encounter this morning with the angry neighbor. He'd already run the background check before I'd even gotten back to the office. Pulling his weight and then some. Hepworth came up mostly clean. Vietnam vet, divorced twice, and on disability for the last decade. He'd tried to sue various people over the years, and there'd been an incident in a grocery store parking lot, a fender bender that turned into a brawl. That was twenty years ago, though. On paper, he'd quieted down. Later, I'd quietly run the background check again, just to see if I could turn up anything else, something Jonah might have missed. I got nothing.

"He's a sonofabitch," Charlie spit out. His sister looked just as surprised as us by the outburst. Jonah slumped further down in his chair. Sweat broke out on his forehead as our client's emotions swamped him.

"Is he all right?" Blake asked. She looked nervously between Jonah and her brother, as if unsure who was less stable in the moment.

"He's fine. He's a psych—"

"Explain what happened with Silas," Jonah interrupted. He leaned into the table and pressed fists to his temples, eyes closed. I flipped my notebook to a fresh page and channeled the paper's blankness—evening out my breathing and wiping my head of any speculation—giving Jonah a neutral place to land if he needed it. I wrote while Charlie talked.

Charlie first met Silas Hepworth the week after he bought his house. Silas had driven the short distance between their properties and, instead of introducing himself or welcoming Charlie to the neighborhood, started in on a property dispute he'd had with the previous owner.

"It was dumb. A damaged tree from my property that fell on his. He demanded I clean it up *and* give him the wood. I did, only to smooth things over. With the grow business, I didn't want asshole neighbors who'd be watching my every move. And when I brought him the wood, he started talking about Vietnam and his back and how he was in pain all the time. Long story short, he became a customer."

Charlie sold him weed regularly for years, stopping by on the second Wednesday of the month when Hepworth's social security payments came through. It wasn't the most pleasant hour of the month. Hepworth complained about the news, the government, the other neighbors, picking apart his limited world in front of a captive audience. Charlie listened, nodded, took his money, and left as soon as he could.

"Who else lives with him?"

"No one. He's alone, rotting in front of his TV."

Fists still pressed into his temples, Jonah explained the face he and Eve saw in the trailer window when they tried to interview Silas.

Charlie shrugged. "I never saw anyone there except Silas."

Jonah nodded imperceptibly. Charlie was telling the truth about the mystery face, which meant we still didn't know who was tracking Jonah and Eve this morning with a shotgun.

Charlie kept talking. Apparently, things with Silas took a turn about a month ago. Hepworth ran into them while they were out on a walk.

"He was getting his mail as we passed and I introduced them. He didn't say much. Neither did Kate. I remembered being happy to get out of there fast before he could go on some rant. Then I went to drop off his stuff the next time." Charlie stopped pacing, shaking his head at the ground. His face turned a darker shade of red and his words were clenched, bitten out. "The crap he said about her . . ."

"What?" Blake was on her feet now, too.

Charlie tried to wave her off, but he was fighting revulsion. "He called her a whore. He said she was using me and I needed to put her in her place."

"What the hell?" Blake looked ready to do violence. "He didn't even know her, did he?"

"I don't see how. He barely leaves his house. He's just—"

"A misogynist," Jonah said without lifting his head.

"Yeah," Charlie agreed. "He was always trashing his ex-wives. Anyway, I told him I wasn't going to listen to his bullshit, especially not about Kate. I cut him off. Said I was done selling to him."

Finally, Jonah straightened up. He was way too pale, even in the half-light of the midnight bakery, but he looked straight at Charlie, understanding the situation more than anyone else in the room could.

"That's when he began blackmailing you."

Jonah

I didn't remember much about leaving the bakery. One minute I was sinking in a vat of shock, fear, and simmering anger and the next I was in Max's driveway as he killed his engine and turned off the headlights. His neighborhood was dark and quiet. I followed the lines of the house, tracing the places where it ended and the night beyond it began, trying to draw the same lines around myself.

Next to me, Max mulled over the interview and everything we'd learned.

"Beer?"

My stomach lurched. "Sure."

We went to the garage. The smell of motor oil and mulch hung heavy and sweet in the motionless air. Max turned on a task light, leaving the rest of the space dark, and set a beer down on his workbench. When he went inside to talk to Shelley, I pressed the can to my head, concentrating on the cold condensation running down my fingers. I could tell, through the fading emotions, that he was lingering inside. Giving me space to breathe. By the time he came back, I felt better. Less like vomiting, at least.

"Was it Charlie?"

I nodded. Set the beer down. "He hadn't considered Silas Hepworth in connection to Kate's disappearance before. It hit him hard and he kept thinking about possibilities, all the things Hepworth could have done to her." I swallowed, trying to keep the images at bay now that they'd started to blur, but I could still see her body, broken, violated, her frantic face reflected in his head. "It was a lot."

"Why didn't you take a break, get some air?"

I shot Max a look. "Why didn't you?"

"Because I don't have the superpower in this agency."

"Stop handling me." I pushed away from the workbench, forcing myself to walk. *Exercise*, Eve had said. Physical exertion to keep my mind occupied within my own body. The swaying, uneven steps around Max's garage were definitely not what she had in mind.

"Then stop trying to prove yourself." Max got up, too. "Fifty-fifty doesn't mean you have to stick it out in an interview like that. It doesn't mean you have to bang your head against this case twenty-four hours a day."

"It got us somewhere tonight, didn't it?"

Charlie had confessed that Silas Hepworth had extorted five thousand dollars and free weed from him, in exchange for not going to the police. A week before Kate disappeared he'd increased his demands. He wanted twenty-five thousand dollars. Charlie told him to go to hell and left Hepworth raging in his living room.

It was a decent motive and a solid suspect, the first we'd had since this case began. I vaguely remembered Max convincing Charlie not to confront Hepworth alone—Max made him promise they would make contact together tomorrow.

"You're not coming with."

"Fine."

Max was surprised. He'd expected a fight.

"I'm going back to the bakery." It hadn't registered until now. Security lights had flooded the property again when Max and I left, illuminating black eyes mounted in the eaves. "Blake has cameras all over that place. She might've caught footage of Kate's car. We could get the plates."

A slow smile spread over Max's face as he shook his head. "Christ, I'm not going to have a job left."

Max set me up on their basement couch with an old quilt and the same unopened beer from the garage. The couch was scratchy and uncomfortable, a nice reminder of who and where I was, but I couldn't sleep. I wasn't afraid to; the furniture would ensure any dreams would be brief, only flashes of some faceless lost person between the squeaks of old springs and constant skin abrasions. But something Max said kept coming back to me, whispering from the places where the nightmares usually lived.

Stop trying to prove yourself.

It crept over me, seeping between my shoulder blades and under my sternum, settling in my bones with a feeling I barely recognized. My body relaxed, felt at ease, and for the first time in a while it felt like I might be enough. That I could do this. The whisper was interrupted by an incoming text.

Steak and potatoes?

The feeling expanded, multiplying inside my chest as I grinned at my phone.

He loved it.
The tofu was in the trash.

I had nothing to do with that.

How was your dinner?

Three dots appeared on the phone and stayed there for an impossibly long time. It felt like my entire existence hung at the edge of those dots. When her message finally came through, my heart leapt into my throat.

It would have been better if you were here afterward.

I left the house through the patio door. The bakery, and my car, were miles away. I followed the river and the moonlight reflecting off the dark slide of water. Shadowy trees loomed around me, their spring leaves rustling in the breeze. Distant engines zigzagged the city, people too far away to sense. My heart thumped strong and steady in my chest, picking up speed the farther I walked. When I reached the bridge to cross into downtown, I broke into a jog. It was still exhausting but I embraced it this time, letting my breath go ragged and my feet pound the pavement. My muscles burned and my thoughts flattened out into one refrain. *Stop trying. Stop trying.*

I passed the bakery and my car. I ran past businesses and apartment buildings, where laughter drifted like smoke off the balconies. I ran down a pitch-black hill, stumbling on the uneven sidewalks as the lactic acid chewed up my legs. I ran until I reached the far edge of town, where the housing developments stopped at a stretch of fields opening into the starry horizon, and slowed to a walk as I reached the street I'd left only hours ago.

I felt drained of everything, yet somehow wired, too. My skin hummed and my lungs ached. I could picture Kate more clearly now—leaving Charlie in bed and slipping out of his house as the sun rose. She'd needed to outrun something, to metabolize the thoughts that found her in the night, to burn them in the sunrise and the proof of a new day. Kate had made a life here in Iowa City. She'd found a friend, a job, a lover. She'd found a home, until something stole her away. Whatever it was, we were going to find it.

My breath had quieted. The thump of my heart returned to a steady, driving beat. On this street, a ring of townhouses circled a pond fringed with cattails. I moved silently to the backyard of the end unit and looked up at the four-season porch. The roof wasn't like any other in the neighborhood. Instead of a smooth line of shingles and rain gutters, it was dotted with instruments, gauges, and equipment with strange arm-looking appendages stretching to the sky. The porch was screened, but a single light emanated from a laptop, illuminating the loveliest face I would ever see.

She was alone. I had no idea what time it was, but Earl would have gone to bed long ago. She was absorbed in whatever was on her screen, eyes darting back and forth as she processed and parsed data, frowning and making occasional notes before continuing to read.

Her mind was like a lighthouse, bright and steady, calling me to shore. Max said I didn't need to prove anything to him. And I realized Eve had been telling me the same thing all along. That I was enough for her. That we could do this, together.

I opened my mouth to say something at the exact moment she glanced up. Our eyes locked. She closed the laptop and slowly stood, dropping a blanket to the floor.

What could I say? What did she need to hear? Her thoughts melted away in a warm, sudden rush of emotion that was answered in the pit of my stomach. She turned and disappeared inside the house. A light switched off somewhere inside.

I was trying to decide whether to knock on the front door or wait when she appeared around the corner of the house. We met in the middle of the yard, stopping a foot apart.

Her eyes were in shadows. Her hair shone in the cloudless, storm-free night. I felt her heart begin to race, the pump of blood and rush of nerves as I cupped her face in my hand, sliding fingers through her hair. She moved even closer, breathing fast.

"What took you so long?"

She was still smiling when I kissed her.

Darcy

It's incredible how one life could become something entirely different. You got so used to going from day to day knowing your limits, memorizing the walls of love and fear that surrounded you. Those walls told you who you were and who you weren't, the things you could and couldn't do.

And they were all lying.

Someone told me a story once about a guy who got eaten by a whale. He'd been recruited by God for some shit job, and when he refused it and tried to run away, God made a whale eat him and bring him back, to rebuild the walls around him. But here's the thing: that story's not true. The real story is that the guy had the courage to run away. He saw the colors on the horizon and knew what his life could be; he wasn't tied to God's will or anyone else. When the whale rose up and swallowed him, he didn't panic or repent or pray. He pulled out a knife and got to work.

I left my life. I broke down the walls. I ate the goddamn whale.

When I left Kate behind, I had no idea what lay ahead. I didn't realize there could be a new home, a new career, even a new name. A friend whose laugh infused me with a kind of buoyancy my body had never felt. A boyfriend who murmured sweet words into my hair at night with his arms wrapped tight around me. That I could smell of cinnamon and coffee and yeast as I took breaks behind the bakery to lift my face to the sun, and when I felt the light and warmth sinking into my skin I could almost imagine I was whole. I was viciously happy despite the ache in my chest when I thought of my mother's last hug. No one else could see the dirt embedded beneath my fingernails, the whale flesh that wouldn't scrub away. I was new. Clean. Joyful. I became a person I never dreamed I could be.

I'd lived in Iowa City for two months now. Been Darcy long enough that I answered to it automatically. Charlie and I became almost immediately inseparable and Blake, although she bitched about it for a while, loved seeing the two of us together.

The first morning he stayed over, he came downstairs in pajama pants and Blake's bunny slippers looking for free coffee. She elbowed him in the gut right as he leaned down to kiss me good morning, making him grunt into my mouth.

"Figures I'd have to do everything for you." She shoved a cup at him. "Feed you, water you, find you a perfect woman."

"Thanks for the slippers, too." He nuzzled me before going back upstairs and I caught Blake smiling dopily at us when he wasn't looking. She wiped her eyes and disappeared to the front room, yelling that she was taking a bigger cut of the edibles money this month for shoe reimbursement.

Charlie slept over a few nights a week and I started taking Tuesdays off so I could spend Monday and Tuesday out at the farm with him. The more time I was there, the more I craved the wide-open space, the endless unbroken horizon in all directions. There were no buildings or turnpikes or forests to cast shadows, no barriers in any direction I faced. For as much as I loved Blake and the bakery, it was still in the city with the constant flow of people in and out all day, and as comfortable as I'd become, my heart still raced whenever I heard a sharp voice or the bang of the front door. I still couldn't bring myself to work the register, staying in the kitchen as far away from people as possible. Not that I expected to know anyone here, or that anyone would know me, but I was uncomfortably aware I hadn't run as far as I should have, stopping nowhere near the mountains or the mindless blue of the sea. I'd left Illinois, but not by much.

I still went to the library every week and checked the local papers and police blotters. There was never a mention of a missing person report or a body being found. The longer it took, the better. All the cop shows I watched claimed that evidence would degrade the longer it was left to the elements. I hoped by the time they found him, there would be nothing left except a broken, ugly skeleton.

"What are you thinking about?" Charlie murmured behind me, stroking my hair away from my face. It was Tuesday morning, and I'd have to drive back into town later today. We stayed in bed longer on Tuesdays, bringing coffee and snacks into the bedroom, sometimes binging shows on Charlie's phone while we snuggled under the covers, or just talking about the news or our days.

I turned to face him, this giant, hairy, sweetheart of a man whose only crime was growing a plant that helped people relax and feel better. It was impossible to tell him what I'd been thinking, to share more about my past beyond what I'd told him and Blake over a bonfire at the farm, that I'd needed to start over. They'd accepted that, like they accepted everything about me, and didn't press me for more than I could give.

"I was thinking about running."

"Running?" He spoke the word like it was the first time he'd heard it.

"It's an exotic, fringe form of exercise."

He made a noise and ran one of his big hands down my ribs, notching it in the dip of my waist. "You don't need to exercise. You're already perfect, so if this is a trick to make me start running—"

"It's not." I snuggled into his side, amazed every time by how perfectly I fit into the crook of his arm. Maybe it was always like this. Maybe people were just meant to fit together this way. I'd had no way of knowing before now. It made me think of the rom-coms Mom always insisted on seeing and the light playing over her face while we watched them. She'd been trying to tell me something in a language I didn't speak until now.

"I like the idea of starting the day outside. Seeing the sunrise. Watching the world wake up." It felt like something Darcy would do, and I suddenly longed for it. I wanted to run through the fields alone and inhale the morning, to do a sun salutation with only the birds and wind for company. And I could. There was nothing stopping me.

"Not much of the world out here."

"This is the best part of the world." I hugged him closer, waiting for a reply that didn't come. When I propped myself back up, he was staring at the ceiling with the strangest look on his face. His jaw was tense and eyes were hard. He looked almost angry. I'd never seen him like this and I instinctively shrank away, retreating to a safe distance at the edge of the bed. "What's wrong?"

"Where will you run?"

"Wherever I feel like it. Why?"

He sat up and glanced out the window. "I want you to be careful. There's someone who . . . One of the neighbors . . ."

"What?"

Then he told me about Silas Hepworth, a guy we'd bumped into once on a walk. He was a customer of Charlie's and had started blackmailing him. I moved closer while he talked, my body slowly thawing as I realized none of Charlie's anger was directed at me. By the time he finished, I was just as angry as he was.

"Does Blake know?"

He shook his head. "I don't want her to worry." Then he cupped my face in his big hands. "I don't want you to, either. But if you're heading out on the roads by yourself, you need to know about him. It's not just the money. He said some things about you the last time I saw him. He's kind of an all-purpose asshole. "

"I know all about those." It was out before I could help it. Charlie looked at me, the anger melting into something closer to concern, but before he could ask any follow-up questions, I redirected the conversation back to Silas and how much he'd taken from Charlie so far.

"It doesn't matter. I'll find a way to handle it. I just want you to watch out for him. You remember where he lives?"

I did. And I promised Charlie I'd steer well clear of Silas. He seemed relieved, but there were still traces of anxiety around his eyes. His hands bunched like they did when he got nervous or distracted. We watched a few reels on his phone, neither of us paying much attention, until I finally crawled out of bed and started putting on clothes I could run in. Charlie's focus suddenly improved.

He hummed in approval of the lacy green underwear and glared at the full-coverage sports bra as soon as I fastened it.

"Running's a terrible sport."

"Oh yeah?" I grinned into the tank top as I pulled it over my head.

"It's bad for your knees. And your skin."

"How?"

He pulled me back onto the bed until I was straddling him. "You could get skin cancer. Here." He ran a finger over my collarbone. "Or here." The finger dipped along the edge of the bra, tracing the route above my breasts and over my heart.

My head tipped back, giving him room to explore. "I'll put on sunscreen."

"I should help you." His hands bracketed my ribcage before sliding further back and unclasping the bra. "So you don't miss any spots."

I let him find a bottle of sunscreen in the bathroom and apply it thoroughly, until my interest in running went from aspirational to nonexistent. Grabbing a condom from the nightstand, I pushed him onto his back.

And that was the most surprising part of this relationship. I'd never been crazy about sex. It had always seemed awkward and messy. I hated how vulnerable it made me feel, exposing myself to someone who might do something unexpected, who could hold me down or hurt me if their mood changed. But Charlie was different. Charlie was careful and eager to please. He acted like I was a gift, like my body was something to unlock and worship every time. If I told him to stop, he did immediately. If I told him to go harder, he leapt to perform. I never thought I could feel comfortable with someone as big as he was and it was honestly strange how my claustrophobia didn't kick in when his hands squeezed my hips, when he closed the space between us. I was safe with Charlie inside me.

He sat up and pulled me against him, our bodies locked, arms winding around each other and holding tight.

"I'm not getting my cardio in like this," I murmured, rocking my hips to make us both groan.

Charlie kissed me, pulled back to look me in the eye, then stopped my heart when he said, "I love you, Darcy."

My shoes hit the pavement in a steady rhythm as each syllable of Charlie's declaration seeped through me. Even out here, with the brilliant blue bowl of sky for company, with oxygen pounding in and out of my lungs, it was impossible not to hear the echo of the last time I'd heard that. My mother's words, wet and fierce, as she hugged me. "I'll love you forever, sweetheart." The press of her cheek to my jaw. The way she'd looked at me as if memorizing every detail of my face. She said *forever*, knowing it was the moment our forevers would part ways and never find each other again. I hadn't believed it. My brain was in survival mode. I couldn't process anything beyond the next moment, let alone the rest of our lives.

Did I say it back? Did I tell her how much I loved her? I couldn't remember. So much of those last few days were a blur, punctuated by sharp flashes painful in their clarity. But every day I spent as Darcy, each tick of the clock that expanded our separate forevers, I thought of more things I hadn't said. How I saw every good thing my mother had done for me, how strong she'd been, how brave. I didn't blame her for what happened. Had I told her that? I'd talked to her every day of my life until two months ago, and I don't know if I said the things that mattered.

I loved my life in Iowa City. I adored Blake and Charlie. But I couldn't ignore the part of my mom I carried inside me. When Charlie said what he did this morning it felt like waking up, like I was an amnesia patient with sudden, awful memories. Because I knew what love meant. I knew what it could make you do.

The road rose and fell like the swell and fade of music set to the sunrise. Birds called to each other and a distant irrigator rained water on a far field. Sweat dripped off my forehead and down my chest as I reached the bottom of a hill and the place where Charlie and I had met Silas Hepworth.

I stopped at the end of his driveway, wiping my forehead with my shirt, my heart pounding. The house at the top of the hill was dark. Without pausing to think, I walked up to it.

Silas answered the door on the third knock. He had bed hair and pillow creases down his face.

"What?" he demanded, pulling himself taller as soon as he saw me.

I smiled, showing my teeth. "Do you remember me?"

He made a noise that I took as a yes.

"I don't think we were properly introduced before." I took a step forward without offering my hand. "I'm with Charlie Ashlock. He's sweet and caring and generous, and he doesn't have any idea how to handle someone like you."

"What's that supposed to—"

I stepped in again, close enough that I could look down at the bristling old man. I could smell his outrage.

"You're the kind of person who destroys people like Charlie. And you enjoy doing it. You think it gives you some kind of power, that it makes you important. But the thing is, deep down, you know," I tilted my head, scanning the quivering folds of his face that were flooding bright red, "even while you're doing it, you know you're not special. You know you don't matter, to anyone or anything. If you fell over dead, your bloating corpse would stink up this house for weeks before anyone cared enough to even check on you. Charlie would probably be the one to call 911. He'd come to your funeral, even after you blackmailed him, and feel bad for you while standing over your sad-ass grave."

Silas edged further back into his house, his face almost purple now. I braced for him to start yelling, but he turned and reached for something behind the door. Before I fully registered what it was, I lunged inside the house, grabbed the barrel of the shotgun, twisted it to the side, and used it to shove the old man to the floor.

He went down with a crash, bouncing off some furniture before landing on the floor. Adrenaline flooded my body as the walls tried to close in around me. The room, already dark, went almost black in front of my eyes, but I didn't run. I stood in the doorway, letting the sunshine heat my back and the breeze cool the sweat on my skin. I held the shotgun like a talisman against the dark place where moans and vicious cursing garbled together.

"Tell Charlie you're done. You're not going to extort any more money from him. If you don't, I'll be back. And believe me when I say no one will miss a piece of shit like you."

I walked out into the morning air, feeling every pulse of blood beating against my veins. The sun was higher now, illuminating the giant rolling fields, green with new life. I could run for miles.

I could bake a hundred loaves of bread. Tossing the shotgun in the ditch at the end of Silas's driveway, I turned to the west and started jogging home to the rhythm of the words in my head.

I love you, Darcy. Love you, Darcy. Love. You. Darcy.

It was going to be a gorgeous day.

Max

As Charlie Ashlock and I walked up Silas Hepworth's driveway, a shotgun blast ripped through the morning air. I ducked, shoving Charlie behind me, and reached for the nonexistent holster at my side. Neither of us had been hit. There was no sign of life in the front yard and all the windows in the house and trailer were dark, no faces or barrels aimed our way.

"What the—" Charlie muttered behind me.

Another blast rang out, echoing off the buildings on Hepworth's property. Charlie pointed to the barn and I nodded. The shots were coming from somewhere behind it. We glanced at each other and moved in that direction, following the weeds that grew at the base of the faded building. When we got to the edge, there was another blast—this one even closer—followed by a wheezy laugh.

"You can't let the butt jump around like that. You've got to brace it."

"I am." This voice was higher, younger.

"Those cans over there say otherwise."

I motioned for Charlie to stay behind me and moved carefully around the edge of the barn. An old man and a young woman leaned over the hood of a rusted pickup with no tires on it. On the other side, about twenty yards across a bald dirt yard, two Campbell's soup cans sat on top of a fence. It was just shooting practice. I took a deep breath and ignored the flood of panic and adrenaline of being on an unfamiliar farm with armed strangers. Sometimes PTSD was an insistent bitch.

"Howdy." I walked forward slowly, hands in sight. The man and young woman whirled around. They didn't aim their guns at us, but they didn't put them down either.

"The hell are you doing here?" The old man—clearly Hepworth—spoke directly to Charlie.

"We need to ask you some questions."

Hepworth straightened with some effort, never losing his grip on the gun. "And I need you to get off my property."

"We'll be happy to, I promise, if we could just have a couple minutes of your time first. You spoke to my partner yesterday." I stopped well short of the truck and extended the business card, which never felt anywhere near as official as a badge. Neither of them looked interested enough to want to read it. "The two of us are trying to help Charlie here track down his girlfriend."

"Already told the other one I don't know anything."

"Grandpa," the young woman turned to Hepworth, "are they talking about the woman who was here the other day?"

The old man flushed red and looked constipated as hell. He grabbed the shotgun out of her hand and told her to be quiet. Ignoring Hepworth, I pulled up Kate's picture and walked close enough for her to see it clearly. "This woman?"

She nodded, shoving long, greasy hair out of her face. "She took grandpa's shotgun. Told him she'd come back and kill him. That's why we're—"

"That's why nothin'." Hepworth cuffed the young woman on her shoulder until she dropped her head and fell silent.

"She threatened you?" I asked Hepworth directly. Charlie stepped up, making a tense box out of the four of us.

"Get in the house."

The young woman hesitated, glancing between all of us. She looked a few years older than Garrett, probably late high school or just graduated. Her eyes were red-rimmed and nervous, and her clothes were as ill-fitting and grimy as her grandfather's. Clearly, hygiene wasn't a big priority on the Hepworth farm.

"Is she . . . ?" the young woman started to ask.

"You heard me," her grandfather repeated. "I said get."

She listened this time, disappearing around the barn in the direction of the house. Hepworth waited until he heard the screen door slam before he focused on me and Charlie.

"Can you tell us what happened?"

He grunted and leaned against the truck, setting one of the shotguns on the hood and keeping the other. "She came here out of the blue, trespassing on my property, and told me to stop, well . . ." He flashed a look at Charlie.

"Blackmailing your neighbor?" I supplied.

"I'm not the one doing anything wrong. He's got the drug operation out here in the middle of the country where good people are trying to make a living. There's kids here." He jabbed in the direction his granddaughter disappeared. "People raising families."

Raising families obviously meant different things to different people. And while calling Charlie's basement a drug operation was technically true, the brightly lit rows marked with careful labels were a far cry from the filthy meth labs and truckloads of opioids I'd seen as a police officer. Charlie had given me a tour this morning, calling each plant by name and excitedly pointing out the properties of "Lenore" vs. "Errol." He was nerdy and kind of irritating, but also nothing like the offenders I'd arrested over the years. Marijuana was legal in most states now, it seemed, and even the feds had backed off on enforcement and prosecution in legalized states. The old man's rant felt like a throwback to satanic panic.

"You're not doing anything wrong?" I flipped open my notebook. "Looks like we've got possession of a controlled substance, harassment, and extortion, from what Charlie tells me."

"Harassment!" Silas exploded, making the rusted truck squeal with his sudden outburst. "That's what you should charge her with. That bitch assaulted me and stole from me."

"Why would she do that?"

"Because this guy's too cowardly to do his own dirty work, that's why."

"What are you talking about?" Charlie stepped closer. Hepworth's hand slid down to the trigger of the shotgun. I moved into a position where I could reach either of them if I had to, and lifted my hands in a let's-take-it-easy gesture.

"Are you saying she stole one of your guns?" I tried to piece the situation together from what his grandkid said earlier.

He grunted. "She knew better than to steal it while I was right there. It was the money she came back for."

"What?" Charlie got in his face, heedless of the gun in Hepworth's gnarled hands.

"The five grand you paid me. I put it in a cupboard in the kitchen until I could take it to the bank. Same place you always saw me put the weed. Well, a few days after that bitch came and threatened me, I go to the cupboard and it's all gone. Every penny. She broke into my house and took it." He squeezed the barrel of the shotgun in a red fist. The finger on the trigger clenched. "And you told her right where to look for it, didn't you?"

"She took the money I paid you?" Charlie seemed confused and overcome.

"As if you didn't know." Hepworth got in Charlie's face.

I wedged a shoulder in between them and snagged the old man's attention. "What happened then?"

"Nothin'. Money was gone and she knew better than to set foot on my property after that."

I nodded and made a noise of understanding. "But what about her threat? You must've been worried she'd carry through with it."

"Worried?" He laughed once, an ugly shot of sound. "I've lived through war. Been married twice and worked these fields for forty years. No little girl's gonna get in my face and make me worry about anything."

"So you didn't talk to her after that? Not even to confront her about the money?"

He spit on the ground, not saying anything. His face looked like bunched leather, something left out in the sun and forgotten.

"And where were you on the morning of June 7?"

"Where I always am. Right goddamn here."

I looked at the open stretch of land beyond the fence and the Campbell's soup cans. Silas Hepworth owned a hundred acres of farmland and a handful of weathered outbuildings. The land rolled gently here, creating pockets of absolute privacy, places where no neighbor could see what he might be doing.

"Sure, Silas."

I picked up the extra shotgun lying on the hood of the pickup, loaded it, took a bead on the tin cans, and squeezed the trigger. Twin blasts ripped apart the air around us. The cans flew off the fence.

"Those charges I read you are real. So if you decide you want to continue blackmailing Charlie, I'm here to tell you that his girlfriend—wherever she is now—was right."

"Right about what?"

I stepped closer until he had to look up to see me.

"You're going to regret it."

Back at Charlie's place, shit hit the fan. He'd been quiet and even docile at Silas's house, letting me lead the interview as he hovered in the background. As soon as we walked back into his kitchen, though, he went into a full meltdown.

"He killed her. God, do you think he killed her?" Charlie paced the yellow Formica, head in his hands like he was trying to pull his own hair out. "Why would she do that? Why would she threaten that asshat and steal back the money? Oh my god, she was trying to protect me and he killed her."

He kept spiraling, ignoring me until I had to physically get in front of him, take him by the shoulders, and push him into a chair.

"Sit down. Breathe. Smoke something."

"But you heard—"

"I did." I sat across from him. "I've heard a lot of people say a lot of things, as a private investigator and as law enforcement. Most of it is bullshit or cover. When people get backed into a corner, they'll say anything they think can get them out of that corner. You have any kids?"

He shook his head.

"Been around kids?"

He shrugged as his eyes filled with water and he backhanded his face with an arm. He was barely listening.

"Interviewing suspects is a lot like dealing with children. You've got to weed through their stories and figure out fact from fiction."

Garrett, poor kid, was especially unlucky to have a dad who was a professional investigator. In his one attempt at outright lying, I'd decimated his story about the events leading up to a broken window at his friend's house and had both him and his friend in tears and confessing everything in under twenty minutes. That was gold-medal parenting, a moment I pulled out and savored whenever I needed a pick-me-up.

"Silas is no different. We've got to weigh the evidence and decide what's true and what's bullshit. That's where I need you."

Charlie blinked and seemed to regain some focus. "What can I do?"

"First: do you think Kate actually went over there?"

He thought about it for a minute before nodding. "I don't see why he would've made that up. And Kate brought up Silas a few times after I told her about him."

"She wanted to know if he was still blackmailing you?"

He nodded again.

"Okay, so that tracks. And it tells us something important about Kate."

"What's that?" Charlie wiped his face again.

"She's a fighter."

He stared at me, wordless, before swallowing and looking at an empty chair on his right. "Thank you."

We moved on to the other crucial point of the interview: Silas's claim that he hadn't seen or talked to Kate after that one encounter. He seemed shifty and triggered by the whole conversation, and he clearly couldn't wait to get us off his land. Was he just an angry old man or did he have something to hide?

"You've known him for years at this point. Is he violent?"

Charlie was back up and pacing again—the guy couldn't sit still—but it came off as less unhinged this time. Maybe Charlie Ashlock thought by the mile.

"Yes and no. He was always talking shit, but I never saw him do anything about it. He liked being angry; it was like he fed on it."

I told Charlie about the assault charge on Hepworth's record. "But a road rage brawl in a parking lot twenty years ago is a long way from premeditated kidnapping or murder."

Charlie jerked at the word. I hadn't spoken it aloud in front of him before now, but it was time. Kate had been gone almost ten days, not by her own choice as far as we could tell, and the incident with Hepworth made it a virtual certainty. She'd cared enough about Charlie to go out of her way to confront his blackmailer. She'd put herself in danger for him. Someone who did that didn't turn around and leave town without even a note. She'd been taken, or forced to leave.

Hepworth could have intercepted her while she was on her morning run and overpowered her, or convinced her to come to his place for another talk. Once she was off the road, he would've been free to attack her. She'd had her keys with the mace on her at the time, but maybe the mace hadn't done its job. After she was out of the way, either dead or still alive and trapped somewhere,

Hepworth could've easily walked to Charlie's house and driven her car to another location, even stowing it in one of the outbuildings on his property. He'd known Charlie a while and probably knew he wasn't an early riser. The odds of Charlie waking up when he moved the car would've been low. Hepworth couldn't get inside the house—so no way of taking her things—but at least by making the car disappear he could give the impression that Kate was somewhere farther away than the neighboring farm.

The scenario added up on a few different levels. Hepworth was the only suspect we had to date, at least now that I'd crossed Charlie himself off the list. He had opportunity and motive. On the other hand, it was hard to draw a straight line from being told "back off my boyfriend" to cold-blooded murder.

"Do you think he did something to her?" Charlie asked, pulling me out of my mental case file. He stood in the middle of his ugly kitchen wearing a stained T-shirt and shorts, arms hanging useless at his sides. His hair was a mess and even his beard seemed weirdly matted. Everything about him screamed lazy stoner, except for his eyes. His eyes belonged to a man five times his age. They were sunken and lined, teeming with a thousand emotions threatening to overpower him.

I faced him head on, which was the only way to deliver bad news.

"It's possible. We're going to need to keep digging."

He nodded, looking down at the floor.

"It's not too late to file a missing person case with the police. They have resources we don't. With enough evidence, they might be able to get a warrant to search Hepworth's property."

"Would they have enough evidence?"

I sighed. "It's mostly circumstantial right now. We'll go back over the route again and see if we can find any physical traces she could've left behind. Maybe there'll be something on or near his property. That could help with a warrant."

Charlie heaved out a long breath. "It's not about the grow operation. I know you think that."

I held my hands up and lied. "I don't think anything about it."

"She didn't want anything to do with the police. Ever."

"And you never pressed her on that?"

"No. It's not like I'm Blue Lives Matter." He winced and shook his head. "Sorry if you are."

"No. That's partly why I left the force."

"Cool." Charlie pulled a crescent wrench out of one of the cupboards and started loosening the hardware on his sink. It was such a random move all I could do was sit at the table and watch. Maybe I'd overestimated his mental state? As he made a pile out of the faucet and water handles, and just as I was starting to wish Jonah was here, he pulled the entire stainless-steel basin out of the countertop and flipped it upside down.

Taped to the underside of the sink were bricks of ziplocked cash, same as the ones he'd brought to the office at our first appointment. The bricks covered the entire basin like barnacles on a boat. Charlie opened the cupboard beneath the sink, showing me another, slightly larger basin that was still attached to the plumbing.

"Smart." I nodded. "Do you have a false tub, too?"

"Too much work." Charlie pulled a brick off the sink and handed it to me. "Here's for this week and next. You said five thousand a week, right?"

Holding the cash pushed a dull weight against my gut, a nagging, gnawing feeling I tried to shrug off. "Plus expenses, but we haven't had much besides mileage so don't worry about that."

"Bill me for them. I told you, the money's not important. I just need to know what happened to her."

It was a subtle and significant shift. When Charlie first walked into our office with a backpack full of kitchen sink cash, he wanted to find Kate and make sure she was okay. Now, he wanted to know what happened to her. The slip into past tense, the slow chokehold of resignation over hope, was a milestone in a lot of our cases. I hated it every time.

I stood up, holding the brick of cash. "I'll send an invoice for expenses when I get back to the office."

Charlie walked me to the door. "Even though you're not a cop anymore, you probably still don't approve of what I'm doing. How I make a living, I mean. There's a lot of people like Silas out here, who lump me in with drug lords and the mafia."

"I've met some of those people. You're not them."

"But I'm sure it's still hard for you. Not reporting me. So, thanks," he waffled, glancing at the upside-down sink, "for not doing that."

Charlie shifted from foot to foot. His face had flushed and he avoided any eye contact. The weight in my gut got heavier.

I wanted to tell him his line of work didn't have any bearing on the case, but if Silas was involved in Kate's disappearance, that might not be entirely true. In the end, I settled on, "Yeah, no problem."

He nodded and tried to smile. Even the attempt looked painful. "You're still going to keep looking, right? Even if I'm . . ." He trailed off.

I clapped him on the shoulder and left my hand there until he looked up.

"We're not giving up on her."

Jonah was still at the office when I got back.

"Working late?" It was almost dinnertime. I'd texted Shelley from the car that I was close to wrapping up and asked if she needed anything at the store. She replied with a kissy face emoji that I took as a no.

Jonah made a half-awake noise, not stirring from his computer. He was hunched over, barely propped on one arm while clicking through grainy black-and-white footage.

"Pastries & Dreams security cameras?"

Another noise, this one sounding even less conscious.

The resolution wasn't the worst I'd seen, but Blake clearly hadn't sprung for the deluxe cameras. At least she'd paid for the thirty-day archive. From the date stamp on the screen, it looked like Jonah had worked through at least a week of footage already.

"Any sightings?"

He flipped to another window, backed the video up fifteen seconds, and clicked play.

There she was.

Kate/Darcy parked in the spot next to the garage behind the bakery. She got out of the car with the overnight bag that was sitting in Charlie's bedroom right now, and opened the gate to the backyard. With the angle of the camera and the position of the gate, the car's license plate would've been visible if Kate and her bag hadn't blocked the entire front of the car. She locked the gate behind her, cutting off the view, before crossing the yard to the back steps.

"Shit. They all like that?"

"So far. She didn't use the car much. I've only found her going in and out six times. No luck on any of them."

Jonah backed it up again and we watched Kate cross the yard, approaching the back door and the camera. She kept her head down, one hand gripping the bag slung over her shoulder, the other holding her keys. She didn't seem to be in any hurry, maybe tired or lost in thought. She looked older than I'd assumed based on the picture Charlie had given us. It was something about the way she moved, a carefulness I didn't associate with anyone under forty. Or maybe it was just because she didn't have a screen glued to her hand.

"I'd still say mid-twenties." Jonah weighed in on my internal debate. "She's got some baby fat left in her cheeks."

"How is baby fat different than regular fat?"

"Gravity."

Before she disappeared inside the bakery, Kate looked around, scanning the yard behind her in a move that seemed automatic.

"Yeah, she does that every time," Jonah said, again talking to my thoughts. "Sometimes she pauses for longer." He flipped back to the other footage, hitting play and slumping further down in his chair.

I went to the safe. "We got another payment from Charlie." The brick of cash had weighed down my coat pocket the whole way back to Iowa City, but I hadn't felt comfortable putting it on the passenger seat. Even now, the pile of bills stuffed on top of the random papers crammed into the safe gave me heartburn. I locked it quickly and went to find some Tums.

"What is it?" Jonah asked.

"Nothing." The Tums jar was empty. Shit. I trashed it and made do with an aspirin. But by the time I came back to our desks, Jonah had turned around and was frowning at me.

"I said it's nothing."

We both knew I was lying. Jonah waited me out, scanning me like an emotional MRI.

Stalling, I grabbed a beer out of the fridge. "Want one?"

He shook his head.

I sat down at my desk, directly across from his, and took a long drink. There was no avoiding this anymore. Frankly, I was shocked Jonah hadn't heard me thinking about it once in the past year. I must have been better at compartmentalization than I'd thought.

"I was worried when we started out. About getting enough clients. Making ends meet."

"That's changed?"

"Christ, just let me say it."

He leaned back, crossed his arms, and waited.

"One day, a few months after we opened this place, I got a package."

I'd been alone in the office, listening to the sound of the furnace heating with money we didn't have, a hundred dollars for each degree, while I went through the books. Every column ended in red at the bottom, and every red number sent my blood pressure rising that much higher. We had some clients, but this was before ACT had come on board with their steady monthly checks and cascade of referrals. We didn't have enough cash to pay rent next month, let alone our paychecks.

The idea of explaining to Shelley that the business had failed less than six month after it started sent me to a new tab on my browser looking through part-time jobs. I skipped past the few private security positions advertised, even though that was the natural fit; the thought of a knockoff uniform and the little self-important desks where those jack-offs sat on their asses doing nothing made me angry just thinking about it. Bartending could have been good money, except I barely knew how to do anything other than open a beer can. I was considering a second-shift warehouse job—the pain in my shoulder had been getting better and I could easily forget to mention it on the application—when a FedEx truck arrived.

The package didn't look like anything special—a cardboard box, blank except for the postmarks. The return address was a rural route in Iowa I wasn't familiar with. It was addressed to Celina Investigations, c/o Max Summerlin. The handwriting looked vaguely familiar, but I couldn't place it.

I opened it and dropped the box cutter on my desk, staring at the contents.

It was cash. Stacks and stacks of cash.

There was no note, no indication of who sent it or why, but in my gut I already knew. I took it to the back room, even though the odds of a client walking through the door were slim to none, and counted.

"How much?" Jonah asked.

"Two hundred thousand."

He made a noise and leaned against his desk, face in his hands. "Kara."

"I think so."

Kara Johnson had been my quasi partner during a DEA task force operation, which turned out to be my last assignment in law enforcement. The DEA had been hunting for the money from a mostly busted drug empire. I didn't know if they ended up finding any after I resigned, but apparently Kara had. And she was sharing.

I traced the return address to an animal sanctuary in the middle of the state. Nothing on their website indicated Kara was there, but there wouldn't be. She lived firmly below any standard radars.

"And you decided to keep it without telling me."

"I didn't want your hands to be dirty, too."

Jonah shoved away from the desk, standing up. "What are you, my father? You don't get to decide that for me, Max."

"I know I—"

"No, you don't." Jonah slammed the laptop closed and pulled the cord out of the wall. He grabbed his coat off the desk, making papers fly. Photographs of missing persons flapped across the office, black-and-white faces landing everywhere. "You don't know what having a partner means."

"Believe me, I—"

"Right." He laughed, shoving the front door open before turning around. "Carrying more than your share is one thing. I knew that was going to happen. But this?" He shook his head, looking at me with an open disgust I'd never seen on my best friend's face, before walking out.

Jonah

Eve's house was always intrinsically Eve. No matter where she lived, whether it was an over-the-top renovated Victorian mansion or an accessible townhouse on the edge of a cornfield, she made every space undeniably *her*. And I needed that more than I wanted to admit right now.

I washed sky-blue dishes and looked out a window lined with delicate beakers holding leaves and branches of all shapes and sizes. A gauge mounted above the greenery measured at least four atmospheric things. I recognized temperature, or at least I was pretty sure it was temperature. The breakfast bar was covered with academic journals, scribbled notes, a pill reminder box, and more vases dotted with single flowers in each one—a black calla lily, a dahlia, and more I couldn't name. Magnets with scientific formulas covered the fridge, along with several pictures—mostly of Eve and Earl. The largest one showed Earl with his late wife, her laughing as he kissed her cheek in front of their apple orchard. Another was a black-and-white photo of Marie Curie working in her lab. There was a picture of me I didn't remember Eve taking. I was facing away from the camera, sitting on the bluff overlooking the Mississippi River in my backyard.

The first time I saw that picture, displayed next to Eve's family and heroes, I'd felt suddenly strangled by a mix of hope and dread. A panic attack clawing at the edges of everything I wanted. I'd tried to ignore it, both the feeling and the photo, and pretend my heart wasn't crashing waves against my chest for the rest of the night. I think we played Scrabble—word games were part of Earl's ongoing post-stroke therapy. I know I lost.

Now, the photo calmed me. I felt centered, focused for the first time since I left the office in the wake of Max's asshole confession. I belonged here, among the formulas and foliage, taped up on Eve's fridge and washing her dishes, with people who didn't lie to me for my own good.

Beyond the small kitchen, Eve and Earl sat at the dining room table together. They'd been huddled in front of my laptop studying the Pastries & Dreams security footage ever since they'd finished devouring the Chinese takeout I'd picked up on the way here.

Earl typed something on his iPad and Eve nodded. "It's like she hears distant thunder." Then, checking an app on her own phone: "No storms that day. Overcast skies, zero precipitation."

"The working hypothesis"—I framed it for Eve's benefit— "is that she was running from something or someone in her past. That's why she had no ID, no phone, no name or any means of tracking her down."

They both nodded and for once Eve didn't question the theory or demand more evidence. She understood, better now than she would have a few years ago, what it felt like to live looking over your shoulder. Not that the drug trafficking ring she'd helped bust had anyone left to hunt her down—the major players were either dead or in prison—but the trauma of watching your husband get tortured in front of you, of being almost killed yourself, didn't dissipate with any application of logic. I could feel the tension in her whenever the doorbell rang, the momentary panic before she smiled at Earl and went to answer it. I knew why she still kept a baseball bat in the coat closet. It was hard not to feel like I'd brought that into her life, even though I knew it wasn't true. Her husband was the one who'd involved himself with a drug lord, who'd gotten himself kidnapped and eventually killed, for money or glory or whatever made people do the shitty things they did. But she'd been oblivious to it until he disappeared, until I'd knocked on her door and told her I could help her find him, and we'd uncovered the whole ugly truth together. It wasn't my fault that she panicked before opening doors now, but guilt was a lot like fear. It didn't fade with logic.

Earl wheeled to the bathroom as I put the last of the dishes away. Eve waited until the door clicked shut before coming to the kitchen and leaning against the counter. Her gaze dropped to my mouth and all thoughts of guilt and fear hazed into something warmer and much more insistent. I moved into her space and braced my hands on the counter on either side of her, boxing her in.

"Hi." She smiled, her face inches from mine. At this distance I could count each individual lash ringing her eyes and feel the heat of her skin.

"Hi." I kept my voice as low as hers. "Are we sneaking around behind Earl's back?"

"That would imply he's a party to this, so obviously no." Her hands skimmed up my arms and looped around my neck. "But I haven't found the right time to talk to him yet, and I'm still reading a few books on the subject."

"How To Tell Your Ex-Father-In-Law You're Dating Again For Dummies."

Her eyes narrowed and her energy crackled dangerously on *dummies*. I bit down on a smile. Sometimes, her reactions were too easy.

"I need him to be comfortable with this. You're one of his best friends now and he's lost so much in the last few years. I don't want him to feel like he's losing either one of us. Or access to smuggled steaks."

Everything I'd sensed from Earl told me he was ninety percent fine with me in his daughter-in-law's life, but I wanted to do this right. It felt more important than anything I'd done. I drew back. "Do you want me to be there when you talk to him? Or ask for some weird patriarchal permission on the sly?"

She smiled again. "Thank you, but no. I want to talk to him alone. I will. Soon."

Before she could start logging mental calendar appointments, I moved back in, feeling the spike in her heart rate and the answering one in my own chest. The freedom to do that, to be this close to her, was like a drug soaring through my veins, only better than any drug I was used to. "Then I guess we should make the most of this bathroom break."

The other night on Eve's lawn had felt like something out of time, slow and deliberate, like we were amazed to find each other in the same dream and doing everything we could to avoid waking up. This was different. This kiss was instant heat—fast and open and hard, both of us twisting closer and looking for more. She pulled me down by the hair, scraping her nails over my scalp. I grazed her temple, her ear, her throat, trying to learn as much of her as quickly as possible. Someone groaned. It might have been me. The need vibrating through her and echoing inside me turned the world into a vacuum where only we existed. And neither of us wanted to come up for air.

She lifted a leg, running it over my hip, and under the white noise filling my brain I heard the idea in her head.

"Like this?" Lifting her, I set her on the edge of the counter and stepped between her legs, bracketing her hips until a start of surprise shocked me into the reality of what I'd just done.

Everything went cold.

"Shit. I'm sorry."

I backed up, putting space between us, trying to redraw non-existent lines between my head and hers as panic filled the edges. She hadn't asked me to put her on the counter. She hadn't made any physical move to indicate she wanted to be up there. She *thought* it, and I'd taken that as some kind of permission. Like any errant thought in her head was mine to consume.

She perched on the countertop, confusion mixing with the haze of need clouding her energy. Her hair looked like she just got out of bed, but her eyes were as piercing as always, cataloging everything. "What's wrong?"

"I don't know how to do this."

"Which part? Because the evidence so far suggests otherwise." She tilted her head and reached a hand out, but I couldn't take it.

"You know which part. The part where you thought something and I acted on it, because I have no boundaries." I paced, trying not to look at her, because looking at her made me need to touch her again. "You won't get to have any boundaries either. I can spy on everything in your head whether or not either of us wants me to."

"Kendrick."

"You're thinking I'm an idiot right now, that we were past all this. But you also like how I'm running my hands through my hair and what it does to my arms." I dropped them to my sides and turned to face her. "Do you have any idea how tuned to you I am? How invasive this is?

"It's like the dreams, the one-way glass where I see people who have no idea I'm there. I'm a voyeur to their misery, drowning in their panic and fear, and what good does it do? I wake up and they're still alone."

The need in her cooled. Her mind started firing again, analyzing everything I said. The arm appreciation was already history. Her fingers drummed on the counter.

"Do you think any of this is new information to me?"

"You were surprised." I stared at the fridge and the picture of me on it. Maybe there was a reason I was facing away from the camera, a sign that I didn't belong with the smiling faces. "I felt it. You can't lie to me."

"And I told you I could handle whatever you are, as long as you're honest about it."

I remembered. Outside a barn, on the verge of a panic attack and a massive, unhinged heist. A painfully white world. Her eyes on mine.

"Come over here."

It was impossible not to do what she asked. If she told me to scale a mountain, I would've died trying. I moved back in front of her and even the proximity made my skin hum, like electrons were jumping back and forth between us. She started to say something, but a crash in the bathroom caught her attention.

"He's fine. The toilet paper bar fell off the wall again. We should move that so it's not getting caught by the wheelchair."

She laughed. "And you think you only invade privacy? If you hadn't been here, I would've checked on him." She waited until my gaze snagged on hers. "You've given Earl his dignity back. You see him."

I shrugged it off, but she wasn't done. She caught my face in both hands. "And I see you, Jonah Kendrick. You were upset when you got here tonight. Something happened with Max."

I hadn't brought up the argument about Max's under-the-table funding. I didn't want to think about it anymore, even though his presumption kept eating at me. He'd always been good at keeping his thoughts and emotions in check. I just had no idea how much he was hiding underneath that blank veneer.

"How did you know that?"

"Observation and analysis. You picked up dinner from Cedar Rapids, which meant you needed a long drive to work off excess input."

"Excess input?" My hands had found her back again. She leaned into them.

"Yes, too much data from the world. Your street racing expels the excess, probably through a combination bath of adrenaline and dopamine. But it didn't completely offset the incident, because you were still upset when you got here, which meant whatever happened was personal—not a random encounter with a stranger. You repeatedly ran your hands through your hair while we set the table, which yes, looks sexy when you wear these black T-shirts. And when Earl mentioned Max, you reacted to the name in an anomalous way."

I stared at her, mouth open, and her voice dropped to barely more than a whisper. "This entanglement goes both ways. I thought you knew that."

I did and I didn't. Eve was a gift I didn't know how to accept, and being with her was as terrifying as it was inevitable.

"I'm tuned to you, too. My methods are different than yours, but some people find them just as invasive."

"They're not."

"My students would disagree. I'll admit I was surprised when you put me on the counter, but I wasn't exactly unhappy about it."

She pulled, slow and steady, until our foreheads pressed together. "Next time, ask. And I'll tell you if I do or don't want something."

"It's not that simple."

"It never is. But we'll start there. Right or wrong, you have to choose a methodology for your data set."

Her lips found my throat and it became difficult to think, let alone talk. "I knew I would end up in your lab someday."

She hummed and wound her legs around my hips, pulling me in hard. I lost track of time until the bathroom doorknob rattled, bringing us up with a start.

"Shit."

Eve barely made it back to the table before Earl opened the bathroom door. I rearranged random things in the fridge until it felt safe to join them.

Neither of us paid much attention to the footage. We shot glances at each other and she thought about what happened in the kitchen until I had to leave the room entirely. She laughed as I escaped to the porch, which is when I realized she was reliving it on purpose. To torture me. Goddamn, this woman was going to kill me.

While I stared desperately at weather instruments and tried to think about nothing but rain and lightning, Earl startled both of us by banging on the table.

"What?"

He pointed at the screen and I felt excitement churn through both of them before I even got back to the table. Eve backed up the footage as Earl typed on his iPad.

You would've seen it if you weren't too busy making googly eyes at each other. Ask her out already.

"Good idea." I clapped Earl on the back and we both turned to Eve, who blushed until her skin matched her hair.

"I wanted to, um, talk to you about that first," she stammered.

Just get on with it. You two are driving me nuts.

Earl shook his head at both of us, eyes twinkling as he jabbed at the screen.

On the grainy footage, Blake was taking the trash out. She opened the gate then stopped, dropping the bags. Pulling her phone out to take a call, she wandered away from the fence, and Earl—schooling us all in investigation—paused the shot.

We had a dead-on view of the license plate of Kate's car.

Darcy

My mom and I always celebrated her birthday the same way. Every year, we went to the movies. She popped popcorn at home and smuggled it into the theater in a giant handbag, along with candy and sodas from the grocery store. We watched at least two movies, buying tickets for the first one at matinee prices and then ducking into the next theater after the first show ended. An entire day's worth of food and entertainment for twenty bucks. As a kid I was nervous about getting caught, but Mom always told me it was about confidence.

"Act like you own the place and no one will know any different."

And she was right, although the employees probably did notice. They just weren't paid enough to care.

We watched kid and family movies when I was young. Disney, Pixar, musicals, Marvel, although the second movie of the day was more random. Sometimes it was a blockbuster or a family drama. Once we watched a Japanese horror film that gave me nightmares for months. When I turned thirteen she stopped covering my eyes during bloody or sexy scenes. Then, she met Ted. For two years, he came along for Mom's birthday tradition, but he did it all wrong. He bought tickets for both movies, paid fifty dollars for concessions, and then complained about them. He talked during the movies and held Mom's hand the whole time, like he couldn't stand it if her attention wasn't at least partially on him.

He was tall, slim, with thick dark hair and a meticulously shaved jaw. His eyes were as dark as coal and when he looked at you, it felt like a laser. He knew how to charm people, how to use his looks in any given situation, and that's what he'd done to my mom. At the time I was sixteen and outraged that she would let this guy into our world. I could see it more clearly now. A struggling, single mom meets a man with a giant house next to an idyllic forest. He seems successful, attentive, the kind of guy who can make impossible things like medical bills and rent increases disappear.

We missed her birthday tradition the year we escaped him, but every year after that we went back to the theater. And we did it our way. Smuggled food, bonus movies. She insisted on comedies and romances, I think, because she wanted me to believe that love existed in the world. That the nightmare of Ted was an exception, and not the norm. I didn't need to watch made-up stories to believe in love. All I had to do was look at her.

At the beginning of June, I told Blake I needed the day off and did something I promised my mom I would never do.

I drove back to Illinois.

I didn't stop until I reached the movie theater with its potholed parking lot and bright marquee. Inside, I bought a ticket with cash, slipped into the theater of the most romantic show playing, and felt my breath catch in my throat when I saw her sitting alone in the fifth row. She was already staring at me, as if she'd been watching the door and waiting. Slowly, I moved up the aisle and into the row. By the time I sat down, tears were coursing silently down my face.

We watched an entire preview, both of us facing forward and pretending this was normal. Mom played with the popcorn in her gallon Ziploc bag, but she didn't eat it. I tried to get ahold of my emotions enough to speak. When the trailer ended, she whispered to the screen.

"You shouldn't have come."

I looked behind us. There were only a handful of people here on a Thursday afternoon, and the closest ones were two rows back. "I haven't seen anything in the news. No body discovered. No missing person report."

"Nobody missed him."

The laugh burst out before I could stop it, high and loud. Her dry humor was exactly what I needed to clear the clot of emotion in my throat, an instant remedy, but it sent fresh tears pricking into my eyes. I'd missed her so much. Angling my head, I studied her profile as she watched the next preview. She looked healthy. Her hair was freshly trimmed in the super-short pixie cut she'd worn my entire life, and she was still dying it the same dark brown. Her hands were steady and she looked like she'd finally put on some weight.

"How are you?"

She swallowed and her hand found mine in the dark. Her slender bones squeezed around my palm. "Better now." I smiled and looked back at the screen. I wanted to rest my head in her lap, to feel her hand stroking the hair away from my face, but I settled for circling her arm with my other hand.

"You look good," she whispered.

"I'm doing so well." I hesitated, not sure how much to tell her. "I've made friends."

"I'm happy for you, sweetheart." I could hear the tears in her voice, choking her with the weight of our choice, the moment we'd separated our forevers from each other.

"I could come back more. No one's looking for me, Mom. I don't think—"

"No." She squeezed my hand tighter as she cut me off. "It's not safe yet. It's only been a few months."

"When will it be safe?"

"Not after two months," she clapped back. I sighed, caught between the comfort of being with her and the frustration of not knowing when I could see her again.

"How long do you think?" She didn't answer, so I pressed. "A year? Two? There's not going to be any physical evidence left on the body. It's only his house—"

"I scrubbed out the kitchen after you left."

"You weren't supposed to go back there!"

"Well, I did."

Emotion boiled beneath my skin. "So, if all the evidence is gone and no one has reported that psychopath missing, not even—"

"Stop."

Her quiet command reminded me where we were. I gave up and faced the screen, letting the argument die for now.

The previews ended and a commercial for the theater came on, the one they always played before the film finally started. Nostalgia caught me low and hard in the gut as all the years we'd spent here came flooding back, from the time I'd thought my mother could do anything, that she was an oracle showing me the secrets and hidden shortcuts through this world, to the last years when things shifted between us. She was struggling to put her life back together, trying to pretend things were okay and that she wasn't a little bit broken, but I didn't need her to be the oracle by then. She was my best friend, and for as much as I loved Blake and Charlie, I knew she always would be.

The movie started—all bright colors and happy music with the kind of beautiful, well-tended celebrities that made you feel like you could step into their world, if only for a few hours.

Next to me, Mom sighed. "When will George Clooney stop being gorgeous?"

"When the Earth stops rotating."

I looked around again, subtly checking out the other movie-goers. I'd been so focused on Mom, I hadn't paid any attention to who was in the theater with us. No one looked familiar, and no one noticed us. They were too wrapped up in the Clooney of it all. I settled back in my seat, relaxing into this stolen moment. If nothing else, I would see her on her birthday next year, and the next one after that. I could keep this much of her.

As the meet-cute played out on-screen, something tapped my elbow. I looked down to see a box of Milk Duds—my favorite—sliding across the arm of the chair with my name scrawled on them. My real name. Smiling, I reached into my coat pocket and pulled out a box of Junior Mints, her favorite, and handed them to her.

We looked at each other, unshed tears shining with flickering movie lights in her eyes and mine.

"Happy Birthday, Mom."

*　*　*

A few days later, I was manning the front counter while Blake went to the bathroom. The students I'd just helped gathered their to-go cups and bags of pastries, chatting as they wandered out. The bell on the front door chimed again and a man appeared in the doorway, wearing a hoodie and a ball cap. As soon as his gaze landed on me, his thin lips stretched back over yellowing teeth.

It was impossible. He was impossible. Dirt clogged my throat and nose, the dirt I'd shoveled into a grave two hundred miles away. My body froze. My heart stopped.

The man moved to the counter, filling the dirt-choked room until there was nothing but him.

"Hello, Kate."

Max

Other than paying for the privilege of driving on the freeway every ten miles, western Illinois wasn't that different from eastern Iowa. The hills rolled easy and long into the horizon, punctuated by cattle, crops, and the occasional church steeple or truck stop sign on the horizon. Jonah drove, which meant it took a lot less time than it should have to reach Peoria, a tidy city on the banks of the Illinois River.

We hadn't said much on the drive and nothing about the two hundred thousand dollars of illegal money I'd accepted and used for the business. It was probably better we weren't talking.

He'd texted this morning with a photograph of Kate's license plate, which came up as being owned by a Katherine Barker. I'd gotten excited about the name until I pulled the record and found it belonged to a ninety-five-year-old woman living in Peoria. Still, it was a lead, the first solid lead we'd gotten into Kate's past, and neither one of us was letting the other take it solo. Fifty fucking fifty.

It starting raining as we pulled onto a narrow residential street lined with oak trees and aging brick duplexes. We parked and walked up the sidewalk to a front door crowded with pots, their flowers dipping under the weight of raindrops. Jonah rang the bell and we waited until the door was opened by a woman who looked about as substantial as crepe paper origami. Huge red glasses perched on her tiny, wrinkled face.

"I'm not buying any." She thwacked the No Soliciting sign taped up in faded letters on her door.

"We're not selling any." I flashed my PI license. "Are you Katherine Barker?"

She made us stand out in the rain while we explained we were looking for the owner of a gray 2008 Mazda.

"I sold that car. She said she'd take care of all the paperwork."

"Who?"

Jonah was already turning around, peering through the rain.

"The girl across the street."

We were two yards short of the door to the opposite duplex when Jonah slowed. He looked apprehensive.

"What?"

"She's watching us."

I didn't know if he meant the old lady behind us or whoever lived inside this place. Was it Kate? Could she have left Iowa City and fled back here? For all the technology and resources we had, sometimes it was as simple as tracking a license plate. I didn't have to wait long. Before we could knock, deadbolts clicked and the door opened two inches—another thick chain still attaching the door to the frame. A slice of a petite woman with short dark hair and a single blue eye peered out at us. She didn't speak and something about her face made me want to see her hands, to reach for my nonexistent holster. Instead, I went through the same spiel.

"I don't know what you're talking about."

"We're looking for someone." Jonah held up his phone, showing the woman the picture of Kate on the couch. "She may be in trouble."

The woman's eye lingered on the phone. Her voice, when it came again, was unsteady. "I can't help you."

Jonah kept the photo in her line of sight. "We might be able to help you."

"Are you the police?"

"No. We just want to make sure Kate's all right."

The woman slammed the door. Jonah took a deep breath and shook his head. "Just wait."

Almost a minute passed before the latch scraped against wood and the door opened. The woman wore sweats dusted with flour and a faded pair of slippers. In her hand she held a knife.

The house was small and bright, with framed abstract art prints on every wall. Knickknacks and plants spilled over the shelves and the whole place smelled of cinnamon. It reminded me of the bakery, and within five seconds I was convinced Kate either was here or had been at one point. There weren't any photographs in sight, but every instinct told me we were on the right track.

Jonah flashed me a look as the woman led us through the house to a covered patio table in the backyard. It said, clearly, *shut up and let me handle this.*

And he was right. The woman fidgeted, unwilling to meet our eyes as she glanced across the fence to the other side of the duplex, where an older Asian couple worked in their garden, despite the rain. Her weapon, an efficient-looking carving knife, lay on the table a few inches from her fingers. She was saying volumes, none of it spoken.

There were only two chairs for the table. I let Jonah sit next to her and hung back in the corner of the patio, trying to seem as unobtrusive as possible. I'd already run property records as we crossed the street. The entire duplex was owned by a Mr. and Mrs. Le, who I assumed were the couple weeding next door.

"Who do you work for?"

"Ourselves." Jonah laid a business card gently in front of the woman. "We run a PI agency out of Iowa City."

"You're really not the police?" Her words and tone were excruciatingly careful. She still didn't want to look at us, but chanced a glance at Jonah.

Jonah jerked his head in my direction. "He used to be, but he got over it."

Another long silence as Jonah read everything in her head. It was starting to drive me crazy, being the only one on the outside of this nonverbal conversation.

"Why do you think Kate's in trouble?" the woman asked.

Jonah twitched suddenly, like a seizure. His hands fisted under the table and he started breathing hard and fast. The woman jumped up, taking the knife with her. "What's wrong with him?"

The truth wouldn't make sense—that the thing twisting Jonah up right now was whatever was wrong with *her*. I stepped forward and laid a hand on Jonah's chair. "He has episodes. Don't worry; he'll be fine."

She looked more worried than ever. "I think you need to go now."

"Are you Kate's mom?" It didn't take a former cop to mark the resemblance between them, and the tone in her voice when she asked if Kate was in trouble all but confirmed it.

She looked at me as if weighing her options before answering. "Yes."

Briefly, I explained our case and how Kate had disappeared a week and a half ago without a trace. She sank back into her chair, staring blindly at the patio tile.

"Do you have any idea where she might have gone?"

The woman shook her head tightly, tears filling her eyes. Jonah looked better—the color was coming back into his face—but like a masochist he stayed at the table instead of giving himself a break and taking a lap around the block.

"Is there anyone in her life who might have wished her harm?"

Kate's mom wiped her eyes. "I don't know how to answer that."

Jonah leaned in, waiting until he caught her gaze and held it. His breathing was still ragged.

"Why don't you tell us about the man you and your daughter buried?"

It took another hour of coaxing, explaining Jonah's abilities and sharing pictures of my family, before Valerie Campbell was comfortable enough to tell her story.

"I raised Kate on my own. I was young when I had her—twenty-three—and her dad didn't stick around long. We got by, though. I worked in daycare centers where I could bring Kate to work with me and then for the school districts so I could have summers off with her. We never had much, but she never needed much. She was always grateful for the littlest things. A trip to McDonald's, a bus ride to see a rose garden in bloom. It was so easy to raise Kate. Sometimes I worried it was too easy, that the universe would tip the other way and there'd be a difficult phase ahead. I was right, I guess. It just wasn't how I expected it. The worst things never are."

"You taught her to bake," Jonah said.

We'd moved inside the house, holding steaming mugs of coffee around a small peninsula in Valerie's kitchen. The knife was back in its place in the knife block. She glanced at Jonah like he was a zoo animal, something he got a lot, and eventually she nodded.

"It was cheaper to make our own bread and cook a pot of soup that could last a week. Kate loved baking. The chemistry of it, turning one thing into something else. She would sit in front of the oven and watch every pan of cookies until they were perfectly done."

The summer Kate turned sixteen, they went to a county fair and Valerie met Ted Kramer. He was at the fair with his son and the four of them were paired up in the same Ferris wheel car. They started talking during the ride and afterward Ted invited the Campbells to join them at a contest he was judging for their church booth.

"I told him I was raised Catholic but hadn't attended in decades. He laughed and said, 'That sounds like every Catholic I've met.' He promised his church was more welcoming. He said it was a good community, a place he'd relied on after his wife left and he had to raise his son alone."

Ted seemed open and charming, buying the Campbell women food and souvenirs as they spent the rest of the day together. He asked Valerie questions about herself, but didn't pry. He pointed out mud puddles around the carnival games so they wouldn't get their shoes dirty. And he offered his sweater to Valerie after the sun set and he caught her shivering. When he asked for her number at the end of the night, she didn't hesitate to give it to him.

"I'd had a few other relationships over the years, none that turned into anything long-term, but I always hoped I'd meet someone like Ted. He was handsome and well-spoken. He mentioned his job, but didn't drone on about it, and was clearly family-oriented."

Valerie went to the living room and pulled a box of photos off the shelf. Finding one at the very bottom, she stared at it, her mouth working.

"There were no red flags, or at least none I wanted to see. He owned a beautiful house with no mortgage and kept it nice, not like some disgusting bachelor pads I'd seen. He took me to good restaurants and sent fresh flowers to my work every week. Even Kate seemed to like him in the beginning. His son, Theo, was a little older than her, and quiet. I didn't realize how quiet at the time, or think about why a teenager almost out of high school would be so quiet. I hardly saw him after that day at the fair, but I never wondered about it, not at first. Ted filled those spaces. He kept you focused on the things he wanted you to see." She kept talking to the photo in a measured monotone, the story carefully, painfully stripped of any emotion.

"We'd been dating a few months when Ted suggested the trip to Las Vegas for the two of us. It was a spontaneous getaway, or so I thought. We stayed in a suite at the Bellagio overlooking the fountains. And when we were walking by a chapel, he pulled me aside and said we should get married. He didn't ask. I remember thinking, *Shouldn't he get down on one knee? Shouldn't I need to say yes to something?* But he pulled a ring out of his pocket and I was dazzled, I guess, by the idea that he'd planned this. He swept me off my feet. I didn't realize that was on purpose. He took my ability to walk away."

She crossed the living room and handed me the photo. In it, Valerie stood in an alcove with a tall, dark-haired man. He had black eyes, a precise mustache, and a thin smile—the kind of guy who ironed his sheets. He'd wrapped an arm entirely around Valerie, somewhere between her sternum and her throat, holding her against him.

"Kate was furious when I told her we'd gotten married. It was the worst fight we ever had. She begged me to get the marriage annulled, and when I refused she said she'd never accept him as a father. I told Ted, of course, because I thought we could work through it together, that we were a family now. I assumed he'd say something like 'Give her time, she'll come around.' But he didn't. His face went hard and blank. I remember how disturbing it was that first time, like he'd turned into a different person right in front of me. He told me not to worry, that he'd take care of Kate."

Valerie rocked back and forth, her arms crossed tightly over her chest, still staring at the wedding photo. "I think I knew then. Part of me deep down went cold when he said that. But I talked myself out of it. I told myself he meant he would talk to Kate, that he'd work on the relationship." She shook her head as her eyes flooded. "Kate should never forgive me for not listening to her."

Valerie and Kate moved into Ted's house, a two-story colonial that backed up to a wooded preserve. Ted's son, Theo, left for college shortly after they arrived, leaving just the three of them in the last house at the end of a quiet road.

Ted's behavior began changing after the wedding. He convinced Valerie to quit her job and take care of Kate and the house.

He complained about his work—he didn't like his new boss, a recent hire who happened to be Chinese—and started spending more time online. He brought his men's group from church over for dinner without warning, and got upset afterward—always afterward, when no one else was around—if the house wasn't cleaned to his standards or the meal wasn't large enough to feed eight men. If she made extra food in case they had company, he said she was being wasteful.

"He never physically hurt me. I think he avoided it just so he could throw it in my face. 'What, do I mistreat you? Do I hit you? Is the house and clothing and food I provide for you not enough?'

"Everything was about Ted. Our lives had to revolve around him. He demanded constant attention; he needed praise, sympathy, sex, gifts. And even with all of that, somehow nothing I did was enough. By our first anniversary I knew I had to leave him. But I was scared. He'd told me once, when I still thought he was being romantic, that he'd always find me. I belonged to him, and he would never let me go."

Jonah glanced over periodically as Valerie talked, but I didn't need a psychic's confirmation to see she was telling the truth. I'd interviewed enough victims to know what trauma looked like. "What happened then?"

Valerie went still and her voice became distant. "A lot of things."

"Where's Ted now?"

"In the woods behind his house." She looked up, suddenly calm. "This past spring, I killed him, and Kate and I buried the body."

Jonah

Without any dreams to guide me, finding a body in the woods was a lot like looking for a needle in a haystack. Or finding a body in the woods.

Max and I hiked through stands of oak, maple, and pine as the daylight faded, turning the weak light filtering down through the canopy into a grayish twilight. After our interview with Valerie Campbell, we'd driven directly to the house that—on paper—still belonged to Ted Kramer. It was two hours away from Valerie's duplex, outside a sleepy town well past the relentless rings of Chicago suburbs, giving Max plenty of time to dig into Valerie's story. He'd pulled as much information as he could find on his phone about Kate Campbell, her mom, and the man Valerie had claimed to have killed.

A standard background check showed Valerie had struggled with bills for most of her adult life, job hopping around Wisconsin and Illinois. A few traffic violations dotted her record and some utility bills slipped into collections. She'd hung on by her fingernails, until she'd met her husband.

"There's a marriage certificate on file but no divorce decree." Max processed everything out loud, filling the car with two hours of mostly one-sided conversation. "The marriage was eight years ago. Her rental history at the place she's at now goes back at least five."

"She didn't want to make contact again, even to serve papers."

"You sensed that?"

"Yeah, my superpower of listening when she said he threatened to track her down no matter where she went."

He let that fly, turning his attention to the alleged murder victim. Theodore "Ted" Kramer had a much larger presence on paper than either Valerie or her daughter. He'd worked as a quality manager for several manufacturers around the Midwest and had a public Facebook page that went back ten years—the posts seemed equal parts criticism of defective products and lax quality standards mixed with quasi-religious posts.

"He liked getting into fights in the comments." Max paused on what looked like a book-length rant. "This one's about that missing Malaysian plane; he blamed shoddy maintenance and belittled everyone who chimed in with other theories." Max kept scrolling. "Really long-winded posts. He starts using all caps on random words—God, I hate that. His last post applauded immigration restrictions. And that's it. The page is still up, but he basically disappeared from the platform."

"Maybe in real life too."

There was no record of Ted Kramer in any active missing persons databases. Then again, no one had reported Kate Campbell missing either.

Ted Kramer's yard was overgrown with weeds and waving white dandelion heads, which didn't match the image of the closely-shaved buttoned-up guy on socials. No one answered the front door and there was no sign of life inside, no waft of emotion or energy

I could sense. But the mailbox was empty—someone must have been checking it—and the house itself was an imposing two-story brick building with every curtain drawn. I couldn't sense much beyond the front door in a place this big. Someone could've easily sat in the shadows upstairs as we prowled the neglected perimeter.

Max paced the edge of the property twice before moving into the woods. I sighed, fantasized about getting in the car and driving away, before eventually following him in. It was the wrong call. We were still hiking through endless stands of trees an hour later when even the sun started giving up for the day.

"We weren't hired to find Ted Kramer."

Max paused the bloodhound search to lift his phone, looking for service. "I know."

"So what are we doing here?"

He gave up on the signal and climbed over a fallen tree, scanning the ground with his phone flashlight. The buzz of one-track, blinders-on energy radiating off him was as familiar as looking in a mirror.

"I don't know. I'll know when I find it."

"Are you going to find it before we have to sleep here? Did you text Shelley about any of this?"

Max didn't answer. I wanted to punch him.

Ted Kramer's property backed up to the Wolf River Bluffs Forest Preserve, an oblong stretch of green on the map that hugged the south side of the Wolf River in a chain of state parks and forests. We could probably walk all night without seeing a single road or building. If Max knew that, he wasn't thinking about it. He barely registered anything that wasn't terrain.

Things moved around us—a creak of a branch, the crunch of leaves as something padded just out of sight. I couldn't sense anyone else in the woods, which would normally be comforting. The farther away from humanity the better, in general, yet the absence didn't bring relief here. Something kept me on edge and it wasn't just my idiot partner. I couldn't stop looking behind us, until I didn't know whether I was imagining the hushed, rustling noises or not. The hair on the back of my neck stood up.

To distract myself, I went over the interview again. Valerie Campbell's mind had been a complicated shell game, each layer hinting at something hidden beneath. Even when she'd thought about her husband lying facedown in a trough of dirt and dead leaves, it was fractured pieces of a memory. Hands bleeding on a shovel handle. Sweat dripping from her forehead to the corpse. A frantic hug, pulling her daughter close as they both trembled with shock and exhaustion. Darkness and short, heaving breaths.

She didn't linger long enough on any one thought or memory to give us a location for Ted Kramer's body. And despite talking for almost two hours, she never thought about his actual murder. It could have been an intentional omission, once she knew what I was, but it didn't feel like it. Everything about Valerie's thoughts screamed PTSD and the suppression of traumatic memories.

After another half hour when more shadow than light surrounded us, I asked Max, "Are we here because you want to find something or because you don't?"

Max switched directions, doubling back on a slightly different path than the way we'd come in. This one was more crowded with trees and underbrush. Branches scraped us on all sides.

"Hard to say." He was eager to start talking it out. The words instantly relaxed him. "If we find Ted Kramer's body, we've got confirmation of why Kate came to Iowa City in the first place. But then we'd have to notify authorities." As he scanned the ground with his flashlight, a branch hit him in the face and he swore. I grinned for the first time since we'd walked into the woods.

"Sure, let's forget our track record on reporting crimes for a minute." He shot me a look, still rubbing sap off his face. "If you did call the authorities to report a murder, that would put Valerie Campbell in jail and Kate, potentially, under more pressure wherever she is. Making her that much harder to find."

"What did you make of that bit at the end?" Max asked. "Was she telling the truth?"

Just before we'd left Valerie's house, Max had asked the question on both our minds. He'd explained how Kate was living under a pseudonym, paying only cash, and working under the table during her time in Iowa City.

"Is that behavior typical of your daughter?"

Valerie admitted it wasn't.

"Why do you think she was living like that? She did everything possible to conceal her identity. Her closest friends didn't even know her real name."

Valerie had already walked us to the door at that point. She gripped the deadbolt as she surveyed the street with careful eyes. "I told her to. I wanted her to start over completely, to get as far away from me as possible. I knew someone would find Ted's body eventually and come looking for me. Kate doesn't deserve to go to prison for the crime of being a good daughter."

Max glanced at me. Valerie didn't miss it.

"They'd call it something else. Accessory or accomplice, I don't know. But that's not what happened. She saved my life, and I would never allow her to pay for that with the rest of hers. I've made my peace with what I did and what I'll have to do when the time comes. I don't have any regrets besides marrying him in the first place."

Without warning, she'd reached out to me, holding my arm and my attention in a vise grip of desperation and love.

"Dream about her. Find her, please. You have to make sure she's okay."

I could still feel her hand on my arm, the sharp bite of her sudden plea. As if I could dream about people on demand. As if my abilities were in any way under my control. I was an unconsenting voyeur to the worst moments of random victims' lives, unable to do anything except watch as they thrashed and screamed or sank into the mire of their circumstances. Lost and hopeless, they didn't know anyone saw them. I had no way of telling them I was there, that someone would be looking for them, and they weren't alone.

And there was another reason I might not have dreamed about her. I never had nightmares about people who were already dead. Kate Campbell had a name now, but she might not have a pulse.

"She was telling the truth about the identity stuff," I confirmed. "She'd told Kate to change her name and disappear. She didn't want her daughter anywhere near the fallout zone."

Max digested that as we came into an open area along a creek bed. The water was dark and stagnant, and the forest swallowed the sucking sound of our shoes in the mud. Twilight was settling in and it was getting harder and harder to see anything outside the beams from our phones. Somewhere behind us, a twig snapped.

"Would you do that?" Max asked.

"Which? Send someone I loved away to protect them or be the one who left?"

"Either."

I had to breathe into the effort of separating myself from Valerie's decisions and emotions. Draw the boundary and think about what lay on my side. The people in my life who mattered could be counted on one hand with fingers to spare. But it was still impossible to imagine. I couldn't see Max or Eve doing anything I told them, regardless of their own safety. And I wouldn't be able to stomach their self-sacrificing bullshit either. "I doubt it."

He stood between a dead, uprooted tree and the water's edge, staring at the black mirror of the creek. The sheen of his head was muted, turning hollow in the shadows and twisting half-light. I felt his answer before he said it.

"That's what I was trying to do with the money from Kara. We needed it or we would've gone under, and I told myself we were doing good work, that the scales would balance in the end. By not telling you, I thought I was protecting you from the consequences, if it ever came to light."

"You hear yourself, right?"

He sighed. "It was wrong and stupid. You can take a swing at me if it makes you feel better."

He didn't think I would, which made it more satisfying when I turned him around and punched him in the face. He stumbled and fell into the fallen tree, cursing as he tried to untangle himself from the dirt, moss, and rotting roots splayed into the air like an autopsy. I wished it was lighter so I could see the frustration and scrambling as clearly as I sensed it from the forest floor.

When he stopped struggling, I offered a hand. He paused before taking it and pulled himself out of the roots.

"We're good," I told him. "Don't do it again."

He clapped me on the shoulder and that was that.

He picked up his phone where he'd dropped it in the hole the fallen tree must've left in the forest floor. The flashlight made a wild arc as he straightened, knees popping like gunshots, and moved on. Something snagged in my brain, though—a dull warning. Somewhere deep in the woods a chorus of crows screamed at each other. I stopped walking, caught on the snag, the thing that wasn't right.

Dread uncoiled in my gut as I retraced my steps and lifted my phone light to the trunk of the fallen tree. Underneath the base of the trunk, pulled up by the tug of earth, were a pair of stained, thick bones sticking out of the dirt.

"What is it?" Max was ten paces ahead, shining a tiny beam of light back at me.

"A grave."

Kate

As soon as he walked into the bakery, I was seventeen years old again. The last seven years of my life—the escape, the townhouse, college, jobs, murder, Blake and Charlie—all fell away. I was a teenager on the verge of graduating high school and escaping the horror show my life had become. Everything would change, I thought, no matter if my mom ever left Ted or not. I could start fresh at the University of Wisconsin–Madison, and reinvent who and what I was. I could become someone new. Maybe it would give Mom the courage to do the same.

The weekend before graduation, Ted came home in a rage because his job laid him off. His "incompetent manager" was moving his work to another department. Ted was already talking lawsuits and civil actions, storming around like the toddler he was and too far into the tantrum for even Mom to soothe him. She'd been baking bread and hovered at the edge of the room with a smear of dough on her shirt. She looked exhausted and wary and that, more than anything else, made me say it.

"Good for them. They should've fired you ages ago."

Ted turned on me and I froze. Fury flooded his face, veins throbbing, pupils eating his eyes. I'd lived the last year and a half knowing with absolute certainty that no matter how bad things got, we hadn't seen the worst of him yet. Looking at his face now, I knew. The worst was here.

I tried to run. He caught me before I made it two steps. The next thing I knew Mom put herself between us and screamed that she was done; she was leaving him. For a split second I was happy. I thought we could finally leave, together.

He didn't shout back. He grabbed her by the throat, deadly calm, pulled her face close to his, and muttered as her cheeks turned red and then purple. "It's over when I say it's over."

I threw myself at him, not even thinking to grab a knife or a pot, something I could use to hurt him. All I could see was the color bloating my mom's face and the desperation in her eyes.

My attack surprised him. He released Mom and she stumbled back, coughing and gasping. Then she was there, all ninety pounds of her flying at him. He shoved me into the refrigerator, knocking the wind out of me, and pushed her into the pantry, slamming the door and moving the kitchen table against it to trap her inside. I crawled to the living room and grabbed my phone, calling 911, but as the call connected and the operator said, "What's your emergency?" Ted pulled it out of my hands and ended the call before I could do more than gasp an oxygen-starved "Help—" into the receiver.

"What's over," he seethed as he dragged me by the back of my shirt and jerked me down the concrete steps to the unfinished basement, "is the disrespect I've put up with from you."

He hauled me across the dark space, through the beams of ghost walls, over the dirt and cobwebs. I heard the screech of a door open and then I was kicked into blackness.

"This is your time-out room, Kate. You're going to sit here and think long and hard about your behavior in my house. And if I hear one single sound from you, I'll kill her." His voice wavered and broke, as if even he was shocked by what he was saying. His hands shook. "Do you understand?"

I covered my mouth, trying to lock the whimper of pain and rising panic inside. Because he might not be bluffing. If he could do this, I had no idea what else he was capable of.

The door slammed and the metallic click of a padlock slotted into place. His footsteps padded away, and then there was nothing.

He locked me in the time-out room for two days. Two days of blackness. Two days of peeing in the corner and stuffing my fist in my mouth to choke off the sounds I couldn't hold inside. It wasn't a real room, just a crawl space three feet wide by six feet long. I could sit up but not stand. It felt like a tomb, a place for bodies to rot and be forgotten.

Spiders and insects crawled over my skin, making me scratch my arms and legs until they were wet with blood. I heard voices that weren't there. I saw things that couldn't exist. The world was dirty concrete and cinderblock.

I hummed to myself, so soft the spiders couldn't even hear, lullabies Mom used to sing to me when I was young. I held my knees and rocked, mouthing the words, feeling her cool hand on my cheek. She always looked so tired, with bags under her eyes, mascara smeared as she perched on the edge of my twin bed, but she never rushed me through our bedtime ritual. She sang and tucked in each of my stuffed animals around me, hugging me twice and kissing each cheek before going back to the kitchen. I fell asleep listening to her get ready for the next day, sometimes with the perfume of baking sugar in the air.

"It's not your fault," I told no one. "You didn't know."

He came back once. I didn't know how long it had been, if I'd been trapped for hours or weeks. I didn't know if my mother was alive or not. I hadn't heard him come down the stairs and when he opened the door, I jumped and skittered backward like one of the bugs on the walls.

He set a chair in front of the door and sat on it, the creak and scrape of wood heavy underneath him. He didn't talk at first. I was afraid to look at him, but I could feel his eyes on me. His breath sounded uneven and his foot tapped a rhythm-less pattern on the floor. I didn't know what he was thinking—what he was *planning*—and the terror of not knowing choked up my throat and made me close my eyes. I waited; mute, blind, and frozen.

"There's a lot of important people in my men's group," he finally said. "The deputy mayor, several police officers and firefighters. They know you through what I've told them and they've counseled me on how to be a father to such a troubled young woman."

It felt like I was swimming up from the bottom of a dark pool. Faces of strange men floated above me, disconnected, meaningless. I didn't understand what he was talking about.

The chair creaked again, closer this time.

"In the group, they study stories from the Bible. Most of the stories are morality lessons, hoops to keep the masses jumping, but

I always liked the one about Jonah. Do you know that story, Kate? Did you ever once listen in all the times I brought you to church?"

I chanced a look, but a bare lightbulb shone directly behind his head. My eyes teared up, blurring everything into a wall of color and sound. "I'm sorry, Ted. I shouldn't have—"

"No, you shouldn't have." His voice raised, sudden and loud like an explosion. The violence behind it cut off anything else I was going to say. Ted sighed as he resettled himself and the chair scraped against the concrete floor.

"Jonah thought he was just a regular man living his regular life before he died his regular death. He thought he was no one until God revealed His plan for him. God told Jonah that he was a prophet—he had been given divine insight—and it was Jonah's fate to go to Nineveh and warn them that judgment was coming. They had sinned and God needed to punish them.

"That was why Jonah was born. He was born to deliver God's message, to be a prophet. But Jonah—ignorant, defiant Jonah— thought he could change his life. He thought he could escape his fate. He ran from God. He boarded a ship to sail to the ends of the earth, but God followed. God set a storm upon the ship, ready to tear it apart until the sailors threw Jonah into the sea, then God sent a whale to eat him and bring him back to Nineveh.

"That's what happens when you try to change things that have already been set in motion, when you think you can exert your little will on forces greater than you can imagine."

Slowly, I sat up. My eyes had adjusted enough to see the loaf of bread and gallon of water he'd set inside the door. That's when I realized he wasn't letting me out. He'd come down here to give me enough food and water to keep me alive, and to hear the sound of his own voice, his favorite sound in the world. It felt like I finally surfaced from the dark water, as white-hot rage filled my entire body and the story he'd been telling shifted into focus.

"Are you supposed to be God in this delusion?"

"You still don't get it." He stood up, making the chair groan. "I'm the whale."

Then he shut me in the dark again.

He came back the next day, shining a flashlight on me that made me scream and skitter into a corner. He dragged me out and made me wash myself and change my clothes. I begged him to tell me where my mother was—the pantry he'd locked her in was open and empty—but he refused to answer. I was too weak to try to escape or make any kind of plan, and suddenly we were in his pickup, stopped in front of the local police station. I surfaced to hear him saying, "—took off with some guy without telling your mom or me. His name was Brad. You never knew his last name. You called 911 at one point when you guys were on drugs. You finally sobered up and came home, and you're fine."

"Where's my mother?"

He leaned in and it felt like his body filled the entire cab of the truck. I could still smell the dirt and dust. I could feel the bugs crawling over my skin.

"You're going to tell them exactly what I just told you. Do you understand, Kate?"

I was terrified of what he wasn't saying, the silences between his words where my mother wavered between existence and non-existence. Nodding, I climbed out of the truck.

I parroted exactly what Ted told me to a bored investigator who spent twenty minutes asking about the drugs and lecturing me on the irresponsibility of running away, skipping my last days of high school, and making a prank call to 911 while under the influence.

"I'm sorry," I mumbled over and over again, as Ted asked them to go easy on me. "Her mom and I are just glad she's home." His hand hovered over the back of my chair, decorated with three long scratches that no one else seemed to notice.

"Get some rest," the cop told me, standing up to escort us out of the station, "and stay sober."

On the way back to his house, I asked about Mom again. He didn't reply and I became more and more freaked out that I'd just done the completely wrong thing. The cops thought I was an unreliable, drugged-out teenager. I was done with high school now. No one would report my absence or even notice I was gone. I wanted to jump out of his truck, run to any of the houses flashing past us and pound on their doors. Or I could grab the wheel and pull it into an oncoming car. He wasn't wearing a seatbelt. He might fly through the windshield. Die on impact. A dozen different ways to escape or attack him flew through my head, but I couldn't make myself go through with any of them. Because maybe my mother was alive. I could still hear the echo of his voice as he locked me in the time-out room, telling me my behavior would decide my mother's fate. And the thing was, it could be true.

I loathed Ted. I'd disliked him the minute he and Mom started dating. He was too charming, too polished. He had all the right answers and he handed them out with the kind of over-the-top love bombing flair that made me question everything he said. Mom told me not to be so negative. She believed in love enough to ignore the red flags and marry him less than three months after they started dating. We moved into his giant house, surrounded by fields and woods, where no one could witness the monster he started to become. Suddenly, everything was about him. Mom had to cater to his every whim and if she didn't, we heard about it for days. He reminded us of the exact words he'd used if we messed up a chore.

"Did I tell you to take out the trash and leave the can behind the garage? I told you, specifically, to wheel the cans next to the mailbox before 7:00 a.m."

If the trash cans were on the wrong side of the driveway, it was a problem. If they were out at 7:01, even though the garbage truck didn't come until after noon, it was a problem. If a single tissue was stuck to the bottom of a trash basket inside the house, he would show it to me, putting the whole basket right in my face, and ask me if I knew what the problem was. *Actions have consequences, Kate.*

Listening to him, paying attention to every nuance and syllable, was the key to surviving in his house for the last year and a half. That's what kept me frozen in the seat as he drove us back from the police station. He'd told me not to make a sound and I'd spent two days in a pitch-black crawl space without once calling for help. He ordered me to wash up and change, and I did. He told me to lie to the police and I had. My behavior, my ability to listen to his exact, unhinged instructions, might actually decide her fate.

At the house, I got out of the truck and hovered out of his reach as he unlocked the door and went inside. He ordered me to my room. Not the time-out room, but the bedroom on the far side of the second floor with sharp eaves that always smelled faintly of gasoline, since it was right above the garage. He followed three steps behind, the stairs groaning under his weight and sending all the hair on the back of my neck up. I tried to listen for other sounds in the house, to catch my mother's breathing or words, but I couldn't hear anything over the wind whistling through the leaves in the woods.

Their bedroom door was shut. I wanted to pound on it, to shout for my mom, but I kept walking down the long hallway until it stopped at my room.

"Sit down on the bed."

He waited until I complied. My heart filled my ears and throat with panicked thuds, but I lowered myself gingerly on one corner of the twin bed, hands in my lap, looking at his stomach so he could see I was paying attention without challenging him. He stood in the doorway, flipping something metal in his hands. I couldn't tell what.

"You'd better hope you did good enough at the station."

I nodded.

"Do you even understand what I had to do to get us through this? The amount of groundwork, the details. Neither one of you appreciates my ability to plan on a master scale. I can see every move everyone will make from a thousand yards away."

He kept raging about his incredible brain, drifting into a rant about getting fired from his job and how it was all a giant conspiracy because his "foreign" bosses were threatened by his intelligence. I nodded and made small agreeable sounds, but my mind had tripped over the words "Neither of you appreciates" and stuck there. *Appreciates*, as in my mother was well enough to not appreciate this whining asshole right this very second. I didn't know where she was, but she was conscious and alive. She was present tense.

He went on for at least another ten minutes, devolving further into how everyone in his life was against him (duh) and how all he wanted was a tiny shred of gratitude for all he did (good luck). The whole time he kept pacing in front of the doorway and flipping the metal tool in his hand, fingering it like a stress ball. Then, without warning, he slotted the piece of metal into the jamb of the bedroom door and I realized what it was. A lock. Another way to keep me imprisoned.

I chanced a glance at the window and saw a fresh line of screws along the bottom of the sill. A bucket sat in the corner of the room, with a small bag of groceries next to it.

This was my new time-out room.

"Actions have consequences, Kate. Things are going to be different around here."

I looked him in the eye for the first time since we'd left the police station. A burning certainty ran down the length of my spine, the gut-deep knowledge of how completely one hundred percent different things were going to be.

"I know."

Max

It took half the night to get the body excavated. Jonah and I hiked out of the woods far enough to get a signal, marking our path on the way out, and waited for a deputy to show up. He took us seriously, followed us to the spot on the edge of the creek bank, and surveyed the scene with a floodlight that illuminated the entire hole of the uprooted tree.

The bones sticking out of the dirt looked like the bottom of a leg. Smaller bones were littered among the leaves, twigs, and moss, but most of the foot had probably been taken by scavengers.

"Did you disturb the area at all?" His floodlight lingered on a smooth indent in the dirt.

"I fell into it and dropped my phone."

Jonah didn't say anything. No point telling the deputy I'd been punched into the grave. That would bring irrelevant questions, and luckily the night hid any damage Jonah had done to my nose. We didn't need to derail the conversation.

He was still suspicious, though. As we hiked out to call the crime scene team, the deputy asked what we'd been doing out here. Jonah showed him the picture of Kate as I gave him the basics—we were PIs hired to find a missing woman—omitting the part where the missing woman and her mother might have buried a body in these woods.

"You think that's her?"

"I don't see how. She's only been missing for ten days and that body is completely decomposed. Been here a few months at least."

"Why were you looking for her out here?"

Jonah took that one. "We got a tip that she'd been seen in this area."

He called in the 10-55 and requested a team, then took all our information and had us repeat our stories before sending us home. I asked to stay and observe the recovery. There could've been some clothing still intact, a clue that might tell us whether this was the body of Kate's stepfather. But even as an ex-cop, I wasn't allowed back on the scene. The deputy was respectful but firm as he sent us away.

The house's dark brick walls and black windows looked even more abandoned at this time of night. Something creaked in the eaves as we walked to the car, but nothing moved inside or out. It felt as lifeless as the corpse in the woods.

"Should we call Valerie?"

Jonah thought about it as we pulled away and drove through the tiny winding streets back to the freeway. He didn't seem angry anymore and if one clock was all it took to get my friend and partner back, I was relieved. He hadn't broken my nose, but I wouldn't have said a word if he had. Now it was on me to not screw everything up again.

"We didn't tell her we were coming here. That already damages the trust we built with her today."

"If she finds out through the media, she'll put two and two together. It'll be better coming from us."

In the end, we called. She didn't sound surprised by what we'd done, and took the news with quiet resignation. When I asked outright if she would flee like Kate had, she shut me down before the question was even finished.

"When they ask, tell them where to find me."

Then she hung up.

I had a standing date on Thursday night, or Therapy Thursday, as we'd started to call it. Shelley and I had begun marriage counseling sessions with a once-a-month schedule in mind, but after the first session, okay, probably less than ten minutes into the first session, our counselor, Angelica, recommended a more frequent schedule. It was eighty bucks a pop after insurance, which Shelley said was a bargain, and I tried not to multiply eighty by the number of times we'd sat on this Zoom call after dinner, telling a woman with multiple nose piercings and a penchant for the phrase "trauma response" about our week.

"How are nightly check-ins going?" Angelica asked, which was how she usually started the call.

Shelley went first and I was nodding along when Angelica interrupted.

"Max, you don't seem very present for your wife tonight."

Shelley laughed. Angelica didn't know it, but we had therapy bingo cards and "not present" was a corner spot. Shelley had stuffed them in my Christmas stocking last year as a joke, and we'd graduated from filling them in after sessions to actively hiding the game from Angelica. The first one to get a bingo won a single demand, no questions asked. Shelley had burned through her honey-do list and banned me from wearing my favorite T-shirt out in public because of a few sweat stains no one at Lowe's would ever notice. In the few times I'd won, I'd gotten my favorite lasagna and made her watch the Die Hard franchise. If either of us ever got a blackout, there were special favors. I didn't know what hers would be exactly, but she told me once it involved a Scottish accent.

Shelley marked her bingo card with a Cheez-It underneath the camera's view and casually popped a few more markers into her mouth.

"You're right, I'm sorry." An apology gave me a center spot. I grabbed a Cheez-It from Shelley. "I've got a frustrating case at work and it's taking up a lot of my headspace this week."

"Are you able to discuss the case with Shelley? Share your frustration?"

"He found a body last night."

Angelica's professional mask slipped and she leaned forward with equal parts horror and interest. "Oh my god, that must have been so traumatic."

I absently added another Cheez-It to my card as the image of bones protruding from the dirt wiped every other thought from my head.

"It is and it isn't." I thought for a second, trying to be honest about this in a way that someone beside Jonah or the guys in ICPD might understand. "I've seen more than my share of human remains and you get desensitized to them. You have to be, to do the job. But it's always a gut punch if you let yourself think about it. Because it's never just a body. It's not just evidence. It's a person, someone who had likes and dislikes, with allergies and maybe a bad back, who had a cluttered desk at work they told themselves they'd clean up one day, and maybe went to therapy just like this and tried to be a better person. And in the end they're a pile of tissue and a case number."

"Was it a murder?"

"We haven't gotten the autopsy report yet, but you don't end up somewhere like that on accident."

"Right." Angelica nodded, looking vaguely sick. "How does that make you feel?"

"I'm trying not to feel anything because I don't know what the right way *is* to feel about this. The body? They were a victim, but I don't know if they were innocent. This person might have been someone's abusive estranged husband, a guy who controlled and terrorized his wife until it literally came to life or death. And if it is—if it turns out to be this asshole—I'm going to feel worse about discovering and reporting it than if I'd left the entire story alone." We were no closer to finding Kate and now, because of me, her only family might go to prison. It ate at me the whole way home from Illinois. All day today, I'd felt restless, uncomfortable, like a sickness about to start. Something was whispering at the back of my mind.

"There's always a body. There's always a crime. What we do— Jonah and I—is built on the worst moments of people's lives. We profit off their suffering. It's not why we do it, but it doesn't change the fact that we do. I think that's why . . ."

I broke off, staring blindly at the bingo card as the words on it wavered in and out of focus. The whisper grew louder, became audible. Shelley's hand found mine. And then it all came out. The mysterious package of money. Siphoning it into the business without telling anyone. Feeling like shit but relieved at the same time, because we could do this job without needing it. We could chase Jonah's dreams without our hands out. I could say yes to Garrett's overnight baseball camp and pay for our office rent and Shelley's favorite Thai takeout and furnace repairs and therapy.

"No matter how many people we've found, it doesn't make it right. I should've told you," I turned to Shelley, "I should've told you and Jonah right away and we could decide what to do together. I didn't have any right to make that call on my own."

Tears filled Shelley's eyes. She nodded toward my face. "Is that what happened to your nose? Jonah found out?"

"Yeah." It was swollen and purplish and throbbed every time I sneezed. "I told him."

"Are you two okay now?"

"Are we?"

She looked away and my heart fell into my gut. If this was the thing that broke us—after everything we'd been through and fought and survived—if this was how I lost the woman I'd loved for twenty years, I would lose my goddamn mind.

"Shelley, you know I'm shit at this. You know I'm going to say the wrong thing. I'm going to screw it up. And after this thing, I'll screw the next thing up. I'm never going to get it right. But you also know that you mean more to me than anything in the world. There's about thirty grand of the money left. I'll go get it now and you can decide what to do with it. You can light it on fire. You can book your bucket list trip to Iceland. You don't even have to take me, but I need you to come home to me."

She still hadn't turned around and the panic started building. I bargained with the back of her head, the messy bun that got in my face at night, the smell of her that I woke up to every morning.

"There isn't a home if you're not here. You're my home. You and Garrett. You're the reason I go out there and screw everything up. Not that it's your fault. I'm not blaming you, Jesus Christ, it's—I'm trying to say . . ."

Digging into the Cheez-It bag, Shelley pulled out a handful. She turned around and her cheeks were wet.

Without saying a word, she slowly covered every square of my bingo card.

Jonah

"Kate Campbell."

Charlie repeated the name and took my phone, studying the senior photo of Kate I'd taken at her mother's house. Kate's hair was shorter and her face was rounder, but there was something missing, that sense of confidence and possibility when a high schooler stood on the verge of graduation. She leaned against a tree, arms crossed and smiling closed-mouth at the camera. Everything else about her was closed, too. Guarded, like she was waiting for the other shoe to drop.

"Do you know what she was running from? Why she used another name?" Blake stared at the phone over Charlie's shoulder. We sat in the dining room of the bakery after closing time, the air heavy with coffee grounds and cleaning products. The music was off, the only light filtering in from the late-afternoon sun. Both of them had become lost in the photo, in the glimpse of one of Kate's other lives.

"We think so." Max and I had debated how much to tell them. It wasn't just Kate's secret; it was Valerie's, too. And Kate had started a brand-new life to keep that secret. Ultimately, though, Charlie was our client. He needed to know we'd found at least a piece of her.

I told them the basics about Valerie and Kate, the single mother and her teenage daughter. Then I told them about Ted.

"He abused them?" Blake's energy went from shocked to murderous in a heartbeat. Charlie wasn't far behind.

"There's no record of charges being brought against him." We'd looked, thoroughly, but Theodore Kramer had come up completely clean in the background check. He'd worked as a quality manager for various manufacturers in central Illinois, pulling a low-six-figure salary before he'd been fired from the last position a year ago. Several of the HR departments divulged that his performance had been "unsatisfactory," but wouldn't say anything else for legal reasons. We couldn't find record of him working in the last year, even though his credit remained spotless.

He'd been active in his church, a place called Divine Light that took over a bankrupt office supply building and boasted a website made of sixty percent adjectives. There was no phone number, only an email address that auto-replied with a generic blessing and the assurance that they'd get back to us as soon as possible. They hadn't.

He popped up in a few local newspaper stories, one about the church and another profiling "lovely lawns" in the area. His parents were dead, his first wife had left him, and his son lived alone in an apartment in the Chicago suburbs. Our attempts to contact the first wife and son had gone as well as the church.

"She was trying to get away from her stepfather?" Blake took the darkened phone out of Charlie's hand and gave it back to me.

"No. Things came to a head with him years ago. Neither Valerie or Kate had any contact with him. Until this spring."

I pulled up the media story about the body being exhumed in the woods behind Ted Kramer's house and pushed the phone back across the table.

"Oh my god." Charlie shoved out of his chair, full of nausea and fear. "Is it Kate?"

"No. The remains are too decomposed. She's only been gone a few weeks. This body was, well, it had been there longer."

"Oh." Blake's face went pale as she made the connection. "Oh, shit."

I braced against the force of their emotions, breathing deep. Yoga breaths. Max had offered to come with me for this meeting, but he would've had to cancel a follow-up appointment with an infidelity client. I told him I could handle it. And I could.

"We don't know whose body it is yet. Identification could take a while, and the authorities might not share information with us."

"Have you talked to Ted Kramer?" Blake narrowed her gaze.

"No. We haven't been able to locate him." Above ground, anyway. Blake seemed to understand the implications.

"Good." She nodded. "But that still doesn't help us find Darcy. I mean, Kate."

Charlie hadn't leapfrogged to the Kate-and-her-mother-might-be-murderers conclusion. His energy had stuttered on the article about the body, and now worked its way into confusion. He'd started pacing again.

"What is it?"

"I . . . nothing."

I closed my eyes, waiting for the image to bloom on the back of my eyelids. A low building with a flat metal roof. Even reflected in

Charlie's head, the place didn't look in great shape. It was missing windows and boards, with weeds chewing in on all sides.

"You're thinking about a building. Somewhere near your house."

"It's just that—"

"He's right?" Blake cut in. "Holy shit, do me next!"

Charlie ignored her and I tried to focus as a bizarre parade of meme-worthy scenes spilled out of Blake's head.

"I've been going to Silas's the last few nights," Charlie admitted. I moved as far away as possible from the table where Blake was grinning and thinking comically hard.

Charlie claimed he went to talk to him—which felt mostly true—but changed his mind when he heard Silas yelling inside his house. Maybe at his grandkid or the TV. Charlie tried listening in, but Silas came outside and walked to one of the outbuildings on the property, the same stubborn, neglected structure I'd seen in his head.

"He stayed there for a half hour, maybe, before going back to the house. I went again the next night and just waited. He came out later, after the news, but he went to the same building and stayed the same amount of time." Charlie stuffed his hands in his pockets. "He doesn't farm anymore—hasn't in years. There's no reason for him to be out there. And I thought, maybe, you know, that Kate—"

I picked up my phone and the box of pastries I'd bought for Earl. "Stay home tonight. Don't trespass on the property of an angry gun owner. Max and I will check it out."

Charlie agreed and the two of them walked me to the Evolution parked out front. Blake looked at me like she was in a staring contest only she knew about. I sighed and shook my head, unlocking the car.

"It's dangerous to ride a unicorn bareback. Even for young Rob Lowe."

Kate

The day after Ted locked me in the bedroom with a bucket and some snacks, I heard a crash on the opposite end of the hall, followed by stomping and short, guttural yells. It sounded like Ted was taking the house apart. Did that mean my mother had escaped? Did it mean she was dead? I didn't know. I had zero information, but I'd spent the entire night dismantling the lamp next to my bed, shattering the lightbulb, and gluing the shards of glass to the end of the brass pipe. I grabbed it and ducked behind the door, praying he would open it and come barreling inside. I visualized the back of his head, the vulnerable skin at his throat, walking myself through each blow. How he might counter, how I would respond.

He thought he was a whale, an instrument of God making me face my fate. He thought he could swallow up my whole life and no one would stop him.

Except me.

This time, Jonah was going to eat the whale.

I waited, gripping the glass-encrusted pipe like a lifeline, listening to the chaos erupting from him like bile as he crashed through the house. Then I heard the front door slam. I crept to the window and watched him rage around the yard. He stopped, looking at the woods as if he wanted to check them, but he didn't. He never went into the preserve. It was too dirty, too disordered. The trees didn't line up perfectly like the shrubs along his sidewalk. He couldn't douse the preserve in chemicals like he did with his fluorescent green lawn. The woods were beyond his control, and he hated that. After a minute, he turned and disappeared around the corner of the house. His truck engine fired up and roared away.

The sound of my bedroom doorknob sent my heart into my throat and I panicked, running across the room, convinced that somehow he'd tricked me into giving up my hiding spot behind the door. I raised the pipe as the door opened—ready to kill him anyway, the hell with the element of surprise, the hell with my sad Pinterest weapon, I would do it with my bare hands—before stumbling to a stop.

Mom stood in the doorway.

A cry tore out of my throat. I dropped the pipe and threw myself at her, sobbing before her arms even wrapped around my back.

"I thought you were dead."

She kissed the side of my head hard, holding me like she would never let go again. But too soon she drew back, bracketing my shoulders and scanning every inch of me. "Are you okay?"

I wasn't. I was years and countless mental breaks and meltdowns away from okay. It would probably take more therapy than I could ever afford to think of myself in those terms again, but Ted was gone and my mom was here. My bedroom door was open and all we had to do was walk through it. I nodded.

She seemed to accept my answer for exactly what it was, her mouth turning into a thin, grim line.

"Get your weapon. Let's go."

The keys to my mom's car were long gone and who knew what he'd done with our phones. With no transportation or means of communication, we did the only thing we could: we escaped through the woods. Once we'd gotten deep enough into the trees to feel comfortable talking, we traded horror stories. Ted had left my mother in the pantry for hours, telling her the same thing he'd used to threaten me—that he'd murder me if she made a sound. He knew exactly how to control both of us, to exploit our love for each other, knowing we would walk to the ends of the world to keep the other one safe.

He must've gotten bored at some point because eventually he dragged her out of the pantry in the middle of the night. He made her cook for him, clean up the mess he'd made in the kitchen, and put the entire house in order. He didn't tell her where I was. She listened to his rants about being fired, raging for hours as she worked and searched for evidence of me. He hovered over her, not letting her out of his sight until she realized she needed him to let his guard down, which—with a paranoid psycho like him—was going to be next to impossible. Gradually, she began layering in compliments, telling him no one appreciated his genius, that he operated on a different level than the rest of us. One of those things was a hundred percent true.

It might've worked. With enough time and lies, she might've been able to soothe him into submission. But the next morning, a police cruiser pulled up to the house. Before she could do anything, he dragged her upstairs to their bedroom, swore he would kill both of us if she made a single noise, and locked her inside.

We pieced together what must've happened next. I'd missed the last few days of my senior year and, on top of that, had made a 911 call. The cop was probably sent out to do a welfare check, which is when Ted came up with the bullshit story that I'd run off with some drugged-out guy. Maybe he said Mom had gone looking for me. Who knew? He was charming when he wanted to be, could convince people he possessed genuine human emotions and he always had answers for everything. He'd probably turned on the concerned-protector-father act and the cop had lapped it up. Maybe they were even in the men's group together. The visit from the cop explained why we had to go to the station, to make the police close their file and validate every bias along the way.

We still would've been trapped if Mom hadn't found access to the attic in the ceiling of their bedroom closet. When Ted locked her in their bedroom, she climbed the closet shelves and hid in the insulation, waiting for him to notice she was missing. As soon as he left to track her down, she climbed down and rescued me.

Walking through the woods felt like a dream, the trees closing green over our heads, shadowing our pain, soothing our shock with birdcalls and the gentle dampened breeze winding through the rolling hills and valleys. We climbed over piles of moss-covered branches, stopped to rest against a giant, sprawling oak tree, and watched the squirrels and chipmunks dart through the canopy. I didn't know what lay beyond the woods, where Ted might be lurking, but it felt like he couldn't touch us here, that as long as we stayed in this breathing, beautiful forest where there was a hundred directions to run, we couldn't be trapped alone in the dark again.

We slept there for one night, but hunger drove us out in the morning. On the other side of the woods, we found a farm with a silver-haired woman working in a massive garden. She jumped when she saw us and I can only imagine how we must've looked: filthy clothes, glazed, exhausted eyes, the brass pipe clutched in my hand.

"My daughter and I need help," Mom said as my eyes darted to the road, the outbuildings, searching for any sign that Ted was going to jump out at us.

The woman stepped forward with immediate understanding in her eyes. Her shoulders straightened and she stretched out a gloved hand to us. "You're safe here."

It took years to rebuild our lives, to come to terms with the fact that the police didn't believe us. Ted had gotten there first, told them I'd gone into a teenage rage and fed my mother enough lies to make her believe that he was a monster. Monsters do that; they twist the story until fiction feels truer than fact. And Ted was a world-class expert in spinning his bullshit until dogs talked, the sky was purple, and the entire world hung upside down around him. No charges were ever filed. In the end, that was Mom's decision and she never said why, but I think she couldn't handle the trauma of seeing him in a courtroom for weeks or months, trying to convince strangers they should believe her over him. Because that's all we had. Our word against his. It's why she never filed for divorce; she knew it would give him a way back into our lives and the leverage to make us suffer even more. She could barely stand going back to his house to get our stuff. We did it while he was at church and two of her old coworkers came with us, standing sentinel at Ted's front door in case he showed up while we packed what would fit in the back of her car. We moved across the state and tried to restart our lives.

Mom rented one side of a duplex from an elderly couple who owned a restaurant and were delighted to discount the rent in exchange for bookkeeping services. I enrolled in a community college and lived at home. Mom wanted me to go to the university where I'd been accepted and live in the dorms, but I couldn't leave her. What if he came back and I wasn't there? What if something happened to her and I could've prevented it? I commuted to my classes and took a part-time job near home. Mom enrolled us in self-defense classes at the Y and insisted on *Great British Bake Off* binge nights. It felt like she was preparing me for the worst while still hoping for the best.

After college, I took a mind-numbing office job in the next town over. I dated a little, but the tiniest red flag had me swiping left so fast it froze my phone screen. Every Sunday, Mom baked a quiche and a batch of muffins or scones, and we spent hours picking at our plates and reading the newspaper. It was a Sunday when the first text arrived.

My mom's phone dinged with an incoming message from an unknown number. It was a picture of the front of our duplex. The text was two words: Nice place.

She dropped the phone like it was a snake and, after I read it too, we both stared at the front door. It had been years, but neither of us questioned for a second who'd sent the text. He was using a new phone line or a burner or whatever, and somehow he'd tracked us down. Despite the sudden rush of adrenaline, the crash of my heartbeat against my chest, and the desperate desire to run far, far away as fast as we possibly could, I stalked to the kitchen counter and drew the biggest cleaver out of the butcher block. Mom was right by my side with a hammer in tow as we opened the front door and walked out to the lawn.

The street looked the same as it always did. It was a residential road, with duplexes on one side and tiny ramblers on the other. A few cars were parked along the curb and it didn't look like anyone was lurking in any of them, but I checked each interior anyway, phone actively recording in one hand, knife in the other. Mom waited by our place, blocking the open doorway with a wide stance as she rapped the end of the hammer against her palm.

I worked my way from one end of the block to the other, scaring a mother out for a walk with her kids, before returning to Mom.

"He could've taken the picture anytime," she said.

We stood there, weapons in hand, guarding our new home, but at the same time I felt nauseous and panicky, like the time-out-room bugs were crawling over my skin. The urge to run, to not get locked inside a small, black cage, was almost more than I could bear.

Mom put a hand on my arm. "He's not here."

"He'll come back."

She didn't reply. We both knew it was true.

Max

When people heard I was a private investigator, they got a very specific image in their heads. It usually involved me in a trench coat and a hat, sitting in a car at a stakeout holding binoculars. I had to explain that the lion's share of PI work was digital. I spent most of my days online, in databases and searching through electronic archives. The old-school stereotype of some PI in a noir movie wasn't true.

Except when I was sitting in a car at a stakeout with binoculars.

Jonah passed me a Red Bull, which he claimed was from Eve, and stretched until his entire spine cracked. "I don't think he's coming out. It's after ten o'clock."

We'd been parked on the side of the road leading to Silas Hepworth's property for over two hours. A large oak tree partially shielded the car, but we still had a decent view of the side of Hepworth's house and were taking turns with night vision binoculars. If he went to the same outbuilding Charlie described, our plan was to drive up to the house and pretend that we needed to ask him some follow-up questions. With any luck, we could get a glimpse of what he was doing out there.

"Charlie said he went out after the news last night. Let's give it another hour."

Jonah grunted and thumped his head on the headrest. He hated the passenger seat. "If he doesn't show tonight, I can't do this again tomorrow."

"Hot date?"

"Yeah, actually." Even the hair falling in his face couldn't cover the smile.

"Good for you, man. You deserve it." I punched him in the arm and focused on the house. "I can't tomorrow, either. Shelley and I have plans."

"So whatever this guy's getting up to, he better get up to it tonight."

We traded the binoculars every ten minutes, yawning and listening to NPR. The security lights flicked on at one point, but it was just a deer wandering through the yard. I was nodding off when my phone buzzed with an incoming text.

Have update on the 10-55. Call this number tomorrow.

It was from Laredo, the officer assigned to investigate the body we'd discovered in the reserve. I hit the button to call immediately. He picked up on the second ring.

"I said tomorrow."

"We're both working now."

He was walking somewhere. The connection cut in and out. "I don't have an ID, but the ME said decomp was advanced."

"Are we talking months?" It had been almost three since Valerie had murdered her husband.

"Years. ME estimates between seven and ten. It's an adult female."

Jonah and I looked at each other. The body didn't belong to Ted Kramer.

"Any leads on the ID?"

"Since you were out on a casual hike in the area, I'd ask you the same thing," Laredo said, which meant he wasn't getting any promising hits in the missing persons database.

"It doesn't fit the timeline of our missing woman. She's only been gone a few weeks." I asked him to keep us updated, which he seemed less inclined to do now that we didn't have any information to offer. The call started cutting out as he rattled off the usual "active and ongoing case" disclosure, which I could recite in my sleep. Then the line went dead.

Jonah swore. "So there's another body in those woods."

"At least one." The Wolf River Bluffs Forest Preserve had a few hiking trails, but no camping facilities, shelters, or other visitor amenities that would make it a popular hiking destination. It wasn't near any major highways or tourist areas. All those factors could make it an ideal dumping ground. The woman buried out there seven to ten years ago was probably completely unrelated to the Kate Campbell case. It was only by chance, and the dumb luck of that tree falling over to expose her grave, that we found her at all.

Jonah disagreed. "I don't think it's a coincidence."

"Who is she then? Laredo's clearly having no luck ID'ing her or he wouldn't be taking my calls at ten-thirty at night."

Jonah grabbed his laptop, but didn't make much headway. The phone hotspot was at one bar and every page he tried loading kept timing out. Cell service in rural Iowa was patchy at best. Hepworth's security lights activated again, this time from two deer running. This stakeout sucked.

The phone rang again with the Illinois area code.

"Laredo?"

"Uh, no." The voice on the other end was higher, younger. "I think I missed some calls from you." The connection glitched, coming back in time for me to hear, "I'm Theo Kramer."

Ted's son, who lived in Chicago. I put the call on speaker as Jonah shut his laptop and sat up straighter.

"Thanks for getting back to us."

"Yeah. Uh, I'm sorry to call so late. I guess I figured I'd be leaving a message." He laughed awkwardly.

"This is perfect timing. My partner's here, too." Briefly, I outlined the reason we'd reached out. He seemed surprised to hear we were looking for Kate Campbell.

"I don't know if I can really help. I haven't seen Kate in years. Not since Valerie left my father. That was maybe 2015?"

"Did you keep in touch via phone? Social media?"

"No." He paused. "I don't think they would've wanted to."

"Why not?" Jonah asked.

Theo seemed to be shuffling the phone around. That, or the connection kept glitching. "They got out. Away from him. Once you get away from him, you don't really want any rem—" The connection shorted again.

"Goddamnit." I got out of the car and stalked up the nearest hill, looking for a better signal. Jonah followed. "Can you hear me, Theo?"

After trying a few different spots, the call cleared up. Theo was still there. I apologized and shifted the conversation to his father. "What's he like?"

"Asshole. Big one. If you've talked to him for two minutes, you probably already know that."

Jonah glanced at me. From the light of the phone screen, I could tell he was wondering the same thing I was. "When was the last time you saw your father?"

Theo sighed. "Two Christmases ago, I guess? He demanded I come home for the holiday. Kept calling and texting. I finally gave in. It was Covid and I couldn't really go anywhere else, but man, it was the wrong call."

"You have a bad relationship with him?"

Theo laughed again, loud and bitter this time. "Cliché, right? Sons hating their fathers, but mine . . . Everything was about how it made him look. My grades, my sports, my friends. And nothing was enough. It's like I grew up with a black hole. I don't know how, but after I moved out and Valerie left, he got even worse. When I saw him on Christmas, he was raging about all kinds of shit. Covid conspiracies, election fraud, tons of racist stuff. He spent half the day online and showed me pictures of Valerie's new place. I was like, what, are you stalking her?"

"Was he?"

"Not in his mind. He doesn't think like that. He threw shade on her house and her car, talked about how much worse off she was without him. I was like, yeah, whatever, this has been fun. I left as soon as I could and I've hardly talked to him since."

"I'm sorry. Sounds like you didn't have it easy," I offered.

"I'm gone now. On two different meds, I barely make rent, and my last girlfriend said I had 'trust issues,' but I'm not under his thumb anymore. I make my own decisions. Living my own life, you know?"

The wind picked up. At the bottom of the hill, the car doors stood open, light spilling out of the cab. I was about to thank Theo and let him go when Jonah grabbed my wrist, holding the phone in place.

"You lived at your dad's house the whole time you grew up?" Jonah rattled off the address.

"Yeah?" Theo sounded confused.

"Did you ever hear about a woman who'd gone missing in that area? It probably would've been when you were in late middle or early high school."

Of course. Theo would have been right there when the woman was buried in the woods behind his house.

He thought for a minute before answering. "Not that I can remember. But I wasn't really paying attention to the news then. That was around the time my mom left. She just left a note one day and was gone."

I looked at Jonah, his face cut into ghostly light and shadow. His eyes went wide with understanding.

I thanked Theo for his time, rushing him off the phone, when a gunshot exploded in the night.

Jonah

I tackled Max, sending us both to the ground.

The blast came from the base of the hill, somewhere near Max's car. I rolled over, crushing rows of young stalks, as Max searched for a weapon he didn't have. The shadow of the oak tree and the cloudy sky hid the shooter from sight.

"Get down here if you don't want to eat lead," the voice barked.

We both hesitated. It was too far away for me to sense anything. "Silas?"

Another gunshot blast answered the question, ringing across the open plain and echoing off distant barns. "I said now."

"Don't shoot." Max lifted his hands, getting up as slowly as possible. "We're unarmed and not causing any harm."

We walked down the hill, hands raised, and met Silas Hepworth at the bottom. He reloaded his shotgun, braced his squat legs, and aimed at Max's chest. Surprise and anger rolled off him when he recognized us.

Max started to explain, but Silas cut him off.

"I could shoot you right here. Nothing stopping me." He would, too. I could feel the urge taking hold. Max shone his phone light on both of us, pausing on each hand.

"We're not threatening you."

"You're on my land. Loitering, trespassing. I got the right to stand my ground." The shotgun didn't waver. The barrel was still fixed on Max's chest. "Two guys hired to harass me, on my property after dark doing God knows what. Probably planting evidence, trying to frame me for that bitch's disappearance."

"We're not—"

He swung the gun on me. The clouds parted for a minute and moonlight cast the old man in eerie shadows. His forehead shone with cold sweat. His eye sockets were as black as the barrel of the shotgun.

"I'm going to call every damn lawyer in the state tomorrow morning. Now get off my land."

Hands still raised, we got in the car and threw it in gear. I was braced, waiting for the gunshot I could feel simmering in his head, but it never came. Cresting the hill of the road, we left Silas, his threats, and his house behind.

Black sky met black land as the headlights cut gouges into the night. Max's energy went from tense to angry to frustrated. The speedometer ticked higher and higher.

"Great stakeout," he finally said.

"Textbook," I agreed. "That's why they're banging down our door. I don't know why you were ever worried about the business."

"Christ." Max wiped a hand over his head.

"At least we've got a lead on the body in the woods." I pulled up the background check we'd run on Ted Kramer. His first wife's name was Andrea.

"You really think he killed her?" Max asked.

"I do."

When the Illinois cop said the body was a woman, I'd gotten a strange feeling in my gut. It wasn't psychic. It didn't feel like the seeping invasion of the world pouring into my skin. This was different, an opposite knowledge that started inside and moved out. The cases—Kate Campbell's disappearance and the woman buried in the woods—were connected. It wasn't coincidence, no matter how much Max wanted to spout about dumping grounds like he was browsing them on Zillow.

I had a better signal on the highway, but internet access wasn't providing any proof of life on Andrea Kramer. No tagged photos on Google. No LinkedIn profiles or social handles. I couldn't find her anywhere.

"She might've just left, like Theo said." Max was in devil's advocate mode.

I couldn't argue the possibility. Maybe she had. I'm sure women wanted to leave their spouses and kids daily. The constant low-level hum of care, exhaustion, and irritation emanating off the mothers of the world could have powered a small country. The fact that Shelley had put up with Max for all these years was honestly mind-boggling.

Then I found it.

On the Facebook page for their church, buried in a landslide of blessings and fundraiser posts, was a series of pictures taken at a picnic. One photo captured a younger Ted Kramer posed with a woman and a boy. Andrea and Theo. I zoomed in and went cold.

Andrea Kramer stood slightly behind Ted, half in shadow as she held her son by the shoulder. She wore a loose sundress and an ill-fitting smile, with the same short, brown hair, the same bird-boned frame and delicate yet sharp features I'd met two days ago.

"We need to call Valerie."

"Why?" Max asked.

I swiveled my screen. He glanced at the photo, then did a double take.

"Holy shit, is that—?"

"Andrea Kramer." Ted's first wife could've been a doppelganger for his second.

Max digested the implications. "We can call her tomorrow. If we still have a company."

"Silas wanted to shoot us, not put us out of business."

Max snorted. "Oh, that's comforting. If he does call a lawyer or lodges a complaint, we could lose our license."

PIs weren't allowed to trespass on private property during surveillance. Parking on the side of the road was fine, as long as we weren't blocking, obstructing, or putting anyone in danger. But we'd clearly crossed that line, walking well within the bounds of his property. And we had no defense.

"I don't like this guy at all."

"What's to like?"

"No." Max pounded the steering wheel, frustration still chugging through him and seeping into the car. "I mean for Kate. He has a confrontation with her, accuses her of stealing the money he blackmailed from Charlie, is out doing weird things in his outbuildings, and spends the rest of the night patrolling the perimeter of his property like some paranoid psycho?"

"To be fair, people are watching him. That's not paranoia."

"Fuck being fair to him. We need to find out what's happening there."

I looked at my phone, the woman frozen on the screen.

"We need to find out what happened to Andrea Kramer."

Kate

The next eighteen months were some of the worst of my life. Ted found ways to torment us that could never be definitively traced back to him. Flowers arrived, lilies rancid in their cloying sweetness. Pictures of us sent from a series of untraceable phone numbers: my mom at work, me at the grocery store, the two of us drinking White Claws on a restaurant terrace. He made anonymous complaints about each of us at our jobs, forcing weeks of humiliating meetings with HR. And he found my only social handle on Instagram, posting as various trolls until I deleted the entire account.

We shrank into ourselves, constantly looking over our shoulders, assuming our every move was being watched. He made us as paranoid as he was. When weeks would pass quietly without any incidents, we questioned our own sanity. Was it happening or not? Had we turned a series of random, bizarre events into a boogeyman? It was exhausting, the constant watchfulness during the day and lying awake in our beds at night, unable to turn off our racing thoughts. Mom started antidepressants and I began antianxiety meds. We met in the dark kitchen at three or four in the morning at least one night a week, silently pulling flour and sugar from the cupboard with zombie-like intent. If we couldn't think or sleep or medicate our demons away, we could always bake them.

"I'm going there," Mom announced one Sunday morning over quiche and newspapers.

"Where?" We'd had zero conversation about any trips or errands today.

"His house."

A cold dread knotted my stomach. I didn't need to ask who *he* was. It was clear from the set of her mouth, the deadness of her words.

"Mom. No."

"He still has my dough cutter. I want it back."

We'd forgotten a few things in the rush of getting the hell out of Ted's house and the dough cutter was one of the abandoned items. It didn't matter at the time; we could always get new stuff. But Mom hadn't found the exact model. I bought her a replacement for Christmas, and she never complained about it, but sometimes she still talked longingly about the old one. And more than its handle or weight or sharpness, I knew it was the fact that it was still there, that part of her was still locked in that house.

"We can't go there." Even the thought of the place filled me with choking panic, the walls closing in, darkness clawing at me. I went to the window and stood in a shaft of morning sunlight, trying to find my balance in the sudden chaos Mom had thrown like a bomb into our Sunday routine.

"You're not going, Kate. I am."

"Neither of us is going."

She stood up, too. The tendons in her neck were taut, her mouth set, not a hint of backing down anywhere in her slight frame. She faced me, squaring off with a quiet, fierce determination.

"I want my dough cutter back."

It was insane. Drive over a hundred miles and go back to that psycho's castle, for a stupid utensil that for all we knew he'd thrown away or burned in effigy by now? I'd rather walk into traffic. But as we faced off across the kitchen, I knew it wasn't about the dough cutter. It was about everything he'd taken from us, everything he held hostage, taunting us with his ghost stalker messages. And Mom was over it. She vibrated with a fury I'd never seen in her, without one drop of the fear that invaded my entire body. I knew she was going to do this no matter how much I argued or tried to reason with her. She wanted her dough cutter and she was going to get it back.

I forced a breath into my lungs, fighting against constricting, overwhelming panic. "You're not going alone."

The house looked the same as it always had. Two sprawling stories, perfectly manicured hedges lining the foundation, the glossy black front door.

His truck was in the driveway. He was home.

We sat in my Mazda a hundred yards down the street, car idling, neither of us speaking. Mom's gaze was fixed on the house, her jaw working like she was rehearsing what she was going to say. I'd tried to convince her that we should go when he wasn't home. Try a Sunday morning when he might be at church. Maybe he hadn't changed his security code. We could slip in, get the dough cutter, and leave. But she vetoed that idea hard. He could get us arrested for trespassing, or worse, catch us in the act and wreak his own revenge. She wanted him to be home, to have it out with him once and for all. I tried to convince her to bring more people. Some of the old coworkers who'd helped us move, a neighbor, or any of the new acquaintances we'd made. I spent a solid half day campaigning for her to ask the movie theater manager she'd been casually flirting with for the last year, but she refused.

"He won't be himself if other people are there."

"Exactly."

"I don't want to see the mask, Kate. I don't want to be gaslit or feel insane anymore. I need to talk to the real Ted."

I hated that I understood. She was calling out the monster, and he only showed himself to certain people. For the first time, I was grateful to be one of them. At least I could stand by my mother's side as she had this out once and for all.

After another minute of gathering herself, Mom looked at me.

"Are you okay?"

"Is that a real question?"

She laughed, breaking the tension in the car a little. "Okay, fair. But I'm ready to do this. I want it over."

"Then let's get your damn dough cutter back."

She pulled into the driveway, blocking his truck in. We got out and walked to the sidewalk, stopping well short of the door. There was no need to ring the doorbell. Mr. Paranoia was aware of everyone who breathed on his property. I had my phone in one hand, recording, and pulled a bottle of mace out of my other pocket, opening it with the practiced ease of someone who'd been stalked for the past year and a half.

Mom stood with her hands empty, but there was a switchblade in her pocket. We'd gone over this plan for days and reviewed every detail on the way here. Despite all our preparation, I still felt a rolling wave of nausea when Ted opened the door.

Unlike the house, he'd changed. He still stood with his chest puffed, wearing a shirt tucked into his jeans, gold belt buckle flashing in the sun. His hair was still trimmed to military specification, jaw immaculately shaved, skin spray-tanned to match the belt. But there were puffy lines around his eyes and forehead. He sagged in some spots and was carved out in others like a cancer had been slowly feasting on him. His eyes gleamed blacker than I remembered them being as he stared at Mom, and the way he looked at her, like a naughty runaway pet had come crawling home, made sickness well in the back of my throat.

"Well, well." The dark, oily words landed like bile.

"We need to talk," Mom said. "Can we come in?"

He glanced at the phone in my hand and I could see the conspiracy theories clouding his obvious pleasure at luring us back here. He seemed to be weighing his options, planning the best way to manipulate and control the situation. He finally agreed, standing back and swinging the door open further.

It took everything I had to follow my mother inside that house. The can of mace turned slippery in my hand and the phone shook as I passed within feet of him. Mom went to the kitchen and straight to a side drawer, pulling out her dough cutter and pocketing it without a word.

"I invited you inside. I didn't give you permission to steal from me." He filled the kitchen doorway, making it impossible to get past him back to the front door.

Like a true queen, Mom didn't even blink. She refused to take the bait. She pulled her hand out of her pocket, but instead of the utensil, it was a switchblade. She opened it one-handed.

"You think any of this bothers me? Your threats, your sad little pictures of our house, your pathetic calls to our jobs. You think any of it makes you matter? Makes you worth responding to?" She laughed again but it wasn't like earlier in the car. This laugh was broad, unmitigated disdain. It was an unleashing, the click of a gate opening that could never be shut again.

"You're nothing, Ted Kramer. You've always been nothing, and you'll always be nothing. I came back for my dough cutter, because it's worth more than a hundred of you."

Her voice was steady and strong. Her eyes were blue fire. She was everything I wasn't in that moment. Hair undone, makeupless, wearing an old hoodie, with the might of a thousand women distilled into her slight body, she faced the monster who'd tried to destroy her and laughed in his face. I'd never loved her more than I did right now.

"If I'm nothing, why is your daughter shaking like a leaf?" Ted leered at me, and I felt the nausea give way to a bone-deep hatred.

"Oh, I don't know," I said, feeling my mother's courage move into me. "Maybe because you kidnapped and locked me in a crawl space for two days."

He shook his head in mock sympathy, performing directly to the camera in my hand. "Hard to kidnap someone in their own home. Which, I might remind you, this was. I provided everything for you, for both of you, and here you are, back for more, aren't you?"

He kept talking, piling bullshit onto twisted bullshit. Trying to spin this situation until he was at the center of the narrative again, making himself the used, tragic hero. I don't know how long he would have monologued, but Mom ended his garbage by yawning right in the middle of it. A huge, bored, over-it yawn and he stopped mid-sentence, a vein popping in his forehead.

"Thanks for showing me what I'm definitely not missing," Mom said, and I couldn't help it. She'd slightly misquoted *Legally Blonde*, one of our all-time favorite movies, and I burst out laughing.

Everything spun out of control. The gate my mom had unlatched flew wide, and the monster barreled into the room. Ted lost it. Face boiling red, he lunged for my mother. Time seemed to slow down. Adrenaline flooded me, replacing the giddiness with burning intent. I stepped between them and sprayed the mace directly in his face. He crashed into me, sending both me and Mom flying back into the stove.

It was that night all over again, only magnified with time and rage. I heard screaming. Bodies thudded together, ripping at each other. Groin. Throat. Eyes. The areas they'd taught us to strike in self-defense flashed through my head, but I couldn't land a single punch. Somehow he had me by the neck. He was too strong. I'd lost my phone and the mace; there was no way out. My vision shrank and tunneled and just as my legs started to give out, I saw it: Mom's knife making a swift, shining arc through the air.

I could breathe again. Blood flew everywhere. He lost his balance and fell. His head smashed onto the floor in front of me, and everything came into focus. I kicked at the back of his head, connecting my boot with his skull over and over again, needing it to disappear, to be smashed into oblivion forever.

There was a crunch that could have been from far away or deep inside my own head. I didn't know, couldn't tell inside from out, waking from dreaming. Vaguely, I felt hands pulling me away from the wrecked, bleeding body and then I was in my mom's arms and we were shaking and holding each other on the floor.

I don't know how long we sat like that. Mom rocked us back and forth, stroking the hair away from my forehead. We stared at Ted's body—the man who'd terrorized us for years, lurking at the edge of every thought—lifeless.

"Is he dead?" I asked.

Mom let go of me and moved to check his pulse. I grabbed the bloody knife and hovered behind her, ready to attack if he reared up and grabbed her.

"I can't feel a pulse," she said after a minute and sat back on her haunches, staring at his bruised and bloated face. "I can't believe I killed him."

Using the knife to lift his shirt, we looked at the long, shallow cut across his torso. It wasn't a fatal wound. There was another stab in his knee, seeping dark into his pants. Also not fatal. We glanced at each other, both of us realizing at the same time that she hadn't killed him. I had. I'd literally beaten him to death.

I ate the whale.

I should have been afraid or worried—anything—at the thought of facing a murder charge. But I'd been afraid for so long. All I felt at the sight of Ted's body was relief, a euphoric lightness running through my veins, lifting everything. When we'd escaped this house years ago and Mom asked if I was okay, I hadn't even known what the word meant. I was so far away from it, looking at it through a dark, distorted ocean. Now it felt like I'd crossed back over the water. I could see it now. I'd murdered my stepfather and I was finally okay.

When Mom told me to go to the garage and touch nothing except two shovels and a sled, I agreed with a smile. I felt like whistling. We wrapped him in a sheet, rolled him on the sled and spent the ten minutes until sundown scrubbing the kitchen with bleach and tossing the used towels onto the body. Ted didn't have any close neighbors, but we still waited for heavy twilight before we pulled the sled into the woods.

It took every ounce of strength we had. We were sweating and cursing and grunting and I would have done it a hundred times, spent every night for the rest of my life dragging Ted's corpse out of our world forever.

We didn't dig as far down as we should have. There were too many tree roots and rocks, and it was barely April. The ground was still hard and it got more compact the farther down we went. The grave we managed to dig was barely two feet at its deepest point, and more like one in the shallow spots. Our arms shook. Our hands bled. Finally, Mom said it was enough. We both knew it wasn't, that we needed to deposit Ted into the bowels of the earth and let the magma incinerate any evidence of him, but I also felt like the night was spinning around me. I heard sounds everywhere, below and above us. Did people come into these woods? I hadn't seen anyone out here when we lived with Ted, but to be fair I hadn't paid much attention to these trees before Mom and I had escaped into them. Now the woods were delivering us again, taking the last part of Ted that could hurt us.

We upended the sled into the grave and Ted fell at a weird angle into the sad, shallow hole. For a second I thought his arm moved, but when I shone the flashlight on him, the body was crumpled and still. He wasn't coming back. We piled the dirt back on until he was covered in a weird mound and dragged a few fallen branches over the top. Then we stumbled away, coming out of the woods farther south than we meant to and having to backtrack to the house.

We stripped down and bagged everything—our clothes, the mace, the knife, our phones, the shovels and sled—and stuffed it all in the trunk of my car. We drove home in bras and underwear, not having the foresight to pack a change of clothes in case we had to murder a man.

Details popped and fizzed in my head. We hadn't worn gloves. The blood on our blistered hands had dripped into the grave as we dug. Our phones had recorded everything, tracking exactly where we'd been all night. I wondered about the difference between first- and second-degree murder and decided not to google it. It seemed serious, all of it, the kind of serious that could ruin our lives forever, but there was only one detail I could hold on to, only one phrase repeating on a glorious loop in the PTSD whiplash that was my head.

"Legally Blonde?"

Mom sat ramrod straight in the driver's seat, her blue satin bra gleaming in the flash of streetlights.

"It came to me in the moment." She turned to me, bags like welts under her eyes, hair dirty and stuck to her head. I'm sure I looked the same or worse. "Maybe we've watched it too many times."

"Better Elle Woods than Elizabeth Bennet."

"'You're the last man in the world I could be prevailed upon to marry.'"

"Meh." I shrugged. "It doesn't work without the accent. And it's about a decade too late."

The laughter started deep in our chests, rumbling like earthquakes until it broke loose. It felt like it would shake the whole car, that we would laugh for the rest of our lives.

* * *

It's hard to cover up a murder when you have no practice or skills in that area. I deleted the video of killing Ted I inadvertently recorded, but I also had cloud service on my phone and we didn't know if the cloud had automatically archived it somewhere, just waiting to be pulled with the right warrant. We checked into a campground the next day, without our phones, and burned the clothes we'd worn. We scrubbed the shovels and sled with bleach and dropped them at three different dumpsters in three different towns. We went to a self-service car wash that had no cameras and vacuumed the back of my car, scrubbing it with more bleach. I was weighing our options for what to do with the actual murder weapons—the knife, the mace, and my boots—on our way home from the dumpster drops and car wash when Mom interrupted me.

"You have to go."

"Go where? Where should I take them?"

"Listen to me. You have to leave, Kate. You can't come back."

It took a minute for what she was saying to sink in. I'd been so focused on getting rid of the evidence. It never occurred to me that we'd have to disappear, too. But wait. No. She wasn't talking about us anymore. She was talking about me, alone.

"Why can't you come?"

"Once they realize he's missing or find his body, I'll be the first person they interview. If I'm gone, they'll know exactly what happened."

"Who's even going to miss that bastard?"

"His church. His men's group. The county when he doesn't pay his property taxes. The post office, when he stops getting his mail. They don't even have to look. We didn't bury him deep enough. Animals could get him—"

"Good for the animals."

"—dogs bring human bones home all the time."

"We don't know—"

"And Theo."

That shut me up for a second. Ted's son had left for college almost as soon as Mom and I moved into the house. He came home the next summer, a skinny, greasy kid with black eyes that didn't blink. He did everything his father told him without a word, too whipped from a lifetime of following orders to ever fight back or even offer an opinion. He'd already learned there was only Ted's way in that house.

He'd found an apartment by the next year and hadn't come home for the summer when Ted imprisoned us. Neither of us had been in contact with him since we'd escaped Ted. Once or twice Mom had mentioned him, hoping he'd gotten away from his father and started his own life, but she hadn't been willing to chance any communication. A connection to the son might become a connection to the father.

"Theo's long gone," I said, hoping more than believing it. Once Ted had control of someone, he didn't let them go. We were living proof of that. "Or," I tried again, reframing, "he'll be grateful that I—"

Mom shot me a look.

"—that someone—" I amended quickly, "took care of his dad for him. He's probably been considering patricide for years."

We argued the rest of the drive home. Nothing I said changed her mind. She was convinced Ted's body would be found and the absence of his still-on-paper wife would lead authorities straight to her. Ted might have even left evidence of his recent stalking, which would make her even more of a suspect. She had to keep living her life as though nothing happened. When I suggested going back to the house to get rid of anything that might point to us, she refused. When I suggested burying him better, she flatly rejected the idea.

"We can't go anywhere near there again."

She was right. I knew she was right, but the urge to go back and do better was overwhelming. If only we'd planned a murder contingency, this could've all been different.

The problem, we both knew, was that if the authorities started to look into Mom as a suspect, what they would find was me. My car at his house. My phone pinging the nearest cell tower practically the whole night. My literal video recording of killing my stepfather.

"We escaped that prison, Kate, and I'm not letting you spend one more minute of your life locked away because of him."

She wore me down over the next few days, until I started believing what she said. It made sense for me to leave town. There was already a record of me being a runaway on file with the local police. On paper, I had a history of disappearing. If they came to question her, she could tell them we'd had a fight and I'd left on bad terms. She hadn't heard from me since. It would hold up, as long as they didn't dig deeper.

The next Friday, she was gone for most of the day and when she came back, she had twelve thousand dollars in cash.

"Where did you get that?" I'd saved less than a thousand since I graduated college. Most of my paycheck went to our rent, gas, groceries, and restaurant takeout.

"It's for you." The bills were bound with rubber bands, not the paper wrapping they used at the bank, and the whole pile was stuffed in a plastic grocery bag. She handed it to me, then she gave me the dough cutter.

"Mom, no."

"I don't need it." Her eyes were suddenly bright. She tucked the dough cutter in my other hand and bracketed my shoulders, holding me in place. "You take it and then wherever you go, I'll be there, too."

"Mom—" Tears welled in my eyes and spilled, making her blurry.

"I couldn't have gotten it back without you. It'll make me happy, knowing you're out there using it. Do you know how many times I've looked at you and marveled at all the things you're capable of, everything you could do if only you let yourself?

"You don't have to worry about me anymore. You don't have to hold yourself back. I want you to fly, Kate. I want you to see the world and fall in love and get your heart broken and know you have it inside you to get up and try again. To do anything you set your mind to.

"You're the best daughter I could have imagined." She hugged me to her chest, hard, and I felt shudders running through her. I couldn't absorb what was happening. We'd been talking about it for days and still I was blindsided, numb.

"I'll love you, forever, Kate." She whispered in my ear before backing away, eyes running over every inch of me as if memorizing this moment. "You have to leave. Now."

Max

"What do you mean we can't leave?"

Shelley dragged me through a room that looked like a warehouse separated into individual metal cages. Giant wooden dartboards hung in the back of every one. We passed a mid-twenties couple, giggling and drinking beer. A table full of axes stood behind them.

Shelley told me to trust her for this date night. She wouldn't tell me where we were going, which usually meant a movie or a restaurant she knew I didn't like. When we pulled into the parking lot for Hatchet Jack's, I was thrown. She smiled like she'd just watched me open the perfect Christmas present.

"I don't feel like axe throwing." She wasn't paying any attention to me as we followed the uniformed guy to our reserved cage. "I don't throw axes."

When we got to our spot, though, I understood why she was so giddy. Jonah and Eve stood inside the cage, the two of them mirroring our expressions perfectly.

"Surprise!" Shelley pulled my arm into her side, practically bouncing. "It's a double date."

After ordering beers and listening to the "axpert" instruct us on how to play darts with axes, Jonah came over and muttered under his breath. "Did you know?"

I shook my head and took a long pull of beer, willing the alcohol into my bloodstream faster. "At least it's not bowling."

Shelley and Eve took turns first, both of them aggressively competitive and not bothering to hide it. Neither landed an axe and demanded second tries. Jonah and I stood at the back of the cage.

"I've been thinking about Valerie."

"Me too."

We'd called her right away this morning and she picked up on the first ring.

"Did they identify him?" she asked before I could say a word. "Did you tell them where to find me?"

Briefly, I filled her in on what we knew of the body so far. She seemed as shocked as we'd been. But not as shocked as she was a minute later.

"Valerie, what do you know about Ted's first wife?"

We sent her the picture and listened to several moments of complete silence on the other end. "Valerie?"

"You think it's her." Her voice was barely a whisper. "You think he killed his first wife?"

We didn't know for sure, but the more we talked it over, the more likely it seemed. We could barely find any records of Andrea Kramer after she'd married Ted. Her employment history ended. No credit in her name. There were a few pictures online at their church's social media, which was where Jonah had pulled her photo, but almost nothing else. And after she supposedly left him, there was nothing. No socials, bills paid, or public records of any kind. Unless she'd pulled a Kate and changed her entire identity, she'd fallen completely off the grid.

"Her name was Andrea. What did he say about her?"

It took a minute for Valerie to pull herself together and when she did, there wasn't much to tell. He'd always claimed Andrea left the family. Theo never went to see her or spend time with his mom. There was no contact, even on holidays or Theo's birthday as far as Valerie knew. "I felt so sorry for him. I tried to reach out at first, not like I was trying to replace his mom. I just wanted him to know I was there if he needed someone to talk to. But he always rejected any effort I made. God," her voice broke. "He must have been so traumatized. His mom disappears and then this woman shows up who looks exactly like her, trying to befriend him."

"You never saw pictures of Andrea?"

"No. Ted never wanted to talk about it. And if Ted didn't want something, we didn't do it."

We ended the call with Valerie and tried Theo again to ask a few follow-up questions about his mom, but like every Gen Z on the planet, he didn't answer his phone. Hopefully, he'd return our call again at some point.

"It's bothering me," Jonah said, after we took our turns throwing axes.

"You want to call Laredo and let him know our theory?" We'd decided not to tip off the authorities in Illinois for the time being. All we had were suspicions, no hard evidence of any kind, and if we implicated Ted Kramer in the murder of his wife, they'd want to question him, which would lead directly to another murder we had no proof of and put Valerie in jeopardy.

"It felt like she was waiting for us to call. And the first thing she wanted to know was when she'd be arrested."

It wasn't typical criminal behavior, but Valerie Campbell wasn't a typical criminal. I'd seen all kinds of reactions and behaviors on ICPD. Some people were wracked with guilt. They wanted to serve time, wanted to be sentenced and pay the consequences, like it would free them from what they'd done. When I said as much to Jonah, he didn't buy in.

"She didn't feel guilty. She's glad he's dead. Her only concern was for Kate. She needed to know Kate was okay. She'd do anything for her, including—"

"Confess to a murder she didn't commit." Jonah and I looked at each other. "Fuck."

"Who's confessing to murder?" Eve asked, handing me an axe.

I took it and walked to the line, testing the blunt weight of the weapon. "Someone who shouldn't."

As the night unfolded and we ordered a few more rounds, axe throwing became surprisingly fun. Shelley found luck with overhead throws and started bellowing a battle cry each time she threw. Eve spent longer than anyone on her turn, calculating distances and velocities and still ending up the worst of the bunch. Jonah and I both threw one-handed and we landed so many that it became a side bet to see who would hit the bull's-eye first.

We didn't forget about Valerie. The realization that Kate had murdered her stepfather clicked into place, humming in the background, and making sense out of everything else we'd learned so far. It felt like we were making progress—in our work and in our lives—despite the fact that we didn't have enough clients, that without Charlie's bricks of cash we might not make rent next month, and that Silas Hepworth might sue us and put us out of business regardless. Celina Investigations could close tomorrow, but this was tonight.

Shelley and Eve had planned well. We were the only group in our area of the building, which I'm sure was by design to keep Jonah away from the brunt of the public. It was a happy place, though, everyone cheering and drinking and egging each other on. Even if he felt the energy of the crowd, it didn't seem like they would sink him. Eve kept tabs on Jonah just as close as I did, watching his expressions and slipping her hand into his when it wasn't their turn. He pulled her in for a hug once, and Shelley flashed me a grin.

"Have you done this before?" Eve asked.

Jonah shook his head. "I've stolen a plane, set a field on fire, confronted a few drug lords, and found more bodies than I want to count. It's kind of surprising I haven't thrown an axe at anyone yet."

"No," Eve corrected. "I meant have you two gone on a double date before?"

I sniggered and Jonah shot me a look. Shelley drained her beer and demanded the story. When I declined, Jonah did the honors.

"He dragged me to parties sometimes when we were undergrads, angling me in front of girls he wanted to talk to. He claimed my face hooked them and his wit reeled them in, but the reality was a little different."

"You don't know that," I objected, even though Jonah absolutely knew it.

"Pottermania was huge. Girls liked us because, with my black hair and Max's red mop, we sort of looked like Harry and Ron."

Shelley and Eve burst out laughing.

"Trust me, Eve. Jonah nailed the 'lives-under-the-stairs' look a long time ago. Whenever girls commented on it, I was like, 'Yep, he's magical.'" For reasons neither of us really understood, we took more than a few Potterheads home from the bar.

"I have to watch the movies now," Shelley said, flashing her doe eyes at me as we paid the tab and headed for the door.

I pulled her in for a kiss. "You would."

Jonah

After the axe throwing, Eve came home with me.

We didn't talk much in the car. She texted Earl, who was visiting a cousin in Des Moines, and had a quick call with her PhD student, Chris, who I apparently still hated, judging by how I fixated on her every word and mood during the brief exchange. After that, she leaned back and watched the few wisps of clouds marring the night sky. Her upturned jaw and the slender column of her throat in profile made my mouth go dry. As we drove from Iowa City to the edge of the state, her energy slowly shifted from content to expectant.

I was just trying not to crash the car.

Like everything else in my life, sex was never as simple for me as it was for other people. Just being near someone exposed me to caverns of emotion and dark, gritty need. Being inside them was to be swallowed by the cavern.

In my twenties and early thirties, I'd opted into the risk of that escape as casually as I could. Bar servers were the best bet, women who showed up at 3:00 a.m., knocked back a shot of whiskey, and dropped a trail of clothing from the kitchen to the bedroom with as little fanfare as serving the next round. Their minds were studded

with all the idiots and assholes of the previous hours, petty grievances they wanted to forget in a tide of alcohol and rush of nerve
endings. They needed the escape as much as I did.

Things shifted, though, as the dreams took over my life, as the
shadows grew longer and drainpipes and ditches and barns swallowed more people I couldn't find in time. Alcohol and pills numbed
me for a while, but the nightmares always waited on the other side.
When I tried to escape through sex, I felt worse. I resented the
women who'd unknowingly given me a glimpse of their functional
realities, the un-haunted worlds they took for granted, and was either
rude to them afterward or sat on the back porch drinking until they
left. I became just another asshole in their night.

I'd never been with someone like Eve, who was so far out of
my league even the staff at the axe place noticed. Tonight she wore
bright sneakers and a jumpsuit that on anyone else would probably
look prison-issue. Eve could have stepped off a runway in it, and
the zipper that ran up the center of the whole thing easily took up
forty percent of my concentration the entire night. I wore a black
T-shirt and jeans, and judging by the tone of her concentration on
me all night, it was the right choice.

I pulled into the driveway and killed the engine. We sat in the
dark for a minute, neither of us making a move to open our doors.
Tension ballooned in the space between us until I was ready to
crawl out of my own skin.

"Thanks for tonight."

"Was it all right?" She seemed strangely anxious. It wasn't
an emotion I was used to from Eve. "I know it was in public, but I
thought it might be better with Max and Shelley there."

"It was great." I had to sit down a few times and escape to the bathroom once, but it was manageable. And it was with Eve, which made it worth any bad moments that came my way. "I'm glad you and Shelley are friends."

"She's going to start a group chat. She mentioned a brewery tour for our next double date. Strictly outdoor patios."

"Max will be on board."

"And you?" She turned to face me, reading me as I read her.

"I'll be there if you are."

The anxiety melted away, replaced by something more restless as she opened her door.

Inside, I mixed drinks while Eve put on music. After bubbling with me during Covid, she knew my house almost as well as I did. It was a strange, domestic feeling, watching her move so easily through spaces I'd kept carefully empty. When I walked out of the kitchen, though, she'd disappeared.

"Kendrick."

The voice came from the loft. The only thing up there was my bed. Blood rushing, heart kicking up, I brought the drinks upstairs.

Eve stood at the railing overlooking the living room. She took both glasses and set them on the ledge, then threaded a hand through my hair and worked her way down to my jaw. I fought the urge to rub against it like a goddamn cat.

She pulled me in, humming her approval. Her thoughts spiraled from my mouth to my arms and chest and lower, before lingering on the two-year journey from her front porch, where she'd shoved me into a pile of slush with a baseball bat, to this moment, where no one else in the world existed.

I framed her face in both hands and murmured, "Who would've thought?" before leaning into her.

The kiss started slow, then shifted and deepened. We moved against the railing, backing each other up, changing positions, fighting to get closer. It was incredible how easily we shifted roles, negotiating the give-and-take like we'd been doing it for years. Breaking away, I brought her hand to my mouth.

"I need you to talk to me. Tell me what you want and what you don't." I bit the base of her thumb. She inhaled and her body dilated, the nerves humming to life.

"I don't want you to stop."

"Let's revisit that one later, because I'm planning to sample every square inch of you." I moved to her wrist and felt her pulse quicken. "It might take a while."

"Good."

I sat on the foot of the bed, pulling that criminal jumpsuit zipper open to her waist and tasting each slice of skin on the way down. When she shrugged the whole thing off, my brain whited out.

The rest of our clothes scattered. She ordered my shirt and pants off, told me where to kiss her, where to bite, moaning when she lost the words and showing me with her hands instead, taking my request for instructions to heart. When I had us both panting on the bed, we paused, eye to eye, a breath apart. An ocean of need churned between us and I couldn't separate which was hers and which was mine. It didn't feel like the escape I'd always sought. It felt like home.

Kate

The darkness had shape. Lines spiraled through it, indigo on black, swirling and disappearing before they took form. I wanted to believe it was nothing, a blank dreamscape that couldn't hurt me, but everything inside knew better.

My heart thudded painfully in my ears. My throat was hoarse and cracked from screaming. The tips of my fingers were jagged and bleeding from clawing at the walls. My shoulder ached from slamming it against the door, trying to break free.

I was locked in the darkness again.

It was every nightmare I'd had since I was seventeen. In the dreams I would rock back and forth as bugs crawled over my skin, knowing absolutely that what was happening was real. I was trapped again. I always knew, no matter how far I ran, that somehow it would never be far enough. That the darkness would find me. And it did. I knew it in my bones. Then, when I woke up from the nightmares soaked in sweat with the blankets and sheets clawed off the bed, I had to lie on the damp, bare mattress and tell myself it was a dream, over and over again. I would pinch my unbitten skin, drag myself outside, and breathe in the light and air until the nightmare faded.

At Charlie's house, the nightmares still came but they receded quicker. I would wake up to his solid warmth, his adorable, oblivious snoring, and hug every inch of myself to him, using his body like an anchor to reality. When my heartbeat settled, I would pull on a sports bra and running shoes and slip out of the house. I ran into the fields, chasing the endless horizon until the blood pumping through my limbs expelled the last of the panic and fear. There was no one anywhere in those mornings. The world distilled to open, rolling land and a perfect blue arch of sky. I could feel myself on the maps, tracing the lines of roads leading everywhere, the endless green stretching from ocean to ocean, possibilities whispering in every direction. I was bound by nothing, trapped by no one. I ran until I believed it again.

Now, everything was inside out. I rocked in the darkness, dizzy with the déjà vu of years of nightmares telling me it wasn't real. I wasn't actually here. And that's how I knew it *was* real. Because the nightmares felt true. And the truth felt like a nightmare.

I don't know how much time passed. I think I slept at one point. The smell of urine mixed with dirt and dust, clogging my nose. I tried to think about Charlie, tried to pull every detail of his face into focus. The texture of his beard, the span of his hands around my waist. I thought about my mother, Milk Duds swapped for Junior Mints in the flickering light of the movie theater. I recited recipes. "Nine cups flour. One tablespoon baking soda. Half tablespoon baking powder. One tablespoon sea salt. Salt quality is key." Blake, winking as she dumped chocolate chips into the mixer. "Never let a recipe tell you how many chocolate chips to use. You measure that shit with your heart."

The room I was locked in felt like a tomb. I'd already traced every inch of it, testing each cinderblock and board, looking for weaknesses. I think I broke something in my shoulder ramming it into the door. It hurt when I breathed too hard.

I was in the middle of the maple cinnamon scone recipe— Ceylon cinnamon, it has to be Ceylon combined with the Grade A dark maple syrup—when footsteps came from outside. He was back. He came every night. I froze at the sound of metal on metal as the door swung open.

White, blinding light shone directly into my eyes. I covered my face and jerked away, skittering as far into the corner as possible.

Something landed on my leg. I yelped and shoved at it before realizing it was a bag.

"Dinnertime."

The word came from nowhere and everywhere, low and menacing.

I lowered my hand and tried opening my eyes. Tears streamed down my face. It was impossible to see around the beam of the flashlight. "You don't have to do this."

I couldn't see anything, couldn't tell if he was even listening or not. There was only a presence, impossibly tall behind the light, the shadow of a skull, the uneven rasp of his breathing.

"No, I don't." The light drifted down to my running leggings, the fabric torn and filthy. Then it flashed to my face again, and the white light stung through my eyes into every corner of my head.

"I don't *have* to do this, Kate, even though you deserve it. You deserve this and worse. And no matter how many questions they ask, no one's gonna find you." The door creaked as he pulled it shut, cutting off the light and leaving me in pulsing darkness.

"I'm doing this because I can. And because I want to."

Metal slapped against the door, the padlock clicked, and I threw myself against it, shoving it open and rolling suddenly free of the room. I dropped, falling to a hard surface. The room had opened, expanded, and I scrambled along the floor until I hit a railing. Where had a railing come from? Bugs crawled over me, biting into my flesh. I swatted at them, slapping my skin until hands covered and trapped mine. I jerked away, hitting my head on the railing.

"Where's the door?"

I twisted toward the light, grabbing the railing like prison bars, and blinked my surroundings into focus. One world superimposed itself onto another. Bedroom over prison. Light onto darkness. Dawn filtered in through the two-story living room windows, the beginning of sunrise over the bluff. I was in my house. I could see it, even as the blackness of the space clawed at my head. My hands gripped the railing, even as broken and bleeding fingers ached at the ends of my arms. Someone was behind me. Kate. Not Kate. I didn't know. I needed fresh air, open skies. Now.

Pushing away from the body behind me, I stumbled down the loft stairs, across the living room, and out to the deck.

It wasn't far enough. I was still trapped. The urge to run tugged at me, to find open land and race for the horizon, but I also knew if I moved any farther right now I would vomit.

Leaning over the deck railing like a life raft, I watched the slide of the Mississippi at the base of the bluff, the dark water always moving, slow and inexorable, to the sea. It was shrouded with pockets of fog. My breathing gradually began to settle and I realized there was a voice murmuring behind me.

"Danica Chase. Angela Garcia." The names of people I'd found. Names that kept the torment of the lost at bay. "Kit Freeman. George Marcus Morrow."

I turned as much as I dared, feeling my stomach clench, and then forgot about my stomach completely.

Eve stood a cautious distance behind me, completely naked, holding a glass of water in one hand and a blanket in the other. I was naked, too. The previous night rushed back, water bursting over a dam, the sudden memory of Eve in my bed, the smell of her, the feel of her, her shimmering pleasure reflecting in me, building exponentially until we were both gasping and spent.

And now this.

Another flash, this time of me trying to escape the nightmare prison and shoving a weight aside before I fell out of bed. Fuck. It had been Eve.

"Are you okay?" I asked.

She stopped chanting the names and lifted both the water and the blanket. "What do you need?"

I needed to rewind this morning, to go back to last night when we were falling asleep and pull myself away from her. Leave the bedroom and sleep in the tub, like I had when the dreams were bad with Celina. I rarely dreamed when I was that uncomfortable. Better that Eve would find me passed out in the bathroom than this. God, I'd woken her with an actual assault, fell off the bed, and ran out of the house buck naked like a maniac.

It was exactly the thing I didn't want to happen.

She shivered and I took the blanket out of her hand and wrapped it around her. "I'm sorry."

"For being who you are? I wasn't expecting breakfast in bed, Kendrick."

She put the water down on the deck railing and leaned next to me, looking over the water. Mascara was smeared under her eyes and her hair stood on end at strange angles. One delicate shoulder poked out of the blanket as she surveyed the morning sky. "Low stratus layer today. Stratus nebulosus at zero altitude." She nodded to the patches of fog on the river. "They rarely last long."

After another minute, the cold had seeped into my skin enough that I could breathe again. I slipped under the blanket and pulled Eve's back against my chest, notching her against me. We passed the water back and forth and watched the sun burn the fog away.

"What do you remember?"

I closed my eyes, resting my forehead on the back of Eve's. I could bring it back now. I'd redrawn the boundaries, anchoring myself in this cocoon.

"She was trapped in a small space. It was completely black. Bugs crawled on her. Biting. Bleeding. Then he came and blinded her with a light. She doesn't know what he's going to do with her. He says she deserves this for what she did."

Eve's energy reflected the horror still churning inside me. "It's Kate? The missing jogger?"

I nodded.

"So she's alive. That's encouraging. And what about the man?"

I could hear his voice, the gloating sneer of it. *No matter how many questions they ask, no one's gonna find you.*

"We've talked to him already."

238

Kate

My favorite time of day was after Blake and I stumbled down to the bakery and turned the ovens on, and before she unlocked the front door and plugged in the neon pink OPEN sign. Neither of us were fully awake, scooping and rolling and kneading side by side as our playlists dovetailed into each other. Flour coated our arms, sugar bloomed in the air, and the sky through the bay window turned from black to gray to lavender to pink. We barely talked, silently exchanging tools and pans and fresh mugs of steaming coffee, moving through each other's spaces with the practice of an old married couple. I could almost feel my mom behind me, nodding her approval at the glossy egg-white finishes and pools of icing melting into a piping hot pan of rolls.

My hair was scooped up in a paisley handkerchief. I wore a tight Fanta T-shirt under baggy overalls with the dough cutter in my back pocket like a talisman. My shoes were glorified slippers, tapping out the Eurythmics under the table. I'd thrifted the entire outfit and, like everything else in Darcy's life, it fit me like a glove. My boyfriend was upstairs snoring in bed while my best friend and I baked for a still-sleeping world.

I picked mint sprigs from the greenhouse by the window and arranged them on a platter of brownies. "If you could be anyone, who would you be?"

Blake drained her coffee, staring at nearly done trays of giant cookies filling the top oven. "Just lead roles or are we talking supporting characters, too?"

"Not in a movie." I finished the platter and slid it into the display case in the front of the store. When I got back, she was still staring at the oven. "I mean you. If you could go anywhere and have any kind of life, what would you want it be?"

We pulled out the cookies and transferred them to cooling racks, working in silence. I didn't need to ask again. She was thinking, treating the question as seriously as a quantum physics thought experiment. No one understood the lure of alternate realities, the importance of all our possible lives, like Blake did.

"We can't time travel?"

"We can't."

She sighed, dumping the last empty pan in the sink.

"Then I'd pick up the entire bakery and put it at the edge of an ocean."

"Beach bakery?"

"Not a scorching-sand-and-palm-tree beach. No one gorges on cinnamon rolls in a bikini. It would be a beach with hidden coves and cliffs, the store nestled right off a hiking trail with the sound of waves in the distance. And this guy runs a bicycle rental shop right across the street." Her grin stretched wider, eyes lighting up as the idea unfolded. "He's huge and bald, with one of those sexy carpenter beards. Full sleeves. Instantly in love with me but it takes him months of coming in for coffee before he says a word. The grump to my sunshine."

"A beach and a grumpy bicycle guy." I could already see her there. Blake was someone who could belong anywhere: a beach, a mountaintop, a city, a submarine. The world would open wider to make room for her.

"You would be telling me to make the first move, because obviously I'm smitten with him, too. I've tried renting a bike and ended up with some hilarious scars. Oh, and I have a moped. The town is so small, I can get anywhere on it. But I still wait for him to make the first move and we end up thrown together in . . ." She ran through a few meet-cute ideas, but I was still stuck on the thing she said first.

"I would be there?"

"You *have* to be there. It wouldn't be my perfect life without you. I suppose Charlie can come too, if he must. But only to keep you happy. He has a different haircut. You'll love it."

My thumping, half-awake heart flooded with more emotion than I could handle at five in the morning. Tears welled in my eyes and I turned away from Blake, embarrassed.

"So what do you think? Beach town? Pastries & Dreams and endless shoreline, just waiting to be walked at sunset?"

"Yeah." I blinked the water back and tried to make my voice sound normal. "I'm in."

An arm looped around my shoulders and pulled me back until our heads bumped. "Good."

I covered her flour-coated arm with mine and we stood there, sleepy and locked together, dreaming a life awake.

* * *

Concrete scraped my skin raw. Dirt, cobwebs, and sticky, seeping fluids coated my hands, my face, my throat. The darkness pitched and rolled, my eyes adding color where there was none. Waves crashed in my head, the white noise of nothingness breaking into patterns. It wasn't real, or maybe it was. My brain clung to anything, desperate for relief. The memory of Blake and I in the kitchen faded, even as I tried to bring it back into focus, to feel the weight of her arm, the lilt of her voice. But the moment was gone. And I was still here.

Caged in a black room.

None of it felt real now. Blake and Charlie shimmered like fever dreams. The bakery couldn't have been an actual place, on the beach or in Iowa or anywhere else. Nowhere was that perfect. I'd never been allowed in a space that light.

All of it felt like a movie I'd watched once a long time ago, when I was young enough to believe another world was waiting, the colors and music and laughter etched in a deep trench in the bowels of my mind, creating a nostalgia for something I'd never known. It was just a trick my brain had been playing on me since I was seventeen and Ted had dragged me down the basement stairs.

This was my life.

This was where I began and ended.

Noises gurgled out of me, shreds of sobs and syllables that lost any meaning. The walls breathed, sucking the oxygen from my lungs and shrinking the edges of the crawl space. They were trying to digest me, to work me into nothing. Or maybe they already had.

A clunk and a screech beyond the door sent me skittering backward. Heavy thumps came closer, the sound of boots on concrete. He came, I remembered. It happened once a day, I'd thought at one point. How many times had he come now? Ten? Twelve?

The metal padlock rattled on the door and then it was opening and the blinding light flashed on my head. I'd already buried my face and closed my eyes, knowing the light was worse than the darkness.

The bucket was dragged out and a fresh one put down. A softer thump—food—and a slosh—water.

"Why are you doing this?"

There was no answer, but the noises paused.

"Why don't you just kill me?"

The flashlight clicked off and I heard the breathing, light and even. I felt his eyes on my back.

"That's not the plan."

The shock of hearing his voice made me raise my head. It was higher, softer than I remembered. Ted's voice had always been loud and animated, filling any space it was in, crowding everything else out. This voice slid into the edges of the crawl space, whispering to the spiders, running finger-light along their webs.

I looked up at the silhouette of the man crouched in the tiny doorway. He was lean, folded up comically small to see inside my prison. The basement light outlined his messy hair, too messy to ever belong to my vain, image-obsessed stepfather.

"You're not Ted."

He laughed and even though it was just as high, just as soft as his voice had been, the sound made my skin crawl.

"Did you forget who found you running on that gravel road? Who visited you in the bakery that day?"

I sat up, my arms shaking from the effort, and tried to make myself think, to separate the real from the not-real.

"I found you the first time when you came to visit your mom. You made such a big deal out of going to the movies with her every year. I knew you'd do it again, even if you thought you could just disappear after murdering my dad."

"Theo." The man's outline wavered into focus, shadows settling into brow, nose, chin. Ted's son crouched outside the time-out room. My stepbrother. My kidnapper.

He was still too thin, still carved out from a lifetime of skirting the edges of Ted's ego, his shoulders permanently hunched and battered by Ted's rage.

"That's how you found me?"

"I followed her to the theater on her birthday and waited until you showed up. It was easy to tag your car and track you back to Iowa City."

I could see him now, the cold shock of Theo Kramer ripped out of a nightmare and thrust into my new life, standing tall and awkward in front of the bakery cases. "Hello, Kate. Long time."

I'd sputtered and struggled for words, trying to keep myself from sprinting out the bakery door and pretending this was normal. He seemed normal, or normal enough for him that I thought he must not know. I waited for him to bring up his dad, mention that he hadn't seen him or maybe what a raging abusive asshole he was, since we were a full state away and far from the shadow of his rotting corpse. But he didn't. Theo ordered a black coffee and watched me while I filled it with shaking hands.

"It's good to see you."

I said something in reply. I have no idea what. We made excruciating small talk for the length of time it took to ring up his order after losing all feeling in my hands. Then he left. As soon as Blake came back from her errand, I told her I felt sick, tore off my apron, and practically sprinted outside. I ran with my head on a swivel to try to see where Theo went, but he'd vanished as quickly as he appeared.

"I wanted to see how you'd react," Theo said. He was still crouched in front of the crawl space door, running a finger lightly along the metal plate of the lock. "When I walked into that bakery, I didn't know if you'd run or try to hide again. Maybe you'd lie and ask me how my father was."

"I knew exactly how your father was." Dead. Rotting.

He didn't act like he'd heard me, still hunching into himself and brushing the lock plate with light strokes of his finger. "Or maybe you'd break down and confess what you'd done."

My mind raced, trying to understand how Theo knew I killed his father. Had he been in the house when it happened, sitting silently upstairs while I kicked Ted's head in? We'd never searched the entire home, too busy burying the body and scrubbing the kitchen clean. Theo could have watched us pull his father's body across the lawn from an upstairs window.

Or maybe there were hidden cameras in the house. A surveillance system we'd never known about. That would fit in perfectly with Ted's controlling, paranoid brand. Theo could've come home, found Ted gone, and watched the recording. But if he'd done that, why hadn't he just handed the evidence over to the police?

"Why?" I sat up as far as the crawl space allowed, studying the backlit shape of the man who'd returned me to the belly of my every nightmare. As a teenager, I'd barely looked at Theo Kramer. He shrank to the edges of the room, existing like a ghost in his father's house. When he wasn't doing chores or eating meals with us, he stayed in his room and there was never any sound of music or videos coming from behind his door. I imagined him googling flight schedules under a blanket, planning his exit strategy. *That's what will happen to us*, I'd thought. If my mom never left Ted, we'd become ghosts, too. When Theo left for college the fall after Ted and Mom got married, I was jealous because he'd gotten away. I never expected to see Theo Kramer again in my life.

"Why did you track me down? Why are you doing this? You're not Ted."

His finger paused on the metal lock plate and his head tilted, considering me.

"Actions have consequences, Kate."

Those words. They were Ted's, spoken every time I'd done something that didn't meet his impossible expectations. Ted, dumping a trash can out on my bed. Ted, locking me in my bedroom after making me lie to the police. Ted, speaking through his hunched, broken son's mouth.

He flicked the flashlight on again, shining it in my face. I flinched and covered my eyes.

"You should know that by now. If you do something wrong, you get punished. That's why you're here. That's why you have to be in time-out."

The light danced away from my eyes and traced a path along the walls. For the first time, I could see the room where I was being held prisoner. The outside wall was concrete blocks, molded and covered in cobwebs. The inside wall was wood. The dark panels looked streaky and mottled, but as my eyes adjusted I could see the streaks were claw marks, dug out by fingernails. Near the top of the wall, four jagged letters had been scratched out.

The light disappeared and the door slammed shut. I barely heard the click of the lock. Crawling over to the wall, I ran my hand over the wood until I could feel the ridges of what my eyes had seen.

THeO.

I wasn't the only one who'd been put in time-outs.

Max

"She's trapped somewhere? In the dark?" Charlie wasn't taking the news of Jonah's dream well. The three of us sat around his kitchen table and for once he wasn't pacing. He had his head in his hands, rocking back and forth, with bloodshot eyes that looked like he'd slept as well as Jonah.

"It's not an exact science. Or a science at all. Sometimes my dreams are echoes or recycled images."

"Have you dreamed about anything like this before?"

Jonah shook his head. "It felt real to me. As real as us sitting here now."

Charlie's voice shook. "She doesn't like the dark. She puts lights on every night. And she can't do enclosed spaces. Even a regular room was hard. I can't imagine . . . Oh god. Kate."

We'd tried calling Valerie on the way here this morning. Her phone went straight to voicemail and she hadn't returned our messages. She was probably still recovering from our last conversation. This one wouldn't be any more comforting, but she'd asked Jonah to dream about her daughter. And he had.

"It's Silas. It's gotta be him. That building out back he kept going to." Charlie shoved away from the table. "He's keeping her there."

"We don't know that." I stood up, too.

"She threatened him and then the money I paid him goes missing, so he blames her. He hates women. And he had the perfect opportunity while she ran by his house."

Jonah glanced at me. He'd taken a Xanax on the way here and was keeping it together, despite Charlie's stress. "The only other person we know who wanted to hurt Kate is in the ground. Silas is our best possibility right now."

It was true. If Kate was being held hostage less than two miles from where we stood, we didn't have a choice. We had to go there.

"Okay, here's the plan."

Twenty minutes later, I hiked through a field of knee-high stalks, their glossy leaves fluttering in the wind. Silas's buildings stood in front of me. The low building with the rusted roof was on the left. I'd come in from the west, keeping the main barn between me and the view of the house. I was blatantly trespassing, breaking the law and code of conduct I was supposed to follow as a private investigator, but it didn't matter at this point. Silas was already planning to sue us. What was one more infraction?

I'd debated taking my gun. If Silas saw me armed on his property, it would only help his "stand your ground" case. But if he really had Kate locked in one of his outbuildings and he found me snooping around, he would shoot regardless. In the end I took it, and I felt better with the weight of it against my chest.

I skirted the edge of the barn, past the rusted pickup where they'd had their target practice and peered around the end of the barn to check the house. The back of the rambler had three windows. I couldn't tell if any of them were open.

Staying low, I ran to the propane tank in the yard and took a better look at the house. The windows were dark and covered. Jonah and Charlie were supposed to knock on the front door at ten o'clock, drawing their attention. I checked my watch. 10:02. It was now or never.

I ran to the outbuilding and tried the door. It wasn't locked, but the screech of rusted hinges carried across the dirt yard. Ducking inside, I eased the door closed and peered through a broken slat. Still no movement by the back of the house.

I unholstered the gun and crept through the dark space. Rows of rotted beams and chicken wire lined the walls, and there was so much mud, debris, and layers of white splatter on the ground I couldn't see the floor. The place had the stench of animal and mold. It had been a chicken barn once, and it smelled like someone had left all the chickens in here to fester and die.

"Kate?" I moved through the space, checking walls and testing floorboards, trying to find a secondary room where she might be locked. At the end of one row was a door. There was no padlock. The arcing pattern of dirt on the floor suggested that this door had been opened a lot, and recently.

"Kate? Are you in there?"

Silence.

I opened the door and shone my phone flashlight inside. The space was empty. It looked like it had been a storage room with broken bins, shelves, and hooks on the walls. I checked each bin, finding nothing until the last one, which held a stack of porn and a baggie of weed. I let the lid go with a bang.

Kate wasn't here. Fuck. We were trespassing, risking our business—again—for nothing. The boards creaked and groaned as I stalked back to the main door, holstering my weapon and trying not to breathe any more of this foul air than I had to. Checking the house through the broken slats, I made sure the coast was clear before opening the screeching door and slipping back outside.

The butt of a shotgun rammed into my face, knocking me into the wall of the barn and onto the ground. Stars burst in front of my eyes. I scrambled to unclip my holster when another blow caught my hand and a foot stepped on my neck.

When my vision cleared, Silas Hepworth was pointing his shotgun at my face.

Jonah

Charlie was a ball of anxiety and fear as we knocked on Silas Hepworth's front door at exactly ten o'clock. Thank god for Xanax.

I hadn't needed to take one this morning, wrapped up in a blanket on the deck with Eve. She'd brought me to a place of stability that usually wasn't possible without a liberal application of chemicals, meditation, or turbo engine speed. I wanted to live in that moment, to take her back to bed for days, to listen to her read radar models over coffee and debate the morning news. And we would. I was only able to leave because I knew I would come back to her—come *home* to her—wherever she was in the world or in the sky. I could chase these nightmares for the rest of my life as long as Eve was on the other side.

The girl who'd aimed a gun barrel at us the other day answered the door on the third knock. She was bleary-eyed and looked like she'd spent the last two months in a dirty bed. Her hair fell into her face as she glared, squinting into the sun. "What?"

I held out our business card. "We'd like to talk to Silas, if he's available."

The girl's energy was a sleepy cocktail of irritation and apathy. She didn't seem to recognize me and tried to shut the door. Charlie put his foot in the jamb, holding it open. "It's important."

The girl swayed. "I dunno where he is."

"Did he go out?" I tried to see past her, to sense anyone else inside the house. Silas didn't seem like the type to let someone else do his talking. Maybe he was gone. But something stuck in my head as the girl kept muttering and swearing at us. Her lethargy bubbled and rolled, the anger piercing through a cloud of fuzzy euphoria. This girl wasn't tired. She was high.

Charlie sensed it, too. Thank god for drug dealers. He switched his approach and pulled a joint out of his pocket. "I'm sorry to bother you. Here, take this for your trouble. We just want to know a few things about—"

A scream tore through the morning. Jerking, I spun around, trying to see where it came from.

"Did you hear that?" But the look on Charlie's face gave me the answer. The scream was in my head.

Max.

Leaving them gaping, I sprinted around the house and across the dirt yard. Outside the low outbuilding, Silas stood on top of Max with a shotgun shoved practically down his throat.

"Stop!" I had no weapons, no backup, and no chance of getting there in time if Silas decided to pull the trigger. I pulled my phone out and hit the camera button. "Silas! I'm recording this, okay? Max isn't trying to hurt you. He's not stealing from you or damaging your property. We're just here to—"

"Trespass. Breaking and entering. I should shoot you both right here."

The camera shook as I got closer. Max was sprawled on the ground, his face bright red. Behind me, Charlie and the girl caught up, both panting and gripped with sudden dread at the scene in front of them.

"Grandpa, what the hell?"

"Get in the house."

"But—"

"Maybe you're the ones who've been stealing from me." He shoved the barrel of the gun hard into Max's face, his finger poised on the trigger. "The other night when you came, my pills were gone. You've been pretending to look for his girlfriend, thinking it would get you on my property to take what's mine."

Max tried to deny it, but the gun pressed harder on his face, turning his argument into mangled sounds. A flush of guilt swelled behind me, a hot flash of adrenaline, and everything clicked into place.

"We're not stealing from you, Silas, and neither did Kate." I grabbed the girl by the arm and dragged her forward. "You need to talk to your granddaughter."

The girl protested as sweat beaded over her face. Her eyes darted everywhere and her heart felt like it would fly out of her chest.

"She's an addict," I told the old man, who started blustering and defending her.

"She took the money you blackmailed from Charlie. It's not the first time your meds have gone missing, is it? Have you lost other stuff? Jewelry? Valuables?" The Xanax shielded me from the worst of the garbage as I combed through the girl's head. "A watch. Gold, right? She pawned it for drugs."

"If you know about the watch, then you must've taken it." But Silas's energy shifted, became less sure.

"When did the watch go missing?" Max asked, able to speak now that he wasn't eating a shotgun barrel.

"Long before Kate disappeared and we got involved. This stuff only happens when she's staying with you, right?"

"Grandpa, you're not going to believe strangers over me," the girl whined, getting desperate.

Silas's face worked, his jowls trembling and pulling tight. He stared at his granddaughter like he'd never seen her before. "You . . . after everything I've done for you?" His face twisted. "How could you do this to me?"

The girl's energy shifted like quicksilver. All supplication vanished, replaced by a deep, scorching anger. Apparently the temper was genetic. She tossed her hair and her dilated pupils flashed pure venom. "How could I? After you've talked for years about how women are evil? What did you think was gonna happen after you told me exactly what you thought of me? Fuck you."

The girl shook me off and ran for the house. Silas looked like he'd aged years during the last several minutes. Max took the shotgun from him and stood up, emptying it of ammunition before leaning it against the building.

"There's nothing here," Max said. "Let's go."

We dropped Charlie off at his house, promising to keep him updated, and were heading back to Iowa City when Valerie finally returned our calls. Her phone had gone dead and she hadn't realized it. Max put her on speaker so I could relay the dream one more time.

"We just checked out Charlie's neighbor. It's not him. Whoever this is, Kate knows him. He said she deserved this."

"She's in a small, dark—" she cut off and Max and I glanced at each other, wondering if the call got dropped.

"Valerie?"

"I know where she is."

Kate

It all made sense now. The kind of sense that wavered in and out of focus, swelling into perfect clarity and then skittering away like bugs in the light.

Every day when Theo came to change my bucket and deliver my rations, he stayed a little longer, talked a little more. He still hunched in front of the door, blocking any path to freedom, and once I caught sight of a crowbar lying near his feet. He wasn't taking chances, but he also wasn't in a hurry to leave.

He was alone in this house where he'd lived as a ghost during his childhood, now with the ghost of his abusive father whispering to him from the shadows. I was the only living distraction inside these walls. Maybe that was why he'd taken me.

I drew him out slowly, planning our conversations the entire time between his visits. It was the only thing keeping me sane, my only tether to this reality, and an incredibly fragile one. The spiders still clawed in. I had visions of a prophet being digested by a monster. Screams that echoed inside my head. But I clung to the knowledge that Theo was coming back, memorizing everything he'd said last time and plotting what to ask next. I traced my questions on the clawed walls, murmuring to myself, rocking back and forth in blackness.

And gradually, it worked. Theo talked about how his dad locked him in the time-out room throughout his awful, literally-tortured childhood. A few hours at first, sometimes for the day while Ted went to work. And Theo wasn't the only one. Ted had imprisoned his first wife, Theo's mom, in here, too. He sounded clinical when he talked about it, his voice blank and dead. When I asked what happened to her, Theo said she abandoned them. But after he locked the door and went upstairs for the night, I pressed my face to the wood and ran my hands over the long, thin ridges that told a different story.

One day he brought a roll of toilet paper. Another day he brought a thin, used bar of soap. I used half my water that day scrubbing my skin raw and sitting in the sludge like a feral hog. I gradually moved closer to the door when I heard footsteps on the stairs, until we were only a few feet apart during our conversations, and I crouched on my feet the way he did, mirroring him even though I swayed and lost my balance a lot.

Eventually, Theo told me he'd come home one day this spring and found the house empty. Ted's phone was there, his wallet untouched where it always sat on a bookshelf in the living room. He didn't tell me how exactly he found out that I'd killed his dad, but the details he dropped were specific. There must have been hidden security cameras, eyes he didn't want me to know too much about.

And I knew why he hadn't taken the footage to the police. That morning, when he'd stepped out of the trees surrounding Charlie's house, there was no more pretending. No more small talk. He knew what I'd done. It shimmered in the morning air, rising in every gasp of my burning lungs. I tried to speak, to hold him off as I fumbled at my pockets, but I couldn't get the mace out in time. He twisted my arm behind my back, bent me over until I thought my shoulder would snap, and leaned down to whisper in my ear.

"If you're quiet, I won't have to hurt him."

It was dumb, so incredibly dumb, but I flashed to an image of Charlie in bed, the covers twisted, a hairy forearm thrown over his face to block out the sun, and I did what Theo told me. I went quietly.

He put me in the trunk of my own car, the same trunk where Mom and I had chucked our bloody clothes and the shovels and sled. I could smell blood and bleach and exhaust. With every bump and jerk of the road, I could feel clods of dirt hitting the body. I thought it was the worst place I could be trapped until the car stopped. Theo opened the trunk and I saw where we were.

Not at a police station. Not in the woods.

He'd brought me to Ted's house in Illinois and locked me in the time-out room because he knew. He understood that I would take jail in a heartbeat over this. That I would beg for prison. He'd been locked in here, too, had probably lost his mind inside these walls as completely as I was losing mine. It took someone who'd been tortured to understand what torture was.

And that meant I might understand him, too.

I was leaning against the door, my ear pressed to the wood for what felt like hours, when he opened the door to the basement. There was a lock on that one, too, but not a padlock. It opened with the steady click of a deadbolt that echoed through my skull. I pulled away, scrambling unsteadily back to a spot a few feet from the door and assuming the crouched position he expected by now.

The padlock opened with a key. I could hear the faint scrape and turn as clearly as if it were an airplane roaring overhead. Then the clunk of the padlock being removed and the squeak of the metal plate swinging away from the door. I counted the movements on my fingers, each broken nail pressing in turn against the concrete. The door swung open, revealing Theo in a mirror image to me on the other side. He flashed his light around the room while I hid my face. The routine was familiar now, almost comforting. I hoped he thought so, too.

"Hi," I said, my face still buried.

He took yesterday's paper plate and water jug and changed out the bucket. He did that first now, removing the smell of piss and shit, or at least the worst of it, before we started talking. The new food and water would come last, after he was done with me. Sometimes he threw them in and slammed the door. Sometimes he slid them across the doorway like an offering. Once, when I tried to ask him more about his mother, he locked the door without giving me anything. That was the first night I hallucinated the prophet and the whale. Today I was determined not to upset him.

"Thank you," I said when the bucket was gone. The light lingered on my face and then jerked away. I dropped my hand and chanced looking up.

He leaned against the door, one hand hidden behind the frame, the other rolling the flashlight back and forth on the ground. It threw shadows across the walls, making patterns too sharp and fast to see.

"I know this is a lot of work for you, Theo. And I appreciate it. The fresh buckets, the food, the water."

The speech was slow and unsteady on my tongue. Even though I'd spent hours memorizing the words, they felt like a foreign language. They could break and split into meaningless sounds at any moment.

Theo spun the flashlight in a circle, making me dizzy. "If you died right away, you wouldn't be punished properly."

I nodded, swaying back and forth. The ground was moving underneath me, distracting me as ants crawled over my feet. The passing spin of the flashlight made their shadows breathe. "I know. I understand that now. But I'm still grateful. And I was just hoping . . ." I faded, putting a hand to the floor to stop the rocking. It didn't help.

"Hoping what?" Theo finally asked.

"Is it too much to ask for tampons?"

Theo froze. The flashlight stopped moving. My hand shook as I took the filthy, blood-covered underwear from where it had been cradled in my lap and dropped it on the floor in front of him. He looked down, disgusted and fascinated, and that's all I needed.

I launched myself at him, springing out of the crouch to hit him squarely in the chest. He fell back, hitting the floor, and I drove an elbow into his throat. He gagged, his eyes bulging white and round, and I rolled off him, sprinting as fast as I could to the stairs and the open doorway at the top.

My heart thundered in my ears. My eyes watered. I didn't know where Theo was and I didn't look back to check. I ran up the concrete steps, stumbling into the wall. A hand grabbed my ankle and I screamed, falling and cracking my shoulder on the steps. The light from the doorway faded as I was dragged backwards.

"No." It was a guttural shriek, an animal rising and snarling to life. There was nothing except the doorway above and darkness behind, no world outside of those two things. I would murder Theo;

I would eat him; I would claw my way out of my own skin before I went back into the dark. My body thudded down the steps, my hands scrambling for purchase, but there was nothing to hold on to. I hit the bottom and saw the crowbar lying next to the bottom step. Grabbing it with both hands, I scissored up and swung it behind me in a vicious backhand. Theo had both hands on my leg and couldn't block it in time. It cracked into his temple. He grunted and let me go. Gasping, I bear-crawled back up the stairs and slammed the door closed, clicking the deadbolt into place. Theo raced upstairs, throwing his weight against the door, but it was solid. He wasn't getting out.

I froze against the door, shocked and panting. Adrenaline flooded my body. My heart felt like it was trying to break out of my chest. The door to the basement was in a hallway off the kitchen, and even though there were no direct windows, it was still brighter up here than anything my eyes were used to. The hallway was a watery blur. I scrubbed furiously at my eye sockets, trying to clear my vision. Another thump from the other side of the door—this one sharper and higher. He'd found the crowbar.

The door was solid wood and Theo was no athlete, but he'd break it down sooner or later. The thumps came steady and fast.

I stumbled up, trying to remember if there was any furniture I could push in front of the door. I felt along the walls toward the kitchen, finding nothing. It didn't matter. As long as I could see, I could grab Theo's keys and drive away. I could take his phone and call 911. I could run into the woods if I had to. They'd already saved me twice. They would do it again.

The kitchen was even brighter, but my eyes were adjusting. I could see the counters, the island. I ran my hands over everything, looking for car keys, begging any God that would listen to help me, to deliver me from this nightmare. My breath hitched, tightening in my chest in smaller and smaller gasps that felt in time with the whacks of the crowbar against the door. He was coming. He was going to get out.

I couldn't find any keys. There was nothing in the kitchen but papers and dirty dishes and moldy food cartons. I swore and begged and cried. A sharp pain in my side felt like it was stabbing me with every breath. Then, something splintered in the hallway.

"No. No, no, no, no." I backed up, facing the direction of the sound. It would have to be the woods. I could still make it to the woods.

I turned, ready to run, and screamed at the sight of a man standing in the front doorway. He took a single step toward me and smiled.

Ted.

My heart stopped. My lungs froze. My vision contracted to a single face surrounded by black.

"No. No." I stumbled against the kitchen island and backed around it, trying to put as much distance as I could between me and the man I'd killed.

This wasn't possible. I was hallucinating. The time-out room had drained the last of my sanity and now I was being haunted by a ghost. It was the only explanation.

Ted walked calmly into the room like he'd stepped through a rip in time. He wore boots, khakis, and a pullover sweater. His hair was combed in the same side-slicked style, but a tennis-ball-shaped line above his temple had the shiny, puffed appearance of skin stitched back together. His nose was different, too—larger and crooked. One eye sunk down further than the other as his black gaze lit on me, watching me like a cat stalking a caged bird.

"Not leaving so soon, are you, Kate?" His voice was the same rolling tenor, the same precise inflections called up from the depths of my nightmares. It eclipsed the sounds of splintering wood coming from the hallway.

"Not real," I chanted, shaking my head. My back hit another counter and I felt along the top of it, searching for a weapon without taking my eyes off the distorted ghost. "You're not here. You're not real."

"Why would you think that?" He closed the space between the island and the stove. "Just because you tried to kill me and bury my body doesn't mean I'm not real. I'm the most real, the most alive person in this house."

I shoved a stack of papers off the counter, knocking over a cup of pens and sending a cereal bowl to the floor with a crash. Shards of blue ceramic scattered across the tile. There were two ways out of the kitchen: through the door to the dining room that he was blocking; or the hallway leading back to the basement door. I tried to ignore what the ghost was saying and focus on the dining room door behind him. If he was really a ghost, I could walk right through him. If he wasn't . . .

I leaned down and grabbed a shard of the ceramic bowl, holding it in front of me. The blue porcelain shook and dug into my hand, covered instantly in sweat.

"Get out of my way."

The ghost stopped talking. His eyes flashed and I remembered—Ted didn't like to be interrupted.

"There's only one way out of my house, Kate. I think you'll enjoy the lesson in it. I've worked hard to make it an experience neither you or your mother will forget."

I took a deep breath, filling my lungs until they almost burst from the pressure, and ran.

I charged the ghost—ready to run right through it—and met Ted's closed fist with the side of my head. His punch sent me reeling across the island, the burst of pain making the lights fade in and out. Ringing filled my ears.

"Oh my god."

I swung wildly with the porcelain shard until my arm was shoved behind my back. The edge of it dug into my own skin and I screamed.

"That's better."

I was hauled up to face Ted, which is when I realized Theo had escaped the basement. He was holding me in place.

Ted stepped closer, his damaged face leering over me, and my heart beat as though it could take flight and leave the rest of me behind.

Ted was real. He was here. He wasn't dead or buried or gone.

"How?" I whimpered.

The smile stretched his scars wide, pulling his skin back from his skull.

"I'll show you."

The woods were dark even in the middle of the day. The full summer canopy let only stray fragments of sunbeams inside, slicing across us as Theo hauled me over the uneven terrain. I tried screaming, but they'd gagged me and tied my hands behind my back. The muffled garbled sounds were trapped in my throat, choking around sobs and squeezed by panic. I thought I heard a car once, and tried to yell before Theo shoved my head against a tree and told me to shut up.

Ted walked behind us, reminiscing about my mother and wondering, in a tone that twisted my gut into nauseating knots, how she was doing.

Once, after Theo dragged me over a fallen tree, I saw Ted struggling to get over it. There was something wrong with his leg, held straight and stiff, and in a lucid burst I remembered the stab wound. Mom had swiped him in the torso and jabbed him in the knee. It hadn't mattered at the time. Dead men didn't need to walk. But Ted was walking, struggling through the woods behind us in a furious, uneven gait.

Theo shoved me forward. I knew where we were going long before we got there. I'd only been there once, but I'd dreamt about the place almost every night since. The impossibly hard dirt, shovels cracking against rock after rock, the form wrapped in a sheet on the sled. I'd thought the body moved at one point while we were digging, hadn't I? And it must have. Ted was still alive when we'd done all that, still breathing as we dug his shitty shallow grave.

"Stop here."

Theo obeyed, bringing me to an abrupt halt and shoving me to my knees at the base of a gnarled, bumpy tree.

I was confused. I didn't recognize the spot, didn't see the brush I'd remembered covering the grave with or any disturbed ground. But it had been dark, and that was months ago. The woods had changed since then, always growing, always shifting, always spitting back the bodies you tried to hide inside them. Maybe this was the spot and my nightmares had twisted it into something else in my head.

Ted walked forward, one sure step, one hesitant one, until he towered over me.

"You remember that night, don't you, Kate?"

I stared into the trees, willing any movement between the shadowy trunks. I would take a human, a bear, a wolf, anything. Before a savior could appear, Ted grabbed my chin and jerked my head up.

"You probably remember it a little differently than I do. I'm sure you and Valerie drove back to that pathetic little duplex thinking you got your revenge on me. That the two of you had somehow beaten me. But in your stupidity, you hadn't even bothered to check my pulse."

We had, though, hadn't we? Mom said he was dead. She'd felt his neck. I tried to remember, but everything was spinning. I couldn't focus, couldn't think.

"Then you make the mistake of burying me facedown with a pocket of air in the sheet you wrapped me in. I woke up feeling branches scraping over my back. I couldn't move, until I heard the two of you hauling shovels away, and I realized what you'd done. That's when I found the strength to pull myself out of my own grave, and crawl my way back through the woods."

"Theo came as soon as I called and nursed me back to health. He wanted to go after you right away, to make you pay for what you'd done, but I knew better. We waited and we watched.

"At first you disappeared and Theo thought we might have lost you entirely. I knew you couldn't stray far from Valerie, though. The two of you are thick as thieves. And I was right."

His hand tightened on my chin until I thought my jaw would snap. I whimpered around the wet cloth of the gag. I hated the sound, and I had no control over it.

"It didn't matter where you went, Kate, or what you called yourself. I would've found you. Remember what I told you about Jonah? About how he tried to flee? You could've gone to the ends of the Earth and I still would've hunted you down and swallowed you whole."

He was in my face now, breathing on me, his eyes as black as the tree branches behind him.

"So I'm going to have to show you—again—what it takes to do things right. You think you can bury someone and walk away?" The hand on my chin moved to my throat, and he started to squeeze. His disfigured face filled my vision, massive and unhinged, and his voice dropped to a guttural whisper. "This is how it's done."

The hand at my throat pushed me backward, choking off most of my air until I fell next to the gnarled tree.

On the other side of the trunk, someone had dug a gaping hole in the earth. Inside was an open, empty box the size of a coffin.

Max

The house looked different in the day. The brick and precise black trim seemed ghoulish in the overgrown lawn, like the lost toy of a giant, morbid child. The windows were all dark, their shutters drawn. I rang the bell and knocked, waited a few seconds, and did it again. No answer. There was no movement or noise from inside.

Valerie, who'd gotten here less than five minutes after us, stood at my shoulder. Her jaw was set in determination. We'd stayed on a call with her most of the way here while she explained the torture of the time-out room. Valerie's description of the room—although secondhand through what Kate had told her—matched exactly what Jonah had dreamed.

The man in the dream said we'd been asking questions. And we had. We'd talked to the only other person who had a key to this house: Theo Kramer, Ted's son.

The pieces all slotted into horrible place.

"Anything?" I asked Jonah, who'd moved into the bushes near a bay window and was listening on his own frequency. He gave a negative sign.

"We can call the police, ask them to do a welfare check."

"Can they enter the house?" Valerie pushed me aside and tried the door. It was locked. She keyed in a number to the combination lock. It beeped and flashed red.

"Yes, if they believe someone is injured inside. We can help them believe it."

"Based on what? His dream?"

"Jonah's worked with law enforcement before. And I'm a former—"

Valerie ran to the garage, leaving me in mid-sentence. She flipped the keypad up and keyed in a code. The garage door engaged and lifted. Jonah and I glanced at each other—at least it wasn't breaking and entering—and followed.

We edged past a white BMW sedan and a CRV. Both were empty and the rest of the garage was military-neat, each individual tool hung on its own hook on a spotless wall.

"So he changed the front door code but not the garage?"

Valerie hesitated for the first time at the door to the house. She glanced at the garbage cans lining the back wall. "The garage code was our anniversary."

Inside, the house was quiet and dark. We crept through a mudroom that opened into a living room with a wall of glass over-looking the backyard and the woods. A single opened Coke can sat on the coffee table next to a can of red spray paint. A fat fly landed on the soda and crawled inside.

Jonah went to the table, picked up the Coke, and immediately put it down. He looked off-balance as he turned back to us. "Where's the basement?"

Valerie led us to a hallway, stopping short when she saw the door leading downstairs. It was hacked open, the wood splintered along the grain and the lock lying on the floor.

"Oh my god."

Grabbing her before she could lunge down the stairs, I pulled my gun from the holster. "Let me go first."

She struggled for a second before nodding.

I flicked on my phone flashlight and started a recording, edging the door further open with a long, high creak. The stairs were concrete. The only light filtered down from the first floor. I descended the stairs, gun first, sweeping the corners.

It was an unfinished basement. The floor was dirty; wooden studs and sheets of plastic marked outlines of walls, and oblong spaces disappeared behind pipes and utilities. Behind me, Jonah's breaths became more and more ragged.

"Where is it?" I swept the light from wall to wall as the hair stood up on the back of my neck.

"On the left. The back corner." Even Valerie's voice was hushed, but she pushed me forward, toward the concrete block wall.

"I can't." Jonah doubled over, looking like he was going to be sick. He waved us toward the corner. "This is the place. God. I . . ." He leaned against one of the wall studs, pulling a pill bottle out of his coat.

We got close enough to make out a half-size storage door set into the wall. It stood open, and an overpowering smell of urine, feces, and unwashed human met us as we approached. Jonah started hyperventilating.

"Kate Campbell?"

I shone the flashlight inside the crawl space. It was maybe three feet wide by six feet long, with enough room to sit up. The floor was stained, the walls dirty and cobwebbed. Other than a bucket, a tipped-over water jug, and some slices of bread strewn across the ground, the space was empty.

Valerie crouched on the floor, shining her flashlight on a crumpled piece of clothing. I stooped down to look—it was a bloody pair of underwear.

"Oh god."

I caught her before she fell backward. "We don't know what happened, Valerie."

"She's not here. I thought we'd find her here." Her voice caught.

"We'll find her. Someone was here, and recently. That bread doesn't have any mold on it."

"She was bleeding."

I moved the light around us, checking the floor, walls, and back inside the crawl space. "I don't see much blood anywhere else. A few smears inside the room, but nothing that looks like a violent crime scene."

"That depends on your definition of violent crime."

Feeling sick, I offered a hand to help Valerie up. "You're right. Let's get out of here and—" Jonah wasn't next to the stairs anymore. I didn't see him anywhere.

"Jonah?" I flashed the light around the empty basement.

He was gone.

Jonah

This house was a scream choked off, a hand squeezing a throat, and all the desperate energy swelling behind it. Everything I touched, everything I looked at was caught in the same vise and the longer I was in here, the more it felt like a hand on my throat, too. I broke into a cold sweat long before we reached the basement, barely staying on my feet as Max and Valerie disappeared down the stairs. The darkness ate them in a cold, greedy gulp.

I needed Eve. I needed Xanax or maybe a two-by-four to the head. I needed anything that would take me out of this reality and I needed it now. Swallowing a pill dry, I fought to stay upright as the world tilted and spun. I didn't want to sit, or hold on to a wall. I trusted contact with this basement like I trusted serial killers.

Max said something. It sounded like it came from the end of a long tunnel. The Xanax stuck in my throat, closed off by the fist of this house. I doubled over, gagged, and waited to pass out. Voices receded. Somewhere, someone was hyperventilating like wind whipping through trees. It sounded like it was coming from upstairs. I staggered out of the basement and through the main floor. No one. The rooms were empty of everything but the grasping energy, ripping at me like fingers. Another staircase. Another hallway, pitching like a ship in a storm. All the doors were closed except one.

"Jonah!"

I tried to answer.

The open door led into an office. Dark wood, heavy bookcases. An empty chair, turned to the side, like someone had just left. Framed pictures hung on the wall. Wedding photos, with Ted and both his wives. A family picture of Ted, Valerie, Theo, and a young, recalcitrant Kate sitting at the edge of the shot. Ted and Theo, both in suits.

I moved to the desk, off-balance, praying I wouldn't have to catch myself and touch something in this room. The work surface was littered with laptops, maps, pages torn from books, and dozens of Polaroids. The photos were all of Valerie and Kate taken at a distance. Valerie in front of her duplex. Kate at the bakery. Valerie's back, standing at the edge of a river. Kate, running alone. One paper was a diagram of the interior of a house, each room filled with doodled stick-figure bodies. A stack of journals sat underneath the diagram. I opened the cover of the top one with my phone. It was filled with cramped, practically illegible handwriting.

A hand touched my shoulder. I whirled, crashing into the desk and the cascade of foul energy emanating off of it.

"It's us."

Max and Valerie stood in the doorway. Max had a gun. Valerie must have picked up a kitchen knife on the way upstairs. She brandished the cleaver, looking sick as she absorbed the shrine.

"You okay?"

The panic attack was still unspooling inside me. Every breath felt like a fight. "Sure."

"I don't think anyone's here. The crawl space was unlocked, no damage on the door."

"Lot of damage on the basement door, though."

It didn't make sense. I could feel Max wrestling with it, too. Valerie, who'd been surveying the desk with mounting horror, picked up one of the ripped-out book pages and read a highlighted line. "'They shall not feed, nor shall they drink.'" She looked up. "It's from the book of Jonah."

"Biblical torture playbook?"

"She was given food and water," Max argued. "There was both inside the crawl space."

"Maybe this refers to somewhere else—a secondary location," I guessed.

Valerie kept reading, her voice flat. "And Jonah said: 'Take my life from me, for it is better for me to die than to live.'"

I leaned on Max, who threw an arm around my shoulders. "If it's in this house, I agree. Either kill me or let's go."

We went back downstairs and out through the garage door. The cars in the garage bothered Max. If Kate—or anyone—had gotten out of here, it didn't seem like they'd driven.

"On foot?"

Max looked at both of us, eyes widening, and detoured sharply to the backyard. The long, unkempt grass showcased a well-worn trail leading from the back of the house into the woods. As soon as I saw it, I knew.

Kate was still here.

Kate

I lay in a box staring at a canopy of tree branches and slivers of flawless blue. I'd spent so many days on Charlie's farm looking up, absorbing the colors, the shape of the clouds, the brilliance of each sunrise and sunset. I'd never taken a single one for granted. I was so grateful now that I'd taken the time to breathe deep, to commune with the unique and perfect beauty of the sky over the rolling fields of Iowa—Charlie's sky—because this might be the last time I saw it.

Two faces sneered over me. I didn't look at either of them. I focused on the blue until I'd memorized it and then closed my eyes.

At Ted's instruction, Theo had dragged me into the makeshift coffin and tied my legs so both my hands and feet were bound. Then he had Theo remove my gag. Now they were waiting for me to lose it, for the tears and panic and begging. They didn't understand I had none of that left in me. And even if I did, I would die before giving them the satisfaction of a single *please*.

Charlie's sky. Bonfires and beers. Laughter and childhood stories. Hot cinnamon rolls dripping with icing. Blake's voice belting out, "Every now and then I get a little bit lonely." I hadn't been, not with them. I'd done exactly what Mom had wanted for me. I'd built a brand-new life that had nothing to do with the man standing over me, and it had been beautiful. It had been everything I wanted. Even if it was all a memory that would die with me today, I had no regrets.

A heavy foot stepped into the box next to my hip and I felt breath on my face. I didn't open my eyes. Sunsets. All the pinks and oranges swirled together. They felt like you could walk right into them.

Something hit me on the cheek and I flinched, as whatever it was rolled off and clattered on the bottom of the box.

"That's an audio recording device. A little something I picked up for you." Although Ted's voice was low, a current of ugly excitement ran through it. He was proud of this. He'd been waiting for this moment. "It's on now. I've already set everything in motion. You see, I thought you might want to say good-bye to your mother while you still have the air to do it. I hear people who don't escape their graves can become, well, let's just say you might want to do it sooner than later." The pressure of the foot disappeared from the box and Ted's voice receded. "And don't worry. I'll be sure she gets your message."

There was a pause while he waited for that to sink in. I could feel his hunger, his anticipation. He wanted to feed on my fear.

I blinked my eyes open and waited for them to adjust. The sky, those tiny shots of blue between the trees, hovered above me like dragonflies. Each one a beacon, irrefutable, no matter what happened beneath them. They would always be there, long after he was dead. What was a whale to the whole of the sky?

"I'm glad I got a chance to tell you this."

The heads froze, waiting. I smiled.

"Blake doesn't use brown sugar. She mixes white sugar with molasses, which is the same thing except it's cheaper and better quality. I can't believe we never did that, Mom. So for a standard chocolate chip cookie recipe, she uses half white and half brown sugar, which translates to—" I turned to my side, curling into a fetal position around the small recorder, and ran through the rest of the recipe, the measurements, the tricks and conversions.

"Shut it," Ted ordered, his voice burning with anger.

I described the vanilla. Water leaked out of my eyes, dripping onto the plywood, but my voice never wavered. The lid scraped over the box and I felt the darkness return, a time-out room shrunk down to barely more than the size of my body. I curled in tighter and kept talking. The trick for grinding oats into flour. The quick salted caramel hack.

Clods of dirt thumped onto the top of the box. It was just the mixer jumping, the front door opening and shutting with the never-ending flow of customers. Ted and Theo talked in low, muffled voices, but no, no—it was the students lingering over their coffees, talking about their weekend plans. I was in the kitchen. I was sitting by the bonfire outside Charlie's house. I was walking into the sunset, becoming part of those oranges and brilliant, blinding pinks.

The dirt kept falling, the thuds growing duller and softer as the box became covered. The layer of earth separating me from the world above grew thicker, heavier. The box cracked and groaned, the air inside became hot and stifling. I leaned closer to the recorder, the tiny red light blinking like a submersible on the bottom of the ocean. My voice dropped low, humming strangely in the darkness, but it didn't break. It came out of me like an animal that knew only one thing: if I was going to die here today, I would have the last goddamn word.

"I know you won't play this for my mother. Because I'm not going to scream for you. I won't beg. You lose again, Ted. You'll always be a loser. You think you're God's messenger, that you've swallowed me up after I tried to get away, but guess what? This will eat you from the inside for the rest of your life because you know it's true.

"You. Are. Nothing."

With my chin, I pressed on the recorder until the tiny red light went out and there was only darkness left. It wouldn't be long now.

I curled up tighter and whispered in time to the dirt falling on my grave.

Eat the whale.

Eat the whale.

Eat the whale.

Max

Even in the middle of the day, the woods didn't let in much light. The trees were dense and towering, the canopy blocking most of the sun. When Jonah and I found Andrea Kramer's body, I'd assumed searching would've been easier in the daytime, that there were probably trails to follow if you could see them.

I was wrong.

Jonah, Valerie, and I walked single file, working our way through underbrush and over the rocks, roots, and fallen trees on the forest floor. It was slow going, and every step we took felt like it could be in the wrong direction. We'd called the police while we still had service, but we didn't even know whether Kate or Theo came in here. Kate could've stolen a third car and left. Or Theo could've taken her somewhere completely different.

"They're here." Jonah answered the question I didn't ask.

"How do you know? Can you sense someone?"

Jonah shook his head and left our trail, hacking his way through two bushes to get to a giant pine tree heavy with branches that scraped the ground. He pointed to a branch at chest level. Some of the needles were bright red.

"What is it?"

"Spray paint."

Valerie followed, pulling herself through the tangle of over-grown shrubs. She examined the branch before looking all around, her head on a swivel until she pointed at a spot through a break in the trees. "There! There's another one."

"It's a trail," Jonah said, touching the paint-coated needles. "Someone's marking their path in and out."

"Why?"

Jonah looked into the shadows beyond the next red marker, and shook his head. "I don't know. But it's them. I'm sure of that."

"Kate and Theo?"

"Maybe he's taking her to his father's grave." Jonah rubbed his head, closing his eyes in what looked like pain.

"Why would he do that? How would he even know where it is? If he got control over her again, why not just take her back to the time-out room?"

"Retribution. He wants her to see it," Jonah said, his eyes still shut. "He wants her to know what it felt like."

All the blood drained from Valerie's face. She lifted the cleaver in her hand and took off toward the next marker without another word, racing to get there. By the time we made it to that tree, she was already working her way to the next one, using the knife to hack away at the surrounding brush. It took two more markers before we caught up to her. She stood next to a sprayed bush, look-ing around frantically.

"I don't see any more red."

We all looked, spreading out in the general direction of where it should be. After a minute of fruitless searching we met up in a small dirt clearing.

"Is this the path you took to bury him?" I asked.

Valerie threw her hands wide. "I don't know. It was night. Everything looked different. All I wanted was to get far enough into the trees to a spot that no one would accidentally find."

"How long did you walk?"

"At least a half hour, I think. But we were dragging him, too, pulling his body on a sled. Oh god," she choked out. Her eyes went wide and white, the panic inching in as she spun in circles. "Where is she? It feels like we're running out of time. That I won't find her."

She looked at me. The knife shook in her hand. I wanted to tell her we would find Kate, we would rescue her before she suffered anything else, but the truth was we didn't always find people in time. It might be a body, and not her daughter anymore.

"When you pulled him, was it more uphill or downhill?"

"Downhill."

"Did you notice anything at the spot where you buried him? A boulder, a creek. Something that stood out in your mind."

"The tree. The closest tree was a giant oak, I think. It had a huge gnarled trunk and twisted branches that stretched overhead."

The woods were mostly flat, with gentle crests and dips. I turned toward a downhill slope. "Okay, we're heading downhill and we're looking for an old oak tree."

Valerie nodded, choked up on the knife, and ran ahead. Jonah and I followed. We hacked through the woods for another ten minutes, bottoming out in empty valleys, running to oak trees with no disturbed ground. No Kate. The woods swallowed every sound. Even the cries of birds seemed muffled and distorted, coming from everywhere and nowhere at once. Panic was setting in for all of us now. Valerie's emotions bled into Jonah and their frenetic searching energy drove me faster and harder. We stumbled to the bottom of yet another hill, finding nothing but packed earth and skittering animals, when Jonah doubled over, bracing hands on knees.

"You okay?"

He shook his head at the ground. "We're doing this wrong."

"What else can we do?" Valerie asked. "I'm not going to sit around waiting for the police, if and when they ever show up."

Jonah looked up. His face was streaked with dirt and tense with borrowed fear.

"We don't have to find them. They'll find us."

Jonah

"Kate! Kate Campbell! Kate, where are you?" I bellowed into the stillness of the woods, zigzagging through trees. Branches cut me on all sides, scraping my face, my hands. I kept screaming Kate's name at the top of my lungs.

Max and Valerie had fallen behind, trailing me far enough back that I lost all sense of them. It was a relief, but it put me on edge, too. If I couldn't feel their presence, I didn't know if they were all right.

Max, being Max, had liked the plan, but of course he wanted to be the one to execute it.

"If anyone's out there being bait, it should be me. I've got the combat training. I've got the gun."

"Which is why you stay back to protect Valerie and cover me when we draw out Theo. Besides," I tapped my temple, "I'm the one with the built-in radar."

He didn't agree so much as I left before he could argue and began shouting into the dark, green void.

I kept jogging, hurdling over fallen tree trunks, powering up hills without losing my breath, not slowing down as I yelled into a world distilled into endless columns of brown and green. Eve would be proud.

I hit the creek at one point, probably the same creek where Max and I found Andrea Kramer's body in the hole of the fallen tree. Valerie hadn't said anything about crossing water, so I doubled back along a different route, yelling until I was hoarse.

The crack of a branch sounded like a gunshot behind me. I faltered and stopped. It could've been Max and Valerie, our paths crossing because I changed my route, but it didn't feel like it. I cut over to a large trunk and pressed my back against it, listening, opening up to whatever was following me. It came in a creeping darkness, the dull crunch of leaves. The bait had worked. There was a predator in the woods, the contracted focus of single-minded intent. I closed my eyes and drew careful lines, staking boundaries between me and it.

The energy paused, hesitating. I turned around, bracing myself against the tree, and yelled again.

"I'll find you, Kate. I know you're out there."

They moved again, getting closer. I looked on either side of the trunk, gauging the distance of the sounds, the clarity of the approaching energy. I could feel it clearer now, the anger of being interrupted, the need to stop me before I interfered any more than I already had. And that desperation gave me a shot of hope.

Because it meant that Kate might still be alive.

A blink of movement came on my left, a shift of color in the trees. I pivoted behind the tree trunk as a painfully skinny young man—barely more than a kid—barreled out from behind a bush and swung a shovel at my head.

I ducked. The shovel hit the tree, sending bark flying. Pulling back, he lunged again. This time I caught the metal with both hands, grunting as the tip caught me square in the chest. The kid's eyes were lit up, red-rimmed and crazed. My head was nothing but a skull to him, something to be smashed and spilled open.

He tugged the shovel, but I held on and used his force to swing him into the tree. He winced and the noise was high, like a child's. He hated it. Self-loathing and rage seethed out of him. Kneeing him in the groin, I shifted my grip and used the handle to pin him against the tree.

"Are you Theo?"

The ping of recognition and fear was confirmation enough. An ugly gash bloomed on his temple, half hidden in his hair. He was taller than me, but weak, held together by tendon, bones, and hatred.

I glanced into the woods. There was no sign of Max or Valerie. Maybe I'd lost them when I doubled back at the creek.

"Where's Kate?"

He smirked. "I don't know what you're talking about."

I shoved the handle harder into his chest, feeling the give of young, flexible ribs. He winced again and one of his hands let go of the shovel, dropping to his side.

"Kate Campbell. The woman you abducted who gave you that ugly gash on the side of your head. Where is she?"

Her image flashed through his head, reflecting in mine. A pale, dirty face staring up from a hole in the ground. Calm. Dissociating from the world above her. Then the face was gone, cut off with a slab of wood and covered steadily with shovelfuls of dirt.

A grave. Oh holy fuck, he'd buried her alive.

I slumped, losing my grip on the shovel as the image assaulted me. I didn't feel him move, didn't register his intent until the blade flashed gleefully through his mind. I jerked back, but it was too late.

Theo pulled a knife out of his pocket and stabbed me.

Kate

Kate!

Kate, where are you?

It was a dream. An echo of a prophet swaying in the belly of a monster. Trying to find me deep inside, past all the light and air. I was afraid to touch the sides. I didn't want to know how close they were, how far down I'd come. I'd tried to eat the whale, but I was so tired, so hot. I didn't know where my feet and hands were. But then I heard it: steps pounding away, feet leaving without me. Voices faded as the other one came again, louder.

"Kate!"

I thrashed up and hit my head against the top of the plywood box.

I was Kate. Someone out there knew me and was looking for me. It all came back with tilted and horrifying clarity. What Ted and Theo had done. Where I was. And the fact that I was still alive. My heart thundered in my chest. My lungs pumped hard and fast as desperation clawed its way up my gut.

"I'm here!"

The scream bounced off the edges of the box, smothering me. I sobbed once and choked the rest back, listening. Willing the person to come. To find me. There was no noise now, no reaction to either of our shouts. Or wait. No. There had been. I'd heard footsteps leaving. And the rhythmic thuds of dirt falling on top of me had stopped. Ted and Theo must have gone to find the person calling my name. And if I could hear them, I wasn't buried very deep yet.

I flipped to my back, lying on my arms which were still tied behind me, and wedged my knees between my torso and the top of the box. A million nerves pinged through my body, asleep limbs screaming back to life. Taking a deep breath, I pushed.

The lid of the box moved.

Barely, but enough that I heard a crumble of something falling inside. Creeping to the edge, I rolled my cheek over pieces of rock and inhaled the rich smell of dirt. I hadn't imagined it. Ted and Theo hadn't nailed the box shut before they started burying me and now they'd left before they could finish the job. If dirt could get in, I could get out.

A shot of wild hope seared through me.

I tried to picture exactly where the box had been positioned and how wide the hole was. Which way to push? My whole body shook. Tears leaked steadily down my face as I tried to think. To remember.

"You can do this."

The whisper came out of nowhere, like warm, broken pieces of pottery, meaningless until I put the sounds together, until I realized it was me. Darcy. Kate. I could do this. I could eat this motherfucking whale.

I

I positioned my knees against the box lid, ignoring the scream of deadened nerves in the arms trapped behind me.

Can

I tensed every muscle in my legs, my stomach, my back. I'd trained for this. All that running, pounding my feet against the pavement, the gravel, the fields. I was strong. I was strong enough.

Do

Grunting, I pushed as hard as I could, shoving my knees against the wood, splinters digging into my skin, everything straining, stretching, screaming inside me.

This.

I rolled hard to the right. The lid scraped. An avalanche of dirt fell into the box, hitting my back and boxing me into an even smaller space, but it didn't matter. It didn't matter at all, because I could see a sliver of light along the entire top-left side. Fresh air seeped inside, cool and full of the promise of more. I gasped and breathed in as much as I could, my chest heaving in relief.

But where were Theo and Ted? They might have heard me. One of their faces could appear in the crack of light at any second. This could all be a game, another way to break me.

No.

No, I'd heard the voice. It wasn't them. It couldn't be them. There must be someone else in the woods, someone out there calling me to shore. I had to get to them.

Scrambling, I turned over and repositioned my knees, pushing, rolling, pushing rolling, working the lid as far over as I could. Each tiny shift rained dirt on me, opened the crack an inch wider. My legs burned. My knees grew wet and sticky, slipping when I tried to get traction. More and more dirt filled the box, burying me inside, making it harder to find room. And each second that passed was another chance that a face could appear, that hands could shove the lid back over me and take the light away.

Fighting against the dirt, I moved all the way to the left where the light came in and pushed as hard as I could, feeling the lift of the wood, the slow and steady rise. I braced it, fighting against the weight that wanted to crush me back down, and inched my toes up to get my feet in position. Then I shoved with everything I had left.

With a giant cascade of earth, the lid swung up and slid back down the outside of the box at an angle that let all the light and air flood back into my grave.

I was free.

Max

The shouting stopped before we figured out which direction Jonah had gone. Valerie and I followed the creek for a minute before hearing Jonah's shouts behind us and had to double back. We jogged along the creek bank, panting and winded by this point, and I worried Valerie would stumble and fall directly on the knife she wouldn't let me carry.

"Where is he?" she gasped. "Why did he stop shouting?"

I pulled up Life360 on my phone and swore as it refused to load.

"Let's stop for a minute."

We slowed down and stood back-to-back, listening to the woods for any sign of Jonah.

"Maybe Theo snuck up on him." Even in the whispered tones we'd been using, her voice broke.

"No one sneaks up on Jonah."

I knew it, but my gut still rolled. He'd been shouting for Kate every thirty seconds, and now quiet minutes had ticked by with only the swish of leaves and creak of branches and mounting dread. I couldn't lose my partner out here. I barely remembered who I'd been before I met Jonah. He'd made me the man I was, kept me in line, put up with all my bullshit. And after years and years of watching him pull away from the world, he'd finally found exactly what he needed in Eve. There was no goddamn way I'd let some sociopath take Jonah. Not now.

I put the phone away and pulled my gun out of the holster.

"Stay behind me."

Valerie did as I asked, falling into single file as I moved into the woods. We crept forward, listening every few feet until I heard a shout of pain echoing off the trees.

"Jonah!"

I ran headlong toward the sound, crashing through brush and bushes, not caring how much noise I made until I heard another cry behind me. I swung around, expecting to see Valerie had fallen, that she'd stumbled into a tree or cut herself with that cleaver. What I didn't expect was to find her caught in a chokehold by a man I'd only seen in photographs. The man Kate had supposedly killed.

He had her by the throat with one arm. The other was hidden at her back, along with most of the rest of him. I didn't have a clear shot and didn't dare take it even if I did. Valerie's hands were empty; either she'd dropped the knife or he'd taken it from her. She looked frozen in complete shock and terror. As I pointed my weapon slowly in the air, he nodded in approval.

"Throw it."

I tossed the gun into the woods a few feet to my right. His eyes narrowed, but he didn't comment.

"Walk forward."

I did until he told me to stop. Behind me, another cry of pain pierced the woods. Ted's eyes flashed toward the sound but if he had any concerns about the life of his only child, he didn't show it.

"How are you—" Valerie started before her body jerked like she'd been jabbed with something from behind.

"We'll get to that. Don't worry, love. We have all the time in the world to catch up."

She was shaking, trembling so violently she might have been having a seizure. Moving by millimeters, my hands still in the air, I inched back toward the gun.

"What did you do with Kate?"

He made a *tsk*-ing sound, a sing-songy noise meant for children even as he tightened the arm around her neck. "You'll find out when I'm ready to tell you. For now," the veins on his arm bulged grotesquely blue as Valerie made a choking sound, "I'll be the one to ask the questions."

A crack came from deep in the woods, followed by a muffled grunt. It was too soft to tell if it was Jonah or not. My chest pounded and I felt sick from not knowing. Ted barely noticed, his black eyes fixed on Valerie's shaking form. I took another undetectable step back.

"So, Valerie, darling," he leaned down to speak directly in her ear. She whimpered, holding back sobs, and closed her eyes. His black gaze flicked up to me even as he spoke to her. "Who do we have here?"

Jonah

For a split second, it was like a movie. I saw the knife flash. I watched his skinny fingers flex and thrust, plunging the blade into my stomach. His gloat of triumph burst over me even before the pain, like a surfer riding the crest of a huge, unfolding wave. When it hit me, it was searing, blinding. I think I cried out. I staggered back, and clutched my side.

Theo picked up the shovel, I'd dropped, a murderous gleam lighting his hollowed-out face.

"Kate," the name sounded like a curse, "is learning what happens to people who fuck with my father."

I stumbled into a fallen tree and braced myself on the log.

"You buried her. You buried her alive."

"An eye for an eye." He spun the shovel like a showman at some deranged circus, while still holding the knife wet with my blood. "She did the same thing to him."

"She—what?"

I could barely hear him, could hardly focus on his sick, gleeful energy. The stab wound throbbed with white hot electricity, keeping me firmly within my own body the one time I wanted to be anywhere else. I felt his intention the second before he brought the shovel crashing down, and rolled away from the brunt of the blow, catching the edge of the metal with my leg.

Kicking, I caught him in the knee and he buckled. I went for the knife first—this little felon wasn't stabbing me a second time—and got him by the wrist. He swiped with the knife and punched the butt end of the shovel at me. I dove at him, sending us both to the ground hard. He grunted and wheezed. Stars exploded in front of my eyes. Sweat poured off me, but I knew one thing: I'd landed on top.

I bashed his wrist into the ground until I was ready to vomit. Finally, he let go of the knife and I shoved it away. Every movement felt like I was going to pass out, but it also kept me in my own head, reminded me who I was and what I needed to do.

He tried to hit me, his pathetic fist driving into my shoulder with all his hundred and thirty pounds. I wrenched the shovel out of his other hand and brought the handle down on his neck. He sputtered and turned red, then purple, grabbing wildly for air.

"Do you like it? Do you like suffocating? Should I put you in the goddamn ground?"

It wasn't until he stopped fighting that I threw the shovel aside. It hit the base of a tree with a crack and he heaved, turning to his side and choking on the oxygen he was desperately trying to inhale.

I pulled his arm behind him, trying to hold him still as he fought for breath. Every jerk of his body sent pain ricocheting out from the stab wound in my side.

"How long has she been underground?"

He didn't answer. I wrenched his arm higher up his back.

"Not long," he bit out, coughing into a pile of dead leaves. "We were still shoveling when we heard you."

We.

The image rushed in, seeping into the corners around the pain. His father. His mentor. The man who'd sculpted him in his own image, down to every last sadistic detail.

"He came to you. You nursed him back to health. The two of you planned this for months." The memories leached out of him and into me, polluting my head. The father's rage. The son's subservience and quiet greed. They'd stalked mother and daughter, watching them from the shadows, memorizing their habits and schedules, deciding when they would be most vulnerable. I saw Kate jogging alone through the countryside, Valerie sleeping through her bedroom window. The curl of anticipation, the rush of adrenaline. Throwing Kate into the back of her own car, driving next to a state trooper while she sobbed and beat against the trunk. He got off on it, all of it—the power, the control. Bile rose in my throat.

"Take me to her."

The knife wavered in and out of focus on the ground. I reached for it and grabbed dirt and leaves, tried again. Max. I needed Max. Where the hell was he? I tried to reach past the rancid pile of emotion to sense anyone else in the woods, but the more I opened up, the more of Theo that oozed in.

"Get up." I didn't know who I was talking to anymore. I staggered to my feet, pointing the knife covered in my own blood. The boy's eyes were black holes, sucking me in. The pain in my side seized, my gut twisted, and I fell back to the ground, vomiting.

By the time I looked up again, Theo was gone.

Kate

I couldn't see anyone but I could hear them.

Muffled sounds: branches breaking, men grunting, the swish of leaves and shouts. I couldn't tell where or how far away. But it wasn't here.

Dragging myself up, I rolled out of the dirt-filled box and onto the ground. My hands and feet were still tied. I couldn't run like this and the panic felt almost worse now that I'd gotten out, now that there was a chance I might live to see tomorrow, to see my mom and Blake and Charlie again. Trying to slow my breath, I checked every direction. The giant gnarled tree where Ted had forced me to kneel was the closest one, and it was too big to see if anyone hid behind it. Other trees surrounded the clearing, their trunks obscured by scrub and bushes. Nothing moved. No color or shape caught my attention, but it felt like someone was here, watching me, waiting for the right moment. I didn't know if it was Ted playing another one of his games.

"Come out," I muttered. "I dare you to come out and try it."

I rose to my knees and fell back at the shock of pain. They were covered in red and brown, scraped raw and oozing. Didn't matter.

Couldn't matter. I looked behind me, terrified that someone had crept up while I was distracted. There was nothing. The distant crunches and groans I'd thought I'd heard had fallen silent now.

Someone was coming. Someone was here.

I frantically scanned the ground for a weapon, a tool, anything I could use. Two shovels lay next to a hollowed mound of dirt and an open backpack sat at the base of the gnarled tree.

Wobbling, I pushed off my butt to balance in a squat on my feet and stood up. My legs throbbed and shook. The deadened nerves around my zip-tied ankles sent bolts of electricity cramping through my feet. I hopped once and whimpered on impact, but stayed up. The backpack was only a few yards away. I hopped again, moving around the uneven hole in the ground as the forest floor tilted and faded in and out of focus. The dirt-filled box looked like an open mouth waiting to swallow. It wasn't going to eat me. It wasn't.

I made it to the tree and dropped to my knees, crying out at the jolt of pain. The bag was open. I knocked it over with my shoulder and picked up the bottom of it by the teeth, shaking until I heard its contents hitting the ground. I tossed the bag aside. On the dirt lay a smaller red bag, zip ties scattered like snakes, a pill bottle, a phone, and a utility knife.

A rustle in the brush snapped my head up. I looked in every direction, flattening myself against the tree. No one. No one that I could see. Leaves swayed and shimmered around me, flashing green and gold, hints of light and darkness. I spun and felt around with my hands until I found the knife and worked to open it. My fingers were numb. They felt huge and awkward, impossible to manipulate. I chanced looking away from the woods to focus on the knife and managed to flip it open. It cut my wrist, slicing a long, thin line that bloomed red and spilled over, trailing down to my hand. I could hardly feel it.

The zip tie was impossible to cut. I juggled the knife awkwardly in my fingers, cutting and nicking my hands, trying to find the right angle, the right pressure so I could hit the plastic and not my skin. Every moment that I was still here was time wasted, seconds ticking closer to being discovered and tossed back into the earth. A branch creaked. I didn't look up. Couldn't. I flipped the knife again and stretched myself into a bow to get the zip tie on my ankles instead. Pressing, gripping against the slide of sweat and blood on my hands. I pushed and sawed and finally, the tie broke.

Grabbing the knife, I stumbled up and looked around. Which way? I circled the gnarled tree, staring down the shadows. There were voices. Birds? Animals? I didn't know. I picked a direction I thought was west, the way Mom and I had gone the night we'd escaped Ted the first time. It had brought us to safety once. Maybe it would again.

I ran and my lungs expanded and began pumping—not in panic but that familiar, welcome bite in my chest as I jogged the morning into being, watching the sun crest Charlie's horizon. I could do this. I could find the shore.

I hadn't gone more than fifty paces when I heard the voices again. This time it was a shout, high and clear, a woman's voice.

My mother's.

Max

"I'm Max Summerlin." My hands were still carefully raised, my voice as casual as if I were making some Keurig coffee for a new client. "I've probably got a business card in my wallet if you want to go through it."

"Max." Ted Kramer's arm tightened even further on Valerie's throat. "New boyfriend?"

He surveyed me with loathing, lingering on the empty gun holster. Valerie gasped and tried to shake her head. Somewhere in the distance, a twig snapped and a bird flapped out of its nest, screeching.

"My wife puts up with a lot, but I think she'd draw the line at another woman. I'm a private investigator. My partner and I had the pleasure of meeting your first wife the other day."

A shadow of fear passed over Ted's face. "I don't know what you're talking about."

"Oh, you didn't see the parade of first responders in and out of the woods a few days ago? You must've been pissing yourself sitting there with another woman imprisoned in your basement. The authorities have already determined that Andrea Kramer was murdered, by the way. Strangled to death, which seems to be your preferred method of torture." I nodded at his arm, still wrapped tight around Valerie's throat.

"The police are on their way again now. They're deploying search and rescue this time." At least I hoped to god they were. "They're going to find you, find Kate, and anything else you've tried to bury in these woods. If you don't want to be shot on sight, I strongly suggest you come quietly now."

Ted cocked his head, shifting a look around the stand of trees. "Funny. I don't hear any sirens, no search parties marching through the underbrush. And I think Valerie can tell you," he nuzzled the back of her head, making her shudder, "I have friends on the force."

"I wouldn't count on it."

The voice came from behind Ted. He whirled, dragging Valerie with him, to reveal a young woman standing between two trees. She was covered in dirt, her hair plastered to her head, clothes torn and bloody. She held a small camping knife in one hand that was scraped raw and dripping red.

"Kate!"

The sight of her daughter jolted Valerie into action. She fought against Ted's grip, struggling to free herself. He pulled a gun from behind her back and pressed it into her temple.

Diving behind the tree, I grabbed my own gun and rolled up, ready to take aim, but the Campbell women had already descended.

Whatever twisted showdown Ted Kramer had planned was drowned in a fury of yells and hacking limbs. Valerie had his gun hand in both of hers, pointing the weapon at the sky. Kate kicked Ted in the knee and he screamed, dropping to the ground. They were both on him in a flash. Kate pinned him as Valerie wrenched the gun away. He grabbed for her, but Kate sliced his arm open and his bellow of rage and pain shook the trees. They rolled him onto his belly, shoving his face in the dirt.

"Kate."

Her head snapped up, almost feral, but her face broke into a savage smile as I held up the pair of handcuffs. "Want to do the honors?"

She cuffed her stepfather and stood up, looking down at the writhing, cursing body in the dirt. Valerie stood on his other side, glassy-eyed and panting. There was a pause, a moment full of dark, malignant intent. I thought they would resume attacking him, and I wasn't going to do a thing to stop them, but Valerie looked at her daughter instead and reached across the space that separated them. At her mother's touch, Kate's face transformed. Hatred melted away, replaced by pure, gripping grief.

"Momma."

They stumbled and fell to the forest floor, forgetting about the man handcuffed next to them. Valerie murmured and rocked Kate back and forth, and they held each other as though they'd never let go.

Jonah

"Nicole put a twenty on me getting shot in the arm again."

Max marked the bet on one of the whiteboards in the back room. It used to be my Kate Campbell board, and as soon as I'd erased it we'd started an office pool: which one of us would be injured on our next case. Max had come out of the woods relatively unscathed on this one, but he'd been shot on three separate occasions in the past. I'd only been shot once, but the stab wound from Theo Kramer almost evened our score. I didn't have precognition—thank Christ—but I had an unsettling feeling in my gut that Max wouldn't keep his injury lead for long.

"So that's eighty on me and sixty on you." He capped the marker and stuffed the money in the mason jar next to the board. I grabbed a beer and considered the spread. The left side of the board listed our names and across the top we'd settled on categories of *shot, stabbed, broken bone(s), head injury,* and *misc. internal bleeding,* which was the catch-all for anything else that landed us in the hospital.

Max had just come back from lunch with Nicole Short, the HR director at ACT. Their hiring freeze was over, which meant a flood of new candidate screening business, and apparently she also favored Max taking another bullet. Considering his history, it probably felt like a safe bet.

The front door opened. Bracing my side, I left the back room and saw Kate Campbell standing in the doorway. The sun sliced her in two, half inside, half out. Her emotions were in a tightly controlled war over whether to take another step.

"Hi." I stopped behind my desk, giving her plenty of space. "Max, we've got company."

We hadn't seen Kate Campbell since we dropped her and her mother off at a hospital in Illinois a few weeks ago. Valerie sent us text updates and we'd gotten a few pictures from Charlie, but I wasn't expecting to cross paths again until the case went to trial.

Ted Kramer was being held without bail on charges of murder and attempted murder. Theo, who the police picked up as soon as he'd fled the woods, had been charged with kidnapping, aiding and abetting, and attempted murder. The trial dates weren't set yet, but the story of a father and son's torture of a mother and daughter had been front-page news as soon as it hit the wire and public attention showed no signs of waning.

Kate looked a lot different than she had that day in the hospital. The dirt and blood and tattered clothing were gone, replaced by clean skin, a few gauze bandages, and a sundress, but there were still dark shadows under her eyes and a knee-jerk anxiety as she surveyed our office. She was surprised by the number of plants and the style of the quirky orange chairs in the front, and guessed—correctly—that one of our wives must have decorated. Shelley had just reupholstered those chairs.

Max came out, stopping short when he realized who it was.

"It's a little stuffy in here," I told him. "Why don't you prop open the back door?"

I did the same with the front, moving slowly to give Kate enough time to decide whether she was coming in or going out. She came in and hovered near the window.

When Max reappeared, he offered her a beer.

"No thanks," she said, but the breeze drifting through the building calmed her and after another hesitation she sat on the edge of the chair closest to the door.

"It's good to see you," Max offered. "How are you doing?"

She shrugged and shook her head, a cocktail of tangled emotions rising at the question. "Better, I think. But some days are worse. I don't know. I think that's the price, sometimes. That doesn't make sense."

"It does." It made perfect sense. I felt it this morning, at the breakfast table with Eve and Earl. Earl and I worked on the Sudoku while Eve checked readouts and weather patterns and told us where the sevens went. It was better, so much better, than the decades I'd spent starting every day alone. But having them meant I could lose them. The brighter the sun, the darker the shadows it cast.

"I'm glad you stopped by. I was going to bring this by the bakery." Max pulled a manila envelope out of his desk and walked it over to Kate. She looked inside, confused, and then a genuine smile bloomed on her face.

"I wondered where it was." She pulled out the dough cutter, flipping it in her hand and examining it. "I don't think I need it anymore, but I still want it." She slid it into a pocket of her sundress. "Thank you."

"You could thank us better with pastries." Max smoothed out the envelope and put it back with the supplies. "Maybe some of that cinnamon bread Blake had that one night?"

"You really are a cop, aren't you?"

"Former," Max corrected.

She nodded and her energy shifted, became more serious. "I'm learning that some cops—and former cops—are all right." Then she turned to me. Another shift. This one was even more painful, treading into the darkness, unearthing fresh traumas.

"I—this is going to sound unhinged—" She glanced nervously out the window.

Max laughed and took a swig of beer. "That's his entire identity."

"I saw you, when I was trapped. In a dream, maybe, or a hallucination. There was a prophet caught in a storm. It was a story that Ted—but it doesn't matter what he said. Sometimes the prophet was me. Other times it looked just like you." The room had gone completely quiet, the only noise drifting in from the open doors, the distant traffic heading home for the day. "Mom told me that you're a psychic, that you dreamed about me."

My throat had gone completely dry. "I did."

"I dreamed about you, too." She stood up and smiled awkwardly, turning to escape back into the sun. "I'll bring you guys some cinnamon bread next time."

She hesitated, glancing at me. "Watch out for storms."

Kate

The fire burned bright, all oranges and licking yellows against the star-crusted horizon. Charlie, Blake, and I sat around the fire pit in Charlie's backyard, beers sweating on the arms of our chairs. Blake and Charlie were arguing about something. It had started with Molly Ringwald, I think, and drifted from there. Their voices wove around the fire, flickering with the same heat and light.

A large tent with only screens for sides sat a dozen yards away, halfway between the fire pit and the house. Charlie had put it up and we slept there on the nights I couldn't be inside. I still woke up in a panic, even with the songs of crickets and frogs around me, even with the sleeping weight of Charlie's arm draped protectively over my side. I ran out of the tent some nights and straight into the field. Other nights I paced the perimeter of the yard with a flashlight and a knife. If we were inside, I turned every light on in the house. Sometimes I could go back to sleep, but even if I didn't I still returned to the warm place next to Charlie, snuggled my head into his chest, and felt the rumble of his snore. If he woke up, he'd pull me closer and kiss my hair, and then I relaxed enough to whisper things I couldn't yet say in the daylight. He always listened and, by not trying to make it better, he made it better.

Blake chucked another log on the fire, smirking when Charlie got up to arrange them in some predetermined formation. Eventually she'd start throwing smaller sticks and handfuls of leaves. It was part of their routine, and the comfort of knowing we would do this again next week—Blake coming here for our movie nights, popping a massive batch of popcorn, and all of us ending the night under the stars—was enough to put a lump in my throat. I was home. This place. These people. This was where I belonged.

When the fire was ordered to Charlie's satisfaction, he sat back down and his hand found mine. He slid our palms together and squeezed.

A half-empty bag of marshmallows sat at Blake's feet. We'd roasted some earlier, prompting a debate about the best way to bring a fresh take on s'mores to the bakery. We'd settled on a bar and decided to experiment with a black cherry compote for a twist. That would be tomorrow, or next week. I hadn't gone back to the bakery full-time yet. I worked two or three days a week and sometimes I needed to leave mid-shift, going to the backyard or farther, walking quickly through campus to the river. I always came back and Blake was always waiting, pulling me in for a flour-coated bear hug, generally with a line of confused and impatient customers waiting to order.

Mom visited last week, staying at a hotel down the road from the bakery, visiting Charlie's farm, and working side by side with Blake and me on a batch of frosted Hawkeye cookies. We messed up enough of them that Blake made us take a break and eat some of the failures with coffee on the back steps.

We watched the sunrise together, steam drifting from our mugs. She broke the silence long after the cookies were gone. "My therapist says I have to stop apologizing to you."

"My therapist said it will be a while before you can."

She huffed out a laugh and put an arm around me. When she spoke again, her voice was thick with unshed tears.

"This is what I wanted you to have."

"I know." I rested my head on her shoulder. It was still so delicate, her bones like some exotic, fragile bird. I knew better, though. I knew her shoulder could support all my weight and then some, and even if it broke, it would heal stronger than it had been before. My mother wasn't just any bird; she was a phoenix.

"I wanted this life, too. But it was missing one thing."

Her head lowered to rest on mine, and we watched the sky light up with the fire of a new day until Blake yelled for help with the muffins.

I'd been sad when she went home, but not as much as I thought I'd be. She had her life, the life she'd fought for, and I had mine. We texted daily, and had started a group chat with Blake that was ninety percent links to recipes and drool emojis.

"What do you think?"

The bonfire came back into focus and I blinked, realizing Blake and Charlie were both staring at me. Charlie's thumb rubbed back and forth on my hand, and his eyes were clouded in concern.

"Kate?"

The name was warm and rich on his tongue. It grounded me, brought me back to them. An old name for a new life. I still drifted away a lot, but it hadn't been to a dark place this time.

I smiled at both of them. "I'm here. I'm good."

The whale was dead. And I'd finally made it to shore.

310

Acknowledgments

Some books start with a hook. Some books start on a dare. This book started with a question: can you ever really change your life? The answer, we found out together, was a resounding yes. Here are a few of the people who have changed my life and helped bring this story to you.

Thank you, first and foremost, to my agent, Stephanie Cabot, who has been my champion and voice of reason in this business for over ten years. Stephanie, I would help you bury multiple bodies; just tell me where to bring the shovel. Thank you to the phenomenal team at Grove and Atlantic Crime, including Morgan Entrekin, Zoe Harris, Jenny Choi, Deb Seager, Natalie Church, and my editor, Joe Brosnan. Joe, thank you for all your insight and for bringing this story to the next level.

Minnesota is embarrassingly rich in bookstores. Thank you always and forever to Once Upon a Crime, Magers & Quinn, Valley Book-seller, the Bookstore at Fitger's, Barnes & Noble Burnsville, Next Chapter Booksellers, and all the other amazing local indies who've championed and hand-sold books by Minnesota authors like me. I'm indebted to so many Iowa indies as well, especially Dragonfly Books, The Book Vault, Beaverdale Books, and Prairie Lights. I'm honored to be on your shelves.

I couldn't have written Blake without wasting a lot of my formative years renting movies from Video Update of Rosemount, MN, and That's Rentertainment of Iowa City, IA. Thank you and RIP, you dingy, glorious video stores. I also couldn't have written Pastries & Dreams without growing up in my mom's kitchen and watching her bake everything from the world's best oatmeal bread to Chocolate Angel Pie™, usually with recipes that read more like vague suggestions. (Sorry, Mom, but "add flour to drop" will never be instructive to anyone except you.)

I'm so grateful to Satish Jayaraj for our Sunday morning writing sessions. Thank you to Angela Mejia, who let me take over her apartment with zero notice as I frantically tried to finish a draft good enough to hand in. Thank you to Liz Hessler and Sean Montgomery, who took turns holding my hand through a roller coaster of a year. I'm so grateful for the support of Lisa Guzek Montagné, who is always ready to break out the champagne, and the entire wonderful LGM team. Thank you, Mom and Dad, for tirelessly working your unpaid PR jobs. Mya, Tara, Katrina, and Angela, you are the best sisters in the world. Shout out to Nick, Melonie, Marc, Kristen, Amy, Michelle, and Claire for all your support and friendship. And of course, my heart will always be owned by my very own chaos demons, Logan and Rory. I can't wait to see where we'll go from here.